BENI

THE GUZZI
LEGACY BOOK 4

BETHANY-KRIS

www.bethanykris.com

Editor: Elizabeth Peters

Proofreaders: Tracy A., Mia B., Tori W. and Felicia F.

Cover Design © Under Cover Designs

Interior Design: Under Cover Designs

ISBN: 978-1-989658-01-7

CONTENTS

CHAPTER
1

Ever wonder what it would be like to have a living mirror of yourself?

Benito Guzzi wasn't curious at all.

"Shots!"

His identical twin's shout danced over the loud bar where they and their friends gathered in the club for most of the night.

"Bene," Ashton, one of their mutual friends, said as he stressed the *ay* ending to Benedetto's nickname, "you're going to give us fucking alcohol poisoning. We can't handle liquor like you two, *fuck*, man."

"Beni?"

Down the bar, his twin cocked a brow in his direction. Some might think it looked like a challenge. Others would take it as a question. Beni—his name differentiating from his twin's with a hard *e* at the end—didn't wonder what that look meant when he shared everything with Bene. From looks to style, and even his behaviors and attitude.

When he said *mirrors* of each other, that's what they were.

And it was their twenty-first birthday.

So ...

"Shots," Beni said with a nod.

Cheers from their group lit up the bar. The party was far from over, and if all went well, they would drink far into the morning. People knew Beni and Bene Guzzi for their desire to have a good time.

All the damn time.

"Where are your brothers?" the guy to his left asked. "Shouldn't they be here celebrating?"

Beni shrugged, more interested in the way the bartender had set up the shot glasses in a perfect line along the bar. Grabbing a bottle from the built-in shelves behind the bar, the glass gleamed from the lights. The bass from the music pumped through the floor, vibrating the soles of Beni's Italian leather loafers while more liquor poured.

Straight vodka this time.

They had to go easy on *some* of them.

I guess, he thought.

Bene, having heard the question posed to his twin, answered for Beni. "Corrado's in New York ... Chris is—don't know, whatever. And Marcus?"

Beni scoffed. "Fucking *Marcus*."

"What's that mean?"

Somehow, unlike the small army of their older siblings, Beni and Bene made friends *outside* of the life. That life being *la famiglia*. The mafia. Despite their interest and involvement in the family business, considering their father was the boss and their oldest brother followed his footsteps, they still surrounded themselves with people who had no idea about the other side of their life.

Beni and Bene shared a look.

A *grin*.

Knowing.

Sly.

Amused.

They liked to keep friends that weren't *in*. The two of them communicated easier in their strange way. The same thing they had been doing since before they could talk, if someone thought to ask their parents. Gestures, silent looks, body movements, or even a click of a tongue.

The two had a whole nonverbal language. It was a hell of a lot harder for them to communicate with each other when they were around their family, and they didn't *want* people knowing what they were saying.

"Marcus is Marcus," Beni settled on saying, "too busy being our father's mini-me to come out and have fun with us."

Marcus used to be fun, though. Then, he graduated, attended a few of years of a university for business, and went straight into the mafia to mentor under their father. Once Marcus was *in*, and got his button for the mafia, he was all the fucking way in. Unfailingly responsible—they counted on their oldest brother no matter what.

And sometimes that was just *boring*.

"Ready?"

Bene held his shot glass high into the air. The strobe lights flickered with a higher intensity in the background of the club, making his brother look like a statue. The club was banging, though, and for more reasons than their friends would understand. It was one that wasn't Guzzi owned, because God fucking knew the twins *hated* when tales of their night out got back to their parents, or brothers.

They worried.

Bitched.

The twins didn't understand why.

It was unnecessary.

Couldn't they just have fun?

Okay, maybe that was a bit of a stretch. Their fun usually included trouble—the *wild ones* their family called them because from the time they were old enough to run, the two never stopped. He figured, hey, at least they ran together.

That was the thing about Beni and Bene.

If they had each other, shit was cake.

Easy.

Life was fucking good.

"Ready," Beni said, picking up his own shot and holding it high, too.

Literal mirrors, he thought as he stared at his brother from the other end of the bar. From the way they held their shot glasses, to the curve of their smiles, and the carved-from-glass line of their jaws. Even the browns of their eyes could be mapped by the gold flakes that they'd taken from their father. That playful, but sly smile came from their mother, though. Standing side by side, the twins stood equal in height at six foot, two inches tall. Their weight was almost the same, too, at a solid, lean one-ninety, give or take a pound.

They were identical in every way.

Their stance.

How they carried themselves.

The style of their clothes.

All of it.

"Drop 'em back!" Bene called.

Beni wasn't sure if it was instinct, or just nature, for him to throw back his shot at the same time as his twin. He often found himself echoing the movements of his twin like they had when they were kids. Bene moved left, and Beni moved right. One smirked with the left side of his lips, and the other with his right.

It could be strange and disconcerting for new people who didn't know the twins. It took getting used to, but the twins had never subdued their strange habits for others. It wasn't in their nature to look out for anyone else but each other, after all. Even like *that*.

Shouts and hollers lit up the bar all over again as shot glasses clinked down to the glossy, red top. Bene was already waving for the bartender who had moved further down to serve a group that came up for refills while the Guzzi boys were taking their round with the rest of the group.

"Another round," he called. "Henny next!"

"*Fuck*," Beni groaned, "now you're trying to kill *me*, bro."

People liked to act as though Hennessey tasted great, but in fact, it was *shit*. Absolute, and total garbage. Add onto the horrible taste of the liquor, and it almost always had Beni puking by the end of the night, but especially when he mixed it with other spirits.

"Are you calling it a night, then? Gonna *pussy* out, Beni?"

Fuck his twin for knowing the right buttons to push.

"Never," Beni muttered, flipping his own hand up at the laughter of their friends to wave for the bartender, too. "Another round—Henny." He pointed a finger at his twin, adding, "But then we're doing Fireball."

"Oh, fuck *you*."

Yeah, exactly.

Because as much as his twin knew his secrets, Beni had all of Bene's locked up tight, too. He could play that game, if his brother wanted. He was good for it, always.

When the bartender didn't come as fast as they wanted, their calls for the man became louder, and more obnoxious. But wasn't that every fucking twenty-one-year-old man, anyway? They were just trying to have fun.

Of course, trouble always followed.

It was the twins' way.

"Fuckin' Guzzis thinking they own every goddamn place they step into," someone from the group down the bar muttered. "Why don't you all crawl into one of your *holes*, and party there?"

Beni tipped his chin up, not bothering to give whoever that was his attention. Instead, his gaze drifted to his brother at the other end of their large group. Bene matched his posture with wide shoulders going stiff, chin raised in defiance, and an almost manic gleam in his eye.

Savages.

Piss off a Guzzi, or bad mouth them, and the savage came out to play.

It didn't matter.

No one said a goddamn thing about a Guzzi without it being answered, and usually, *violently*. Beni didn't know if it was a pride thing, or what. A thick rush of rage filled his bloodstream with every beat of his heart because *fuck all of that*.

The guy wasn't just insulting him and his twin—but to be honest, that was enough to make him want to break the fucker's neck—but his entire clan. His father, the other three Guzzi brothers, and their *mother*, too. He didn't even have to name Cara Guzzi; didn't have to breathe a single word about her. He simply had to lump *all* Guzzis into one bunch, and they were insulting the boys' mother, too.

And *no*.

That would not fly over.

Ever.

Bene, who had still been toying with the empty shot glass in his hand, set it down to the top of the bar a bit harder than was necessary. Beni turned when his twin came around their group of friends who had all gone suspiciously silent.

They knew what was about to happen.

The guy—Bene knew which one made the comment, given he had been staring that way—didn't even see the twins coming for him. Fists flew after they yanked the fucker from his bar stool to the floor.

Soon, a whole crowd was fighting. Their friends. The fucker's friends. Some random guy that got knocked sideways during the scuffle. Even the club's security that rushed in to try and break it up.

The wild Guzzi twins struck again.

You'd think people would learn.

"Call the fucking cops!"

∿

"Hungover, wrinkled suits, and smelling like jail," Marcus said to his brothers as Beni and Bene stepped out of the back of the Mercedes, "that's not a good look on the two of you."

Bene grunted under his breath, saying nothing.

Beni, on the other hand, rolled his eyes. "*And?*"

Marcus sighed, and hit the roof of the car, a silent signal for the driver to head out. The driver showed up at the jail that morning, waiting for when the twins were released with orders to *bring them home*. Which they knew, instantly, did not mean their shared penthouse in the city.

No, it meant their parents' massive mansion outside of the city limits where they would have to go through another round of lectures from their brother, father, and maybe their ma, too. Who fucking knew?

Beni just wanted to go to sleep.

"That looks like it's raw," Marcus noted, gesturing at the busted lip Beni sported. "And you're not in any better shape, huh?"

Bene made that noise under his breath again. "Face hurts."

"Yeah, it looks like it."

They weren't exaggerating.

A night in jail did nothing for bruises and cuts. Beni couldn't smile without feeling that split in his lip rip open again. Each time he flexed his hands, his bruised, busted knuckles protested to no end. He was kind of sure he had a bruised rib, if not broken, but the hospital wouldn't do shit for that.

"Should see the other guys," Beni muttered.

Marcus shook his head. "What is wrong with the two of you?"

"Uh …"

Bene looked over at Beni.

He shrugged.

That was not the response Marcus wanted.

Color me fucking surprised.

"What caused the fight at the club?" Marcus asked.

"People using their mouth for shit they shouldn't."

"Excuse me?"

Beni eyed Marcus, and the tailored, pressed suit that covered his form. What was it—*nine* in the morning? Why was he already at their parents' mansion, dressed in a three-piece suit, looking like he was ready to start his whole day?

"Do you ever sleep in?" Beni asked. "Or … I don't know, do what *you* want to do instead of just business for Dad?"

Marcus arched a brow. "Do the two of you ever go out and *not* cause a fucking scene?"

"Not really."

"See, that's a problem. Because that's all the two of you do—*cause problems*, Beni. You can't even control yourselves at a club we don't own. And then you get yourselves arrested. You're fucking lucky Papa has connections to the RCMP, and managed to get those charges dropped. Had it worked out last night, actually."

Bene's brow furrowed.

Beni matched his brother.

"Wait," the two of them echoed at the same time, another strange occurrence for others where the twins were concerned. They could *speak* in tune with one another, without any prior knowledge of what the other would say. "The charges were dropped last night?"

"Yes."

"Why did we only get out this morning?" Beni demanded.

Marcus smirked. "Dad thought you two would do well to sober up in a cell."

Perfect.

Just fucking great.

Beni glared at the mansion at the end of the paved, circular driveway. It was cold as hell—January offered no reprieve in Canada, that was for sure. And yet, he had little to no interest in going inside the warm mansion now because he didn't want to hear his father *bitch*. The sloped, Swedish style of the mansion's eaves brought back familiar memories of his childhood looking out the windows, and the downhill drive in the crisp winter air made him think of sledding down it with his twin.

All good things.

He loved this place.

Just not right now.

"Can I go home?"

"No," Marcus deadpanned.

He wished he was surprised.

Then, Marcus spun on his heels with a wave of his hand, saying, "Let's go, better not keep Papa waiting any longer on the two of you."

The twins shared another look.

Still, they followed after their oldest brother in silence, even though Marcus continued chastising them up the driveway, and into the mansion. His bitching didn't stop even as they walked through the grand foyer, taking one of two curved staircases to the second level of the mansion where their father's office sat overlooking the front yard.

Nostalgia.

That's what it felt like to step foot inside his father's office. There was something about the rich tapestries imported from France, the darkly stained desk and book-shelves his father ordered from Italy, and the handmade rug his mother brought back from India after a trip that just reminded him of times long past.

And *several* trips to this office.

For reasons just like this morning.

Gian, an older reflection of his sons, stood at the front of his desk. He used his thighs to rest along the edge, and folded his hands on his middle. Like his older brother, his father was already dressed in a three-piece suit, his hair slicked back and ready for a day of business.

It was Saturday, right?

Work for the mafia didn't stop.

Only on Sundays.

"A sore sight, the two of you, *oui*?" his French-Italian father asked.

The smartass he was, Beni decided to reply the same way they had retorted to Marcus outside with, "You should see the fucker that tried to slander our name."

It was *not* the right thing to say.

Even though Marcus often mirrored his father in appearance and behavior, he did not have the same attitude that Gian did. Marcus had a much *longer* string of patience that could take a few tugs from the twins before it snapped altogether. Gian was not the same.

His father drew in a steady breath, pursed his lips, and gave them *that* look. A silent, *excuse me, do you want to try that again?* It was the only second chance their fathered offered now that they were grown men out on their own. He wasn't sure when that changed—around seventeen, he supposed, when they graduated high school and decided to go into the family business. The dynamics of their family had to change with their circumstances.

Gian was no longer *just* their father.

He couldn't be when he was also their boss.

Out of all five Guzzi brothers, it was Beni and Bene who struggled the most to make the change. Marcus did fine, ready to take his place at their father's side in business. The other twins in their family, Chris and Corrado, didn't have much of a problem differentiating their father from the man who raised them, and the one who ran a criminal organization, either.

The younger twins, though?

A constant struggle.

Beni was never more aware of it than now.

Bene shuffled on his feet beside Beni. "Listen, Papa, we were only making a point, okay? People can't run off at the mouth about—"

"Made men don't fight, and certainly not in a public club where it causes them to be arrested."

"We're not made yet."

"And you won't be, if you continue this behavior," Gian returned.

Ouch.

That stung a little.

Marcus cleared his throat, coming further into the office to take one of the two high-back leather chairs that faced their father's desk. Gian looked to his oldest son, considering something before he asked, "And what did you have to say to them about all of this?"

"Nothing we say to them matters. That's half the problem."

"*Pardonne-moi?*"

"They're spoiled," Marcus returned in English, knowing the twins had always struggled to learn French like their father spoke more often than not. "And because we've spent more time and effort cleaning after their messes than correcting them, this is the problem we face."

We, Beni noticed.

Not *you*.

Marcus took responsibility for his brothers as much as he placed blame on his parents. It wasn't lost on Beni, and he wasn't shocked to hear Marcus say as much, either. Always the responsible one—he looked out for everyone in their family. He felt an innate sense of duty toward his younger brothers, and for his parents. Maybe it was because he was the oldest, or it could have been the fact he was the only Guzzi brother that was a singleton without a twin to match him, and better him.

After all, Beni always said Bene was his better half, and his brother would reply in kind. When he was nervous, Bene was there to push him. If he went to far, Bene would rein him in. It was the same for him with his twin.

Chris and Corrado were the same.

Marcus, though?

He had to do it all alone.

His need to protect and look after his family came from a different source than theirs, but it was there, nonetheless. It was why they loved him. Even if he *was* just like their dad.

Some days, Beni found himself wishing all his brothers could go back to a time when they were nothing more than *teenagers*. Before the mafia swept into their life to determine how they behaved and treated one another when the doors were open to the public, and even when they were closed. He missed the times when Marcus was *easier*, more carefree. That seemed so long ago, really.

"They're selfish because we've allowed them to be," Marcus continued like the twins weren't sitting right there, "and that's the other half of the problem. Spoiled, and selfish. They don't consider the *family*—their need to protect our name comes from a self-centered place, and not for a selfless reason. They don't consider the mess they make, only the instant gratification from their outbursts."

Gian shifted on his feet, letting his arms fall to his sides. "And so, how do we correct that?"

For the first time since entering the office, Marcus glanced the twins' way. Beni could plainly see the concern warring with duty in his oldest brother's gaze. And yet, Marcus hardened his expression because that's what he needed to do. And he was nothing if not *reliable*. He got shit done, even if it was hard.

Like now.

Beni respected it.

Even if he hated what came next.

"We have to stop letting them run wild, and then cleaning up after them when something goes wrong. We can't continue to expect them to learn when all we've taught them is *someone else* will be there to take care of them, Papa. That's all."

Gian nodded, his attention going to Beni first, and Bene second. "He's right, you know."

The twins said nothing.

They didn't really need to.

Gian pushed away from the desk, standing straight before brushing invisible dust from his pant legs. He took the time to fix the gold *G* cufflinks on his suit jacket, and then lifted his head slightly so that the twins were forced to meet their father's gaze.

"I want to say it's because you both are young, but I think a bigger part of the problem is that you both feed off one another. Is it made better or worse because you are in home territory, and you know someone will be there to catch you when you mess up, or fall? That's yet to be determined, but we're going to find out."

"What does that—"

Gian held up a single hand, quieting Bene. "No, it's my turn now. I have given the two of you more than enough chances to correct the issues you seem to have, but that clearly hasn't worked, Bene."

"Come on, this isn't a *big thing*," Bene muttered. "We just had some fun, and got into a fight. It wasn't like we killed someone."

"Yet." Gian lifted one shoulder, his tone cold and flat as he continued on with, "You have not done something I cannot fix *yet*, and I do not want to reach that point with the two of you. I need you to learn to respect and value your place in this family and business. Apparently, I am not the right man to teach you. I thought the two of you would be like your other brothers—this is what you wanted, and so you would fall into line, and settle out of your wildness. Instead, you've used your status and privilege as an excuse to become worse."

Beni knew exactly what his father was saying.

And how he would fix it.

Correct an issue before it gets worse.

That was the Guzzi way.

"We'll start with a year away, and go from there," his father stated.

Even Marcus looked up at that, although their oldest brother stayed quiet.

Gian nodded. "A year away, mentoring under a different organization. Your uncle in Chicago is willing to make a place for the two of you in the Outfit. I will reconsider after the year is up, depending on how well the two of you have done."

"*What?*"

"We've never worked for the Chicago mob," Beni said.

Bene scowled. "I fucking *hate* Chicago."

They did have a lot of family there, though, being as it

was where their mother came from, and where her family remained. Or rather, what was left of it.

Gian shrugged, a faint smile curving his lips as he replied, "In case you didn't get the memo, boys, it's no longer about what *you* want—I'm doing what's best for you. Otherwise, the more you both act out, the worse my fears become about what will happen to the two of you when I'm not looking. I can't always watch over you. *Marcus* won't always have time to look out for the two of you. And you're scaring your mother."

That did it.

Just the mention of hurting their ma.

It was enough to set them straight.

Or, mostly.

"So, Chicago," Gian said, "you'll leave within the week. Do make sure to spend *as much* time with your mother as possible before you go. Understood?"

What choice did they have?

"It's not so bad," Marcus said over his shoulder, "Chicago, I mean."

Beni didn't believe that. Not for a second.

"And it'll be good for both of you," he added quieter, "even if you don't think so right now."

Right.

Time would tell, wouldn't it?

CHAPTER

2

"The most important lesson a woman can learn in business," a smart woman once told August Rivera, "is that she will always have to work twice as hard to be viewed as even *half* as good as a man in the same position. You'll always have to work for it. They never will."

That woman?

Her ma.

Ada wasn't wrong, either. Her mother liked to hand down those little tidbits of information whenever she thought August was listening. Truth be told, she listened far more than she didn't. Her drive to be successful was in the fabric of her being. All she had to do was look to her parents for the reason why, too.

Her mother, now a fine jewelry designer who immigrated from Nigeria with a small savings and a hope and dream, built her company, *Ada's*, from the ground up. She was the very definition of blood, sweat, and tears.

Her father, half Italian and half African-American, grew up in the projects of the Bronx watching people struggle against injustice and oppression. He saw a need, busted his ass through his college years while donating what time he had left to his community, until passing the bar and becoming a defense attorney.

August was meant to succeed.

If anything was written in her stars, it was *that*.

Maybe that was why, at twenty-two, August already felt like her career had come to a complete standstill. The general rule of thumb for someone who wanted to move up in any company was to refuse to stay in the same position for more than two to three years.

Well …

She had been the assistant to the editor of Bared Brands magazine since she was eighteen. What had been a temp position as an intern for the editor turned into a part-time position while August worked her way through three years of college. And then, after graduating with her degree in business and journalism, her boss offered her a full-time position as her assistant *with* the promise of more.

She wanted to work *on* the magazine. On the editor's team.

Somehow.

Just once, she wanted to see her name listed in the credits of a spread as part of Michelle Coss's team. It didn't seem to matter that, writing for the online publication, she had hit viral status at the age of twenty, or that she had clearly proven herself as a good writer capable of handling the workload on the team. All the gatekeepers at the company saw was her age on paper, and that she hadn't *put in her time*, as they liked to say.

But that was her goal with the magazine, and the reason for her *mistake* of agreeing to move to full-time assistant for the editor. Because here it was, a whole year after continuing this job full-time, but several doing the job, but she still hadn't gotten the chance to pitch an idea for a spread to the editor's team.

You might, though.

Right.

Which brought her back to the current conversation she was having with her father while sitting at her desk. From her position, she could see the frosted-glass walls that made up her boss's office, and the stylish gray and green, modern décor that covered the space where she did most of her office work for the magazine.

In all honesty, her boss was pretty good. Michelle didn't mind if August took an extra half hour for lunch, or if she sat on her phone for an hour when she was supposed to be running errands. The job itself wasn't *bad*. And there was nothing hard about the work—but that was also the problem. She wasn't being creative, and she wasn't challenged pushing papers, running errands around the city, or taking calls.

That's not what she came here for.

She wanted *in* on the editor's team.

Simple as that.

She was going to have her chance, though.

Finally.

"Are you all set for your trip?" her father, Cameron, asked.

August nodded, although he couldn't see it. "Yeah, I just have to grab my bags at the door, and head out in the morning."

Cameron made a noise under his breath before saying, "Be careful, hmm? Don't let those TSA workers feel you up, and watch your step while you're in Chicago. Can't trust any—"

"I'll be fine, Dad."

God knew she had to speak up before her father could really get started. If there was anyone who knew how to have a good panic, it was her dad. Another time, and August might find it amusing and cute. Not today.

The trip to Chicago was more than just a vacation to her. It was the chance for her to finally make a move with her job here at Bared Brands.

"Have you figured out how you want to present your spread to the editor?"

August sighed. "Put me on the spot, why don't you?"

A laugh answered her back.

That was all she got, though.

After an entire year of asking if she could present an article spread on the culture of a brand in communities or cities to her boss, the woman finally agreed to let August have a shot at it. She had written a few short articles for the online version of the magazine, but like a lot of internet publications, those were submitted without the expectancy of pay. The magazine depended on journalists, writers, and opinion sections to fill up their content spaces, drive traffic, wherein they proceeded to make money through ad revenue, and otherwise.

It was the paper magazine where space was *coveted*.

In more ways than August could explain.

Her online publications, two informational pieces and one opinion piece, had gained her a bit of notoriety online, and about fifty-thousand followers on her socials. You would think that should be enough to prove her weight to the magazine, but she swore they only saw her as an artist willing to bleed her passion on glossy paper that they would take for all it was worth … without, of course, giving her much worth in return.

"Well?" her father pressed gently.

August sighed. "I thought I knew how I wanted to present it, but I think it'll be better to scrap any plans I might have until I get to Chicago, and can actually walk the streets. Talk to some people. See how *they* feel about the brands that have changed their landscapes, and influenced the culture around them. You know?"

"My smart girl, hmm?"

She smiled, unable to stop herself.

Always her biggest fans.

And cheerleaders.

It was what she loved the most about her parents. It never failed.

Her boss *suggested*, if all went well, that there was possibly a six-page spread waiting for her take on the influence where brands were concerned in the urban sectors of Chicago. That was, as long as she could pull it off, the content was engaging enough, and her message was clear in the article she had to produce for it.

All things August could do.

Undoubtedly.

She just had to get out of her head to do it.

"Ada thinks the trip will be good for you," her father said, referring to her mother. "And she wants you to take lots of pictures with Camilla while you're there. She misses her."

Yeah, August bet.

August's best friend from the time she was a young teenager, Camilla Donati—now a Rossi, as her friend married a man connected to the Chicago mob a couple years back—was one of the things she was looking forward to the most in the windy city. She didn't get to see Cam nearly as much now that she had moved out of New York, and it always felt like they had a ton to catch up on whenever they got together again.

At the same time, it felt like they picked right up where they left off, too. That was one of the better things about having a best friend, even if she was several states away from August now. Time and distance didn't really make a difference to their friendship.

They were still Camilla and August.

"I will," August assured her father, "because I am sure Ma won't let me forget it."

Likely text her a dozen times a day.

Cameron chuckled. "You know it. And how is Ian treating you?"

Speak of the devil, and he shall appear ...

A truer statement had never passed her mind before.

Ian Bared wasn't actually the devil, but he could come damn close to it sometimes. People working at the magazine called him a tyrant, and he about looked like it, too, in all his six-foot-four-inch glory, carrying around a solid two-hundred-twenty pounds that he stuffed into a tailored, Armani suit day in and day out.

At her father's mention of his acquaintance—she wouldn't call them friends, all things considered—Ian's shadow darkened her desk, making August look up from the magazine she had spread out across the glossy top. She was quick to give the man a smile, and used a sticky note to keep her place in the magazine before closing it up.

Ian smiled back, a little too widely maybe, before waving a finger at her in a silent demand for her to hang up the phone. He wasn't her boss—per se—but he was the CEO and majority owner of Bared Brands. And if not for her father's connection to the man through a case he litigated on behalf of the magazine a few years ago, August likely wouldn't have gotten the internship that started her career at this place.

For whatever reason, Ian *liked* her. Maybe a little too much, all things considered. His office was four floors higher in the large skyscraper, and yet he made an effort to come down to visit her at least once a day.

He wasn't entirely inappropriate, but he also didn't have to be. Some guys just gave off *that* kind of vibe. Maybe their stare lingered a little too long, or their words offered too much room for suggestion.

August found herself between a rock and hard place with Ian Bared. He was closer to her father's age than her own, and for whatever reason, seemed to like her. She wasn't interested—at all. She also felt like because her position here had been determined by his relationship to her father, not to mention Bared Brands didn't exactly foster the greatest environment for women to speak up when they were uncomfortable with the attention of a man at the company, that she couldn't tell the CEO to leave her alone.

Fucking perfect, huh?

As her mother once said … *work twice as hard.*

"He's great," she lied to her father. "I will call you back tonight, okay?"

"Everything good?"

"Yep. I just have to get back to work."

"All right. *Try* to make it to dinner tonight, yes?"

"Absolutely. Love you, Dad."

"Love you, too, August."

Ian's smile became impossibly wider after August hung up the phone, and gave him all her attention. That's what this man seemed to want the most, after all. The attention of women, and men, depending on the situation, entirely on him.

He was the God around this place.

"Mr. Bar—"

"Ian," he interjected smoothly. "How many times have I told you to call me Ian?"

A lot.

She also figured that keeping it professional would help the man to understand she was not interested in dating someone who could be her father.

It didn't.

Clearly.

"Ian," August said, measuring her tone for politeness— no need to make a scene, after all. It never ended well for women who did that, but especially not at this magazine. "I was just about to head out for the day. I was off a half hour ago. Did you need something?"

He stuffed his hands into the pockets of his slacks and rocked on his heels at the front of her desk. Now, she was wishing she had just left instead of sitting at her desk and flipping through that damn magazine for inspiration.

Hindsight, and all that.

"No," he said, "I just heard you were heading out on an assignment and wanted to say goodbye as I won't be seeing you until you come back."

August shrugged as she stood from her desk, making quick work of packing up the few things, like her laptop and clutch, that she hadn't put in her bag earlier. "Yep—a month, maybe more, in Chicago for this spread pitch to the team. Well, I'm taking my three weeks of vacation, but the extra week or so … Michelle allowed me to work on this."

"Finally seeing your potential, then."

Maybe.

"I just want to see what comes out of it. This idea has been in the back of my mind for a while."

"I bet."

Then, Ian reached over the desk and caught one of August's loose box braids in his fingers to curl around one digit. It was a purposeful move, and it all but made her freeze on the spot. That was the problem with this man—a simple conversation could *quickly* cross over into inappropriate territory before someone blinked. One couldn't prepare and avoid it when he behaved this way.

Typically, she kept her hair, but especially when it was done in the protective style of braids, plaited neatly down her back, or tied up. Today, she had worn them down, and she was regretting that choice.

Although, she shouldn't have to regret it at all.

Her hair was not a *toy*.

"I miss your curls," he said.

For several years, August had gone a natural route with her corkscrew head of curls. Sometimes, she still did when she wanted to give her roots a break from the intensity of braiding.

"Maybe," August said lowly, although her tone remained firm, "but I like the braids, Ian."

He dropped his hand instantly.

August dragged in a quick breath.

"Well, I do miss them."

August said nothing.

"Enjoy your trip to Chicago," he added, finally taking a step back, "and I will see you as soon as you are back."

Right.

Ian's little visit reminded her that this trip to Chicago was more than just the spread in the magazine, and visiting her old friend. Like the job offer she had been given a year ago that she hadn't entertained. She was sure as hell entertaining it now.

August practically bounced on the balls of her heels after ringing the ornate doorbell wrapped in brass on the front doors of a three-level Melrose home. The expected windiness of Chicago wasn't that bad, so she didn't mind standing there on the porch while she waited for the doors to open.

Even before she saw the cloudy, dark form take shape in the frosted glass of the French doors, she could hear her friend behind it. Camilla's loud footsteps pounded down the entryway hall of her home, and then the squealing started.

It didn't matter that they were now in their twenties.

Or that Cam was married.

The fact they were grown ass women, essentially, with

jobs, lives, and all the other good stuff that came along with adulthood didn't factor in to their excitement to be together at all. And she was grateful for that because more than anything, sometimes August just needed to *relax*. Say screw all the adult responsibility, throw caution to the wind, and have a little fun.

Cam was *perfect* for that.

When the two of them were together, it reminded her of being seventeen again, having crazy weekends with her best friend, and sitting hungover in church because of it.

Good times.

The cream-painted doors were thrown open in a rush, no grace to it. Camilla darted out before August even had time to appreciate the silk wrap dress her friend wore, never mind the man who darkened the doorway behind her.

She didn't mind, though.

Camilla's arms locked around her neck, and squeezed tight enough to take her breath away. August hugged her friend right back, their squeals lighting up the porch, and surely drawing attention from any neighbors that happened to be outside of their houses currently.

She wished she cared.

Pulling back, Camilla grinned wide enough to show off perfect white teeth. Her pixie-like appearance was only aided by her light skin tone and small features, and white-blonde hair that was currently streaked at the roots with a deep purple shade. The contrast between the two women, August with her nearly six-foot in height, and Camilla in all her small, pixie glory couldn't be denied.

And yet, they were a perfect match.

Best friends 'til the very end.

Always.

"Oh, my God, I missed you so much," Camilla said.

August blinked away the tears that had clouded her eyes. "Yeah, me, too."

Behind her friend, Cam's husband lingered in the opened doorway of their home. Tommaso didn't step in on the girls' moment. He never did. It was one of the things August liked best about him. Despite the fact that this had been the man to finally settle her wild friend down into married life—or as settled as Cam could be—never mind convincing her to move all the way to Chicago to be with him, August liked Tom.

He was a good man.

Good to Cam.

That's what counted.

"Tom," she greeted.

He grinned, winking. "How was your flight?"

"Who *cares*," Camilla crowed, still holding onto August, "she is here for *a whole month now!*"

August laughed, hugging her friend to her side again. "It was good."

Tom nodded. "Perfect. Did you settle into your hotel before coming here?"

Cam waved a hand, dismissing that notion. "She'll probably stay here more, anyway."

"Yeah, I did."

Camilla was already moving to a new topic, which also wasn't anything new for her friend. "We have to do something. You know, to celebrate you being here, and all. Dinner, maybe? Oh, or a *club*. Yes, let's go drink and dance."

Actually, that sounded pretty good.

"Let me settle in for a few days, and then we can do whatever. I have a couple of interviews set up for this week, and I do not want to be hungover for them. This assignment could finally get me a better position at Bared Brands, and I don't want to screw it up for anything, Cam."

Cam pouted. "*Fine*. This weekend, then?"

"That'd be perfect."

"Oh, there's a new club opening on the east side. We should—"

Tommaso made a noise under his breath, drawing in the women's attention. "Not sure that's a good idea, babe. There's been some … bad activity on that end. Gang movement, and stuff. A crew having trouble. Better not to be caught up in something on that side, you know?"

Without even asking, August knew Tom was talking about the Outfit. *Mafia* business. The mob had come on her radar when she met Cam as a young teen, and people whispered that the girl's father was a mafia boss. Of course, she hadn't believed it until her father confirmed it later when he took on a job litigating a set of charges for Camilla's father, Calisto.

Still, the mob hadn't *touched* August's life.

Not really.

And still, she understood that it was very real and present for her friend. Camilla's family was saturated in mafia business. And her husband? The son of a prominent mob boss, too. August always figured, as long as she didn't ask questions or get directly involved, then she was safe.

Right?

"It should be fine, it's just a club," Cam pointed out. "What's the worst that could happen?"

Tom gave her a look before muttering, "We'll see. But have a backup club in the plans, got it?"

"Done deal." Then, Cam turned her attention back on August. "Speaking of a better position … although let's forget Bared Brands, have you considered the offer Alessa gave you a year ago?"

Tommaso's aunt, Alessa Conti, owned Manic Media. The job offer, although she would have to start over and work from the ground up in her career, still lingered in the back of her mind even though she refused it the first time around.

Yes, she was considering it.

No, she was not telling Cam just yet.

Her friend would get excited, wouldn't leave it alone, and would then undoubtedly affect August's decision to make such a big change in her life and career. Not only would it mean starting over, but also moving away from her family.

She needed to figure it out on her own.

"Not really," she lied. "I'm here for other things."

Camilla sighed. "Breaking my heart, Aug."

"Impossible."

A smirk answered her back. "But is that a problem?"

CHAPTER

3

"Wake up," Beni snarled.

He was fed up with *kindly* telling his twin to roll his lazy, hungover ass out of bed. Bene barely reacted beyond a displeased grunt under his breath before rolling over in the black sheets that covered his bed. In fact, he even went as far as dragging the matching black comforter with silver accents over his head to block Beni out. Like that was really going to work. *Come on, you know me better than that.*

Beni grabbed the comforter, and ripped it away from his brother. Along with the flat sheet, and the pillow he was using. That left Bene blinking, dumbly and probably still a little drunkenly, against the bed.

"Next is gonna be cold water on your face," Beni said, amused.

"But *why?*"

"We have shit to do. Get up."

He'd been telling him that for an hour now. On and off, as he got up and around, readying for the morning and the rest of his day. He kept coming back to his brother's room in their shared Chicago apartment in the Heights—the place wasn't amazing, but it also wasn't a shit hole. Given they were two bachelors and mostly just needed a place to sleep considering they rarely did anything else at their place, it worked for them.

"I'm too hungover for your shit today," Bene mumbled, smooshing his face into the mattress. "Go away."

Nope.

Beni stayed put.

Six months working and living in Chicago, and you would think Bene might have learned by now *not* to over-drink. They always had shit to do the next morning, usually early. No one needed to be feeling like a walking, talking ball of puke while doing it.

Except for Bene, it seemed.

"I told you not to get smashed last night," Beni said, picking up a few of the stray pieces of clothing on the floor to throw over the chair in the corner. "And now look at you."

"Shjhf jhjd nknksj."

"What?"

All he heard was unintelligible mumbles.

Bene turned his head, so he faced his brother with closed eyes. "I said, *it's fucking Saturday, Beni.*"

"And we have to be at the gym in an hour. So …?"

"That's … that's a no from me, bro. I'll puke all over the mats if I workout today."

"And I don't workout alone, so get your ass out of bed. Your hangover isn't my problem."

"I fucking hate you."

"But do you *really*?"

"Right now," Bene said in a disgusted sigh, "more than you will ever understand."

And yet, he was still getting what he wanted. It took a bit of effort, and some time with Bene sitting on the edge of his bed with his head between his knees to soothe the rising vomit. He did eventually get his twin out of bed and looking like he *might* be ready to hit the gym.

Yeah, he could have gone alone.

Except he didn't want to.

He watched Bene's bare back—uninked, like his; their father always clear on his great disdain for tattoos—disappear into the bathroom across the hall from their bedrooms that were situated side by side in the small apartment. The door slammed closed behind his twin; another sign Bene was not in the mood for this today.

Oh, well.

Behind the door, he heard flushing before water started to run. Bene's unhappy grumbles continued even after he came back out of the bathroom, glaring at his brother the entire time while he passed him in the hallway.

Beni smirked right back.

"Clean up the attitude," he told Bene, "because it's not going to help you when I decide to kick your ass in the ring later."

Bene groaned from the confines of his bedroom. "We're *boxing* this weekend? I thought we were just ... *why?*"

"That's what Tank wants us to do."

Tank, their personal trainer. It wasn't like the twins needed one, but the guy helped to keep both of them on track with their busy schedules. He made sure they found time to come into the gym, and regularly had plans ready for them when they showed up.

"And if you make me tell him we're going to be late, I will beat your—"

Bene came out of the room with a scowl that could rival the devil's. His fist struck out, smashing Beni right in the shoulder before he passed him in the hallway. Beni rubbed his now sore muscle.

Shit.

"Just so you know, your hangover isn't going to stop me from beating your ass later," Beni warned.

"Only have yourself to blame if I puke on you."

Right, right.

A risk he was willing to take.

There was something about a good competition with his twin that always had Beni revving and ready to go. It never changed in all their years. For some, the competition wasn't healthy, but for him and his twin, it worked to keep them motivated.

Separately, and together.

Because they were a team.

Always had been.

"Are you hitting that club tonight?" Beni asked. "The new one Joe opened on the east end with Cory?"

The Rossi brothers were famous for their businesses. And the two had a *ton* of them. Everything from restaurants to bars and clubs, and even a couple of random ones like laundromats and fucking barber shops. Good money, sure, but he bet that was a lot of upkeep. Being in the mafia should have been enough to keep the Rossi brothers busy, but apparently, they needed more.

"If last night didn't kill me, then probably," Bene said, heading down the hallway.

Beni followed behind. "You're looking alive now."

"*Barely.*"

Well, whose fault was that?

He kept his mouth shut.

As Bene worked his way into his clothes, punching his arms through a custom Frankie Zombie hoodie that was actually *Beni's*, while the two of them headed for the front door, the landline in the apartment started to ring. With traffic, they were already cutting it close to hit the gym before they would be late, so he didn't bother to run and pick it up. Whoever it was could leave a damn message, or call one of the twins on their cells if it was that important.

"Probably Dad," Beni said as his twin slipped on his shoes. "You talked to him last night when he called, right?"

"Yeah."

It wasn't so much the reply his brother gave, as much as it was the way Bene said it. He drawled the word out slowly like he considered not saying it at all. Not to mention, his twin was now avoiding his gaze as he stood straight, and grabbed his gym bag off the hook designated for his shit amongst the many lining the hallway.

He didn't know what that was about.

That *yeah*.

Or the way his brother said it.

Fuck it.

He would figure it out later.

They had other shit to do now.

Being hungover didn't mean shit when Bene was in a mood, and needed to work out all the frustrations he'd been carrying for a week. It was what Beni appreciated the most about his twin when put in a ring against him for a sparring match.

He'd landed one good punch to his twin's kidney before Bene fucking *snapped*. He'd only been faking his interest in working out up until that point in the ring. He came because Beni forced his still-drunk ass out of bed, not because he truly wanted to be there.

Now, though?

He was raining punches down on Beni like he fucking *meant it*. Beni was feeling every single one of the punches that landed, too. He always did know just the right buttons to push to get his twin pissed in no time at all.

Zero?

Meet *one hundred*.

That's what Beni and Bene were for each other.

Under the mouthguard, Beni laughed sardonically when his twin backed him into the ropes, and those punches moved from his face to his kidneys. *Shit*, that hurt, but whatever. It was the twin thing again—his brother didn't need to say he had shit on his mind, or that something was bothering him.

Beni just knew it.

Could *feel* it.

Those bonds he shared with his brother were unexplainable to those who didn't have the same thing with someone else. Even their other twin brothers, Corrado and Chris, didn't share the same intuition and knowledge about their twin the way he did with Bene.

Hey.

At least Bene was working it out.

Or getting there.

He gave his twin all of a good solid minute and a half to beat the hell out of him before he came off the ropes swinging right back. Bene was expecting that, though. Another thing about the two of them being mirrors of one another.

There were no surprise moves here.

Not only did that make it easier to spar in some ways, but it also made it harder. They could prepare for the others' moves, and at the same time, strike out with the unexpected.

Of course, with their gear on to spar, there wasn't much damage they could do to each other except for some sore ribs, and maybe a headache. The trainer watching from the floor kept the match clean, for the most part, hollering to force the boys apart when they started crossing a line.

Beni was huffing like hell when Tank finally blew his whistle to call it a round. Bene wasn't in any better shape. The two twins took a step back from one another, gloves already up and ready to tap each other with matching smirks and glinting eyes.

Stares that said *not this time, but next.*

It was always the same.

"Get some water, you two," Tank said from down below. "Take a breather. Jesus, ya'll be given me fucking heart palpitations with the way you go on sometimes."

Beni laughed as he turned his back to his twin, and in two strides, was jumping over the ropes to land on the mats below. After pulling off his gloves, and spitting out his mouthguard, he reached for the water bottle he'd set on the floor earlier, tipping it up and squeezing it hard to get a steady stream of cold water into his mouth that he could gulp down like it was the air he really needed.

Water was good, too.

Hydration, and all that shit.

Tank, a six-foot-six Latino with shoulders that seemed as wide as he fucking was tall, handed Bene's bottle of water up to him when he didn't come out of the ring. At his feet, Bene's gloves sat, forgotten.

"We need to work on your defense of your head," Tank told him. "Tuck those fucking elbows in, get your fists high and close to your face, you know."

Beni arched a brow at his twin. "Got a point."

Because the head was *always* Bene's weakness. Beni's was the fact he didn't like fast-footed people in a ring. They both had their spots that could be better. And sure, while they used boxing as a form of working out, they were still pretty serious about the technique of it all.

You know, when Bene wasn't hungover and in a mood.

"Or I just don't care as long as I can get the job done."

"Won't be able to get the job done," Tank returned, "if you get knocked the fuck out, *amigo.*"

"Right," Bene muttered around the rim of his water bottle. "I'll keep that in mind."

"Finish that water, and we'll go another—"

Tank's directions came to a halt with the muffled ringing of Beni's cell. He gave the man an apologetic shrug, bending down to dig the phone from his bag.

"Take your call, no worries," Tank said behind him. "I'll get your brother ready for another pounding."

"Gee, thanks, asshole," Bene grumbled in reply.

"It's what I do."

Beni found his phone with a triumphant grunt, and didn't bother to check the caller ID before picking up the call with a fast, "Yeah, Beni here."

He kept his back to the ring.

"Busy?" came a familiar voice.

His uncle, Tommas.

Or rather, his new boss.

Beni found it easier to differentiate between the boss and family aspect with his uncle than he ever had with his father. He wasn't sure why, but Tommas drew that line clearly in the sand, and expected it not to be crossed. It didn't matter who it was, any made man in the family, or Tommas's own son, Beni's cousin, Tommaso … the line was always clear.

No exceptions.

"Boss," Beni replied, "never busy for you. What's up?"

"I have a job for you to do. When can you come to the mansion and have a chat?"

See, this was where Beni's privilege came into play where the mafia was concerned. He didn't have his button—he wasn't *in* technically. He wasn't a made man, by any standard. He was nothing more than an associate of the business with a mafia boss father, and an uncle who ran another organization. If he was any regular fucker, he wouldn't have a direct line to the boss. His orders would come through other lower fucks on the totem pole.

Instead, he was afforded this respect.

He was starting to understand what his father had meant.

Beni was learning to respect his place.

This *status*.

"Give us five minutes to shower—we're at the gym—and we can drive over," Beni said.

Tommas clicked his tongue, murmuring, "Just you today. Bene will have another job with someone else, I suspect."

That was … unusual.

Beni knew better than to question it, though.

"All right, I'll be over, boss."

"See you then."

Tommas hung up the call without a proper goodbye, but Beni didn't care. Turning on his heels to face the ring, he found his brother was already leaning over the ropes with an inquisitive eye locked on him.

"What's up?"

"Boss wants me over at his place for a job, or something."

Bene nodded. "Okay."

Okay?

No questions about the job, or why he wasn't included?

Whatever.

Beni had work to do now.

"Meet up later at the club, then?" he asked.

Bene slapped the ropes with a gloved hand. "You got it."

"How was traffic?"

Beni scowled, but instantly fixed his face to something more respectful and pleasant when his uncle looked up from the stack of papers on his desk as he darkened the doorway of the boss's home office. "Shit."

"That's Chicago on a Saturday afternoon, for you."

"Hmm."

He didn't mind, really. To be honest, other than the almost constant presence of wind, he thought Chicago was a lot like Toronto. The accents were different, and people weren't as kind, but Canada was Canada. And this was certainly *not* Canada.

All in all, Marcus hadn't been wrong months ago. Chicago wasn't half bad, he simply didn't like the reasons for why he had been sent here. That was the difference.

"Lucky for you," Tommas said, closing the folder he'd been perusing at Beni's entrance, "I didn't have anywhere to be today, and I could afford to wait for you."

"I can't control traffic."

Tommas's gaze lifted to meet Beni's, a question—or was it a warning?—lingering there. His uncle said nothing, simply stared and let that look do the job for him.

"Sorry," Beni said, checking his attitude. "I apologize for making you wait."

"Thank you." Gesturing at one of two black leather bucket chairs in front of his desk, he added, "Take a seat, and we can discuss this job I have for you."

All right.

Beni did as he was told, and it was only once he was seated that Tommas leaned back in the office chair to steeple his fingers while regarding his nephew over the tips. Under the scrutiny, he had the strangest urge to fidget. He always felt strange when people stared at him, and he was without his twin. It was easier to defer the energy back to Bene, or even, the identical nature of the twins and their behaviors often distracted people in a way.

Alone, it was just him.

Sometimes, he didn't know what to do with that.

"What?" he finally asked, edgy enough to risk it.

"How are you liking Chicago?"

"Just fine."

Tommas lifted a brow. "That all?"

"I think Papa made the right choice sending us here."

"Oh?"

Beni shrugged. "Don't tell him I said that."

Tommas smirked. "We'll see."

He suspected—and rightfully so—that his uncle would run that information back to Gian, or his sister, Beni's mother, as fast as he possibly could. There was nothing their generation liked more than saying their kids admitted they were right.

Tommas sighed and turned his chair slightly so that he could stare out the long, rectangular windows that filled up a good portion of one wall inside his office. "Have you heard about the issues on the east side?"

"A bit."

"And?"

Beni made a noise in his throat, not wanting to overstep his bounds. The problems circulated around a crew ran by a *Capo*. That meant, men of Beni's status had no business bad mouthing—even if it was just business—a made man.

"Beni," Tommas prodded.

"It sounds like the crew is problematic."

Yeah, that sounded fine.

He mentally patted himself on the back.

Tommas nodded. "Yes, all their issues with the gang, not to mention the things that haven't been put out for public consumption."

"I beg your pardon?"

"The thieving."

Beni's brows shot all the way up. "Someone is stealing within the crew?"

"The Capo running it believes so. Problem for him is that it's being done in such a way he isn't sure *who* is doing it. And that's where you alone come in."

"How so?"

"I'm going to place you inside the crew as a new member. It was the Capo's idea. Jerome does occasionally have good ideas, even if he drives me crazy most of the time. None-theless, you'll take a spot in the crew, run with them, work … all normal things, and while you're at it, find out why they're having all the issues with the gang nearby, and *who* is doing the stealing."

Tommas waved a hand, adding, "See, that's part of the reason why I wanted only *you* on this job. It would be best if you integrated as much as possible into the crew, and you know how they can be about new people."

"Yeah, distrustful, and—"

"Imagine *two* of you taking spots."

Right.

"Bene and I would be … distracting."

Tommas chuckled. "To say the least. Put the two of you together, and you can't help but draw attention with the way you go on."

"We don't *go on*. We just … are."

Yeah.

That worked.

"If you say so, *nipote*," Tommas returned. "So, what do you think? You up for the task."

Sure.

Why not?

"What about what I have been doing with Bene? That's a two-man job."

Since they arrived in Chicago six months ago, their uncle

put them in charge of looking after the streets, and those working for them in the city. Daily, they were running from one end of the city to handle dealers, or inside a bar picking up messages or money from bookies. It was a lot to keep track of, but it also allowed the Capos of the Chicago Outfit a bit of legroom with their people. They didn't have to be everywhere all at once when they could focus on their crews and let Beni and Bene do the heavy lifting elsewhere.

"We'll have others take that over," Tommas said.

"*With* Bene?"

"No, two new people."

"What will Bene—"

"As far as I know," his uncle interjected calmly, "he'll be heading back to Toronto soon. Something he worked out recently with your father. Homesick, I believe. You would have to ask him. You didn't know?"

Suddenly, that strange *yeah* comment from his brother that morning made a hell of a lot more sense. They were supposed to be here—*together*—for at least a year. Here it was, six months in, and already his brother was leaving.

Arranged it behind his back, apparently.

Why?

Why hadn't he told Beni?

"So, he's going home," Beni said quietly, "and I'm staying here?"

"Looks like it. It wouldn't hurt for the two of you to spend some time apart, Beni."

"It's not about being *apart*."

Mostly.

Kind of.

He didn't want to be separated from his brother, but that wasn't why he was pissed off, either. That was because Bene hid it from him.

Tommas raised a brow, murmuring, "If you want me to

believe you're not angry about being separated, perhaps you should stop looking at me like you're going to come over my desk with a tone that suggests the same, yes?"

Fuck.

Beni said nothing.

Tommas seemed to be okay with that. "You'll begin work with the crew soon. And stop to say hello to your aunt before you leave, understood?"

"Yeah, I got it."

But now he had a lot of shit on his mind, and he didn't know how to deal with it. Not the first clue.

CHAPTER

4

"Only you could pull that look off in a club."

August glanced down at her attire at Camilla's comment. "What's wrong with what I'm wearing?"

"I didn't say anything was wrong with it. I said *you* are the only person who could pull that look off in a club, hon."

"Do you know how much I paid for this jacket?"

Just to make a point, August did a little twirl right there on the spot. Holding the jacket open all the while, so that Camilla could get a good look at it while the two of them got ready in her bedroom for the evening.

Camilla laughed. "I *do* like it."

"A *custom* Frankie Zombie."

And *shit*, she loved the damn jacket. It was probably her favorite piece in the whole look, and there was no way she wasn't wearing the hell out of it as much as she could. She would be burning up after a few minutes in the club because of the leather, but oh well.

Beauty *was* pain.

The contrast between the two girls couldn't be more obvious with Camilla in her slinky, black club dress that fell tightly against her curves, and showed off all kinds of leg. Her pixie-like features had been painted seductively with dark kohl and mascara lining a smoked-out eye, and a bright, red lip. Letting her light hair hang loose, it settled in soft waves down her back.

The red-soled six-inch stilettos on her feet, showing off freshly painted toes, would have more than one person giving Cam second looks in the club, and her husband a raging headache from glaring right back. That was the thing, though, Camilla *loved* attention.

Lived for it.

Men or women, she was game.

Well … August supposed that Cam *used to be* game for it. Now that she was married, Camilla stuck to one man, and didn't chase a good time as much as she used to.

As for August, she went with distressed, black skinny jeans that she had rolled up around the ankles to show off the black, strappy three-inch heels on her feet. Under the custom, leather Frankie Zombie jacket with graffiti covering every single inch, she settled for a spaghetti strap, black silk camisole that hung loosely around her body, and showed just a sliver of her stomach.

She had chosen to go for a similar, dark, smoked-out makeup look, but with slightly less kohl lining her brown eyes than her friend, and a russet lip to compliment the golden undertones of her dark skin. As for her braids, she had gathered them with a snag-less tie at the nape of her neck, and secured it in a thick pony.

She wasn't dressed in *typical* club apparel, but that was fine, too. Normal was *boring* … well, as long as you weren't Camilla, because that bitch could make anything fucking work for her, and still turn heads while she did it.

"You wanna pick something from my collection for jewelry?" Cam asked. "I've got more than enough to share."

Understatement.

Camilla's walk-in closet could make a boutique store jealous. Any woman who appreciated the finer things in life would give their firstborn for the chance to go on a free shopping spree in Cam's things. She had expensive taste, too.

August shrugged. "Better not. I drink, and things start getting lost."

Her friend wouldn't care, she knew, but August did.

"I mean, that's fair."

Their laughter in the bedroom must have gained the attention of Camilla's husband down the hall in his office, because soon enough, he darkened the doorway. August noticed him first from her position sitting on the end of their four-poster, canopy bed. A small, amused smile tugged at the corner of his lips as he watched his wife lean over her dresser to get a better look at the line of her lipstick in the mirror.

"Can't draw a straight line on this bottom lip to save my fucking *life*," Camilla muttered.

"Just like the good old days, yep."

Tommaso chuckled darkly in the doorway, gaining the attention of his wife when she swung around in those towering heels of hers. "Now, don't go getting her worked up and remembering *that* time in her life, August, or she might run off on me to do it all over again."

"I would *not*, Tom."

"Mmhmm."

Camilla gave him a simpering smile. "And even if I did, you would chase after me."

"This is true. Are you nearly ready? Your lipstick looks fine."

All it took was a compliment from her husband for Camilla's dark eyes to light up, *pleased*. "Just about, yeah."

"Good." Stuffing his hands in his pockets, Tommaso used his shoulder to rest against the doorjamb as he added, "We should go over the ground rules for tonight."

Camilla gave him a look. "This *again*?"

"What does that mean?"

Neither of the two glanced August's way.

"It's just a club, Tom."

Tommaso nodded. "And at the same time, I want to be safe. Or rather, *you* to be safe, and you know, have a good time. We can't do that if someone causes an issue, right?"

"Don't patronize me."

"I'm not."

"A little," Camilla retorted.

"*Cam.*"

Her friend rolled her eyes, and waved a hand. "*Fine*, go over the ground rules again, if it makes you feel better."

"It will." Tommaso raised a brow, daring his wife to reply with one of her smartass comments to that statement, but Camilla chose to keep her mouth shut. August was still sitting on the edge of the foot of the bed, trying to understand what she had missed. "All should be quiet on the east end—we put word out, so nothing should happen. The streets have been quiet over there the last week, anyway."

"And those *rules*?"

"Cam."

"Just say them, Tom."

"No leaving the club without the group. Not for a smoke, or a breather, or *anything*. Someone goes to the bathroom, then someone else has to go which shouldn't be a problem for you women, because you piss in packs, anyway."

"*Tommaso.*"

He shrugged. "Deny it, Cam."

Well … *he was right.*

"Don't accept randomly sent drinks," Tommaso continued on, "and try not to wander off alone. That'll keep everyone mostly together, and we're less likely to be a target for the gang that has been causing issues with the crew on the east end while we're at the club tonight."

Ah.

Right.

Now it made more sense.

The mafia.

Again.

Camilla looked August's way, clearly noting her silence on the matter. "He's just being … overly precautious."

"Yeah, I know."

It wasn't that as much as it was the fact, they had to be careful at all. Yet another reminder to August that while she was around her friend, and their people, she couldn't pretend like that other side of life—the darker side—didn't exist.

It was very real.

They were living it.

Camilla hung halfway over the bar as she waved at the female bartender down the way. "Hey, Marci, can I just—"

"All on the house, Cam," the chick called back. "Get whatever you need, girl."

A sly smile light up Camilla's features as she glanced at August from the side. "It pays to know people."

August nodded. "Or it pays to be the wife of the next Outfit boss."

"Well, that too."

Their laughter was drowned out by the loud scratching coming from the DJ booth when the man started a new record. The place was *banging.* Even August had to admit that, and she wasn't much of a club-goer since Camilla left New York after getting married. She focused more on college, and her career, than drinking and having fun.

Now, with the swaying lights overhead, the strobes pointed on the DJ in his large, glass-encased booth, the music pumping a familiar tune under her feet that made her want to dance, and the promise of liquor coming soon … well, August was happy to be back.

Camilla practically climbed over the bar, drawing in a whistle from a couple of men—who looked like frat, fuck boys, to be honest—down the way. Her friend ignored the catcalls, and August bet Tommaso was nearby, seriously considering if he could get away with murder in the packed club.

Nothing new to see here.

August took in the club, and the layout again while Camilla found the specific brand of whiskey she wanted on the built-in shelves behind the bar. Glossy, hardwood floors vibrated under her heels. Although up high, the club had an industrial look what with the exposed metal ceilings, and pipes running overhead. Large, bare bulbs provided some light, but the rest was compliments of the light setups over the twenty-five-foot-long bar, and the DJ booth.

At the back of the club, one could find hallways that led to bathrooms for the patrons, a set of offices, and storage. On the east side of the club, the VIP section sat on a raised platform, secured by the same kind of silver, metal bars that crisscrossed the ceiling. There was very little sitting area outside of the VIP, which seemed to be fine for the patrons, because they were much more interested in drinking and dancing.

August knew the feeling.

The club was designed for fun—all kinds of it.

Her stare was still scanning the people dancing on the floor when it came to a stop on a group near the entrance of the club. She recognized two faces in the group that flooded the space—Joe and Cory Rossi, the owners of the club, and cousins to Tommaso, Cam's husband. August met them once or twice, in previous visits to her friend, not to mention they had been in the wedding party when Cam and Tom married.

But it wasn't the Rossi brothers—who were impossible to miss with their impressive sizes, inked skin, and severe stares that said they were appreciating their hard work in front of them—but rather, the two men to their left.

Identical men.

Twins.

August blinked again.

My God.

They were handsome, the twins. Their dark brown hair had been cut in matching high fades, which only accentuated sharp cheekbones and chiseled jawlines when they turned their profiles to the side—at the same time, although in opposite directions. Their identical mouths, pulled down into a frown, showed full lips, and just a day or two worth of scuff.

Leather jackets.

Dark wash jeans.

Converse.

Oh, their clothes didn't match exactly, sure, but they still wore a similar style. And when the one on the left raised his right hand to run his fingers across the nape of his neck while he surveyed the club, the twin on the right did the same with his opposite hand. Except … they hadn't looked at one another. They didn't know either of them were doing that gesture.

Wow.

August had never been more interested in watching other humans until that moment. And yet, despite their matching good looks, her gaze was drawn to the twin on the left more than the one on the right. He filled out that leather jacket and jeans *fantastically.* That was an understatement, really. Strong thighs, a broad chest, and wide shoulders.

Shit, yeah.

Handsome really didn't do him justice. And she bet he would look even better if he was wearing nothing at all, and looming over her in a bed.

Yep.

Damn.

She went there *fast*.

She couldn't help but notice how the two brothers' body language spoke of discomfort. They angled their stances toward one another, and yet turned their heads *away*. As though they didn't want to look at one another, or talk, and yet they still wanted to be together at the same time.

Strange, she thought.

And kind of cute.

She wondered what that must be like—to have an identical twin; to look at your face in someone else's every single day of your life.

Different, she imagined.

Then, all at once, as though he felt someone staring at him, the twin on the left turned his head slightly, gaze cutting to the bar, and *August*, in a breath. His stare landed on hers, holding tight enough to make her chest constrict with the intensity she found behind his dark irises. She sucked in a quick breath, electricity dancing over her skin when his stare lingered a beat longer on hers before he then took in the rest of her.

A *slow* perusal.

He didn't try to hide it at all.

And every inch of her felt it.

By the time his gaze lifted to meet hers again, August was sure there was a red flush to her cheeks. She hadn't meant to stare at him, but with his twin at his side, it was hard *not* to notice the gorgeous man. And it didn't seem to matter because he clearly didn't mind her staring. Not when he had no problem with looking right back, and appeared to enjoy what he found.

Or, that's what his sexy smirk said.

Goddamn.

Was it hotter in here?

It felt like it.

The man across the club quirked up a single eyebrow, tilting his head to the side with an almost silent question that she swore whispered over her skin without him ever having to say a single word. It sounded like *do you like what you see?*

August cocked a brow right back at him.

The response prompted the twin on the left to flash perfect, white teeth in a grin that had her stomach doing flipflops. His tongue peeked out to touch the corner of his upper lip that curled in his amusement.

And *wow*.

Her heart skipped beats.

"Found someone you like?"

Her staring contest with the strangely beautiful twin across the room was broken when August turned to find Camilla grinning at her side. A bottle of her favorite whiskey in hand, and a whole line of shot glasses already lined up on the bar, she must have been standing there enjoying August's little show for a while.

She wasn't even ashamed.

"Who is *that*?" August asked, not bothering to look the twins' way again.

"The one on the right is Bene—Benedetto. The left, or rather, the one now coming your way looking like he wants to take a bite out of you, is Beni—Benito."

"How can you tell the difference?"

"The leather bracelets they wear. Bene's is always on his right, Beni on his left. The same position they always stand next to each other. And he really is coming your way. Use their nicknames, they prefer it. Oh, and don't mention the strange twinness things they do. They really can't help it, and don't even realize when they're doing it."

"Coming my wa—"

"Smile, Aug," her friend murmured, "because he looks like he's a man on a mission, and from the rumors I have heard ... you want to be the woman his attention finds. *Smile*."

"Cam—"

"I'll just leave this with you, and go find Tom," her friend interjected, handing the bottle of whiskey over but taking two shot glasses full of the amber liquid for herself. "And have fun!"

"Cam!"

Her friend was already walking away.

August watched her go until—

"*Ciao*."

Oh, wow.

His voice.

She knew it was him without even needing to turn around to *see* him. Because his voice caused her skin to pebble with goosebumps, and her heart picked up speed all over again. His close proximity had her body heating up like nothing else, and a grin started to form on her lips as she nibbled on her bottom lip.

"You here with someone?" he asked.

August squeezed her eyes shut for a moment, still not ready to turn around. If she did it before she was ready, she would probably embarrass herself, and that was not what she wanted to do here. Not by a long shot.

"Just my friends," she said.

"Cam, yeah. Her husband is a friend. Your name?"

August finally decided to turn around, then, coming face to face with a man who looked like the gracious and good God above had spent just a little more time creating him. Up close, it was far more apparent to her just how beautiful he was.

Strikingly so.

"August Rivera," she said.

He held out a hand.

She took it.

And that heat?

Only burned *hotter*.

"August," he said, as though he were tasting her name in his mouth. And goddamn, it sounded good coming out of those full lips. "Beni."

"Cam let me know."

"Did she?" He winked. "Can I get you a drink?"

She waved that bottle. "On the house—I'll get you one, how about that?"

"I do like a woman that wears Frankie Zombie, *and* gets her own drinks."

Yeah, wow.

She was fucked.

August knew it already.

"How much did that custom cost you?" he asked.

August turned a bit, showcasing the strap near the buckle on the side of the leather jacket with Frankie Zombie's custom graffiti that spelled out PAY FOR ART. "Exactly what the artist thought it was worth, you know?"

Beni nodded. "I respect that."

"So, a drink?"

"Absolutely, *bella*."

Beautiful.

She knew just enough Italian to know a compliment when she heard one, thanks to her father, and Camilla's family.

"And then," he said, leaning in a little closer while his grin deepened into something wickedly sinful. His position gave her a better whiff of the cedar and smoky scent of his cologne mixed in with the leather of his jacket. The smell was mouth-watering—*intoxicating*. Everything this man was all rolled into one, delicious scent. "… what might I be able to do to make this night better for *you*?"

August didn't even have to think about it. "A dance."

"You got it, baby. Whatever you want."

~

Beni was *gorgeous*. No doubt about it. His body fit perfectly to August's as they moved together on the dance floor, his hips swaying to the beat alongside hers as she held her drink high when their group cheered as the song changed to something with a sexier tempo.

But it was his hands that August liked the very most. The way his hands grabbed tightly to her body, long, strong fingers flexing on her waist or hips … fingertips dragging her cami higher so that the pads of his fingers could skim over her overheated skin.

Yeah.

His hands had her thinking naughty fucking thoughts. Like what he might be able to do with them, if they were between her thighs. Or how his fingers might taste sucking on them while he was fucking her into oblivion. Better yet, if he was using those hands to hold her down as he made her scream into the bedsheets.

Yep.

Those hands of his were made for sinning.

And she wanted to be a sinner.

They ran in the same circles, she realized soon after he dragged her to the dance floor. That's why he and his twin had come to the club—because Tom, Cam, and the rest of their friends were going to be there.

It was great because she didn't have to leave the safety of her friends to chill with the guy she had met. Although, to be fair, she didn't feel unsafe with Beni *at all*. She didn't know where his twin had disappeared to, and he didn't mention him.

So, she didn't ask.

Besides, she was too busy enjoying *this*.

August turned a bit, spinning away from Beni to face him, but he didn't let her get far. In a blink, his hand wrapped firmly around her wrist, that heat from his touch lighting up fireworks all through her body when he dragged her close again.

Only this time, they were face to face.

He came *closer*.

She stared at his eyes, the way they darkened when his gaze drifted to her mouth, and he swallowed hard. He wanted to *kiss her*. And fuck her—*God,* she wanted that, too.

"Do it," she whispered.

It had been a long time since August partook in the club life. Well, since Camilla had been living in New York, and clubs were their scene even while they weren't legal to drink. Fake IDs got them in, they'd have fun, pick up a guy, and head home either with a partner, or alone with each other.

She hadn't done this in a while.

Didn't know if she was doing it right.

Not that it mattered.

It *felt* right.

"If I kiss you," Beni murmured, his tone thick with a promise that sounded oh, so wicked, "I'm not going to want to stop until I get you out of here, and in my bed, baby."

That *baby* again.

She didn't like that, usually.

And yet, she did from him.

August dragged her teeth over her lip before using the tip of her tongue to wet the seam. "That sounds like something I definitely want to do."

"Don't tempt me, woman."

"Scared you can't handle me?"

A warning flashed in Beni's eyes.

Sexy, and dark.

"Is that what it is?" she pressed.

How much more would she have to push before he snapped?

Apparently, not far.

That comment did it.

He tipped his head down, closing the distance between them to get his lips *on her*. And damn, she felt that kiss every-fucking-where. She felt it the moment his mouth crashed with hers, the way his lips moved along her own, coaxing the seam open so his tongue could slip in to war with hers. He dominated the kiss, and she didn't mind letting him, the taste of him and whiskey heavy on her tongue while the noise of the club faded into the background.

She'd *lick* that taste from him.

Suck it from his tongue.

His hand on her waist tightened, dragging her even closer, letting her feel the hard ridge of his erection straining against his jeans, and pressing into her body. His other hand came to rest on the length of her braids, although he seemed to know better than to tug on her hair.

Thank fucking God.

A sexy moan escaped his lips, vibrating into their kiss, and surely making her wet between her legs. How was it possible for her body to feel so needy and *ready* from nothing more than a kiss? That heat had taken over, threatening to drag her under the warmth of this man, and the scent of him soaking into her lungs with every ragged breath she took.

Hungry.

That kiss was hungry.

Between them both.

Beni pulled back a bit, baring his teeth, bottom lip trembling as he murmured, "Are you coming home with me tonight, or not?"

"If I say no?"

"Then, it's no."

She heard his unspoken *but* in there.

"But?"

"I'd still like to see you again, either way."

All right.

"I guess you're taking me home, Beni."

He grinned, mouth opening to speak. It was the sounds of bullets shattering glass over the sound of the club's music that stopped the words from coming. That, and the fact that he took her to the floor, covering her body with his own. Screams echoed all around them.

Friends calling out names.

The music scratched violently before stopping.

"Beni!"

"*Camilla!*"

"*Beni!*"

August was silent.

Shaking.

Beni was quiet and calm in her ear, though, those strong hands of his holding tight, even through her trembling. "It's okay—we're okay."

Were they?

CHAPTER 5

Yup.

Nothing like bullets to make a man's dick shrink.

Although, his cock and dwindling lust was now a background thought as Beni pulled August up from the floor. Mostly because, in his haste to get her on the ground when he first started hearing the gunshots, he had forgotten she was holding a glass with a drink.

"Ow," August mumbled.

He grabbed her hands, pulling them away from her chest so he could see the damage. For the moment, he was more worried about her than the moving people around them. The familiar voices of their friends doing a roll call, checking in on everybody, passed him by as he looked over the scrapes on August's palms.

Not bad.

Not bleeding, really.

Just … *there.*

And that pissed him off.

Not thinking about it, he raised her palms, and pressed quick, soft kisses to each. "Sorry, we'll get these cleaned and wrapped up. I didn't mean to—"

Her shaky breath stopped him from saying more, his gaze drawing upwards to find her staring at him. "It's okay."

Beni still didn't let her go. "Does it hurt?"

"Stings a bit."

"They have creams at the hospital—"

"I don't need to go to the hospital."

"Oh, my *God*, August! Are you all right?"

Beni dropped August's hands, and stepped back in just enough time for the tiny tornado that was Camilla Rossi to step in. His friend's wife was a force to be reckoned with on her good days—he didn't want to find out what she was like in this situation.

He took the chance, while the two girls hugged and whispered between one another, to scan the crowd now getting up from the dance floor to look for his friends. He didn't see his twin right away, but he knew Bene was close.

Just that *feeling*.

It always told the truth, even when his gaze didn't.

Tommaso took over Beni's vision, coming his way with a knot in his brow, and a scowl affixed to his face. "Cops have been called."

"Shit."

To say the least …

"Cory and Joe are making calls," his friend added.

Of course.

"Bene?" he asked about his twin.

"Just headed outside. We're all going to meet on the sidewalk as the cops and shit start showing up. It'll be easier to handle them, if we're in a group together. Less chances of them splitting us up when we're showing a united front."

"Right, right," he agreed.

Tommaso made good points. They always had to consider the official side of shit whenever something bad went down. The less time they spent with cops, the better.

"You good?" Tommaso asked.

Beni nodded. "Yeah, I'm fine."

August, though …

He turned to face Camilla and August who were no

longer hugging. Instead, Camilla was looking over August's scrapes, her lips puckering in her displeasure.

"You should get them checked out," the shorter girl said.

August's flushed, her cheeks tinting red. It was one of the first things he noticed about her—how she *blushed*. No, that was a lie. The first thing he noticed about her as she stood across the room from him was the way she stared, and how, despite probably already being nearly six-feet without heels, she still wore a pair that made her legs look shapely in her skinny jeans.

He loved a woman with confidence enough not to care that she was already tall—nah, she had to put heels on to stand *taller*. And he wanted that kind of woman to be at his side. She had kept staring, though.

So curious, and unashamed.

Beautiful, and *sexy*.

The second thing he noticed was that jacket.

Frankie Zombie.

He'd recognize that piece of art anywhere—even from twenty feet away, in the darkness of a club. And the fact that it was draped over the art that was that *woman* … yeah, shit, it only made it better. His hands had itched to be closer, to *touch* her all the way across the room. And when he cocked a brow at her, wondering if she might invite him over?

Her cheeks pinked.

And she answered *perfectly*.

So, he supposed the blush was the third thing he noticed all in the span of seconds while they stared at one another, but none of it stood out more than the other to Beni. That woman, with an outfit that screamed *edgy* and sex, her curves calling for him, and confidence wafting from her had been more than enough to make him approach her.

And then this happened.

Fuck.

"I don't need to go to the hospital just for a couple of scrapes," August muttered. "Stop it, Cam."

"She's right," Beni said, inserting himself into the girls' conversation whether they wanted him there or not. She *was* going to get her hands checked out because only then would he be satisfied that he hadn't truly done any lasting damage when he took her to the floor. Damn, he hadn't really thought about it; just did it because it was his first instinct to protect her. "You should get them cleaned up, and looked at just in case."

"I'm fine," August told him.

He lifted one shoulder. "It would make me feel better to be *sure*."

August sighed.

Cam shot Beni a smile over her shoulder. "See, even *he* thinks so."

"This is ridiculous."

"*Cautious*," he returned.

August gave him a look.

He returned it.

"Hear that?"

Beni turned at Tommaso's question, listening over the sounds of crying people, and feet crunching against glass. The familiar wailing had him sighing.

"Cops are almost here."

"We need to head outside," Tom told the rest of their small group still inside the club. "Stay together, didn't see anything, don't know anything, and didn't hear anything. Got it?"

Nods answered him back.

Beni and Tommaso followed behind the women in silence as they headed out of the club. Outside, he found the Rossi brothers, still snapping shit into their phones, and his twin. Bene leaned against the brick wall of the club, next to a busted window. One of several, it seemed. Apparently, that must have been the main attack for the drive-by. The front windows of the club.

Bene barely even glanced in Beni's direction when he approached.

"Hey," he said.

Bene grunted under his breath, more interested in glaring down the block.

"You all right?"

His twin hitched a shoulder.

That was it.

Beni might have been annoyed on another night, but today had been bad enough between the two of them. He'd made sure his twin knew he wasn't very fucking happy to find out Bene was leaving through their *uncle*, and not him.

Bene, on the other hand, said nothing.

And now?

Now, he looked pissed.

"What the fuck is your problem?" Beni asked him as the wailing sirens came closer.

Bene glanced his way, but still, said nothing.

"*Well?* Are you going to speak, or keep looking at me like you're stupid?"

"I guess I must be *something*, huh?"

What?

His twin pushed off the wall, passed him by, their shoulders slamming together in his haste, as Bene muttered under his breath, "Whatever, man."

What was going on?

Beni didn't have time to figure it out. Flashing lights colored the streets.

Ah.

The cops had arrived.

～

The murmurs of men in the hospital waiting room lowered to nothing at all when the Outfit boss stepped into the space, his right and left hand men flanking him on either side. It was rare, that outside of a private family dinner, one would get the chance to see the three highest men in the Chicago mob in a room together.

And yet, there they were.

Theo DeLuca stood on Tommas's right. Damian Rossi, the father to Joe and Cory Rossi who owned the shot-up club, stood on the man's left. Despite it being close to twelve at night, all three looked as though they were ready for a full day of business in their three-piece suits.

Beni cleared his throat to gain Tommaso's attention, and nodded toward the man's father—their *boss*—when Tom looked his way. Tommaso whistled low, gaining the attention of the others who hadn't noticed the shift in atmosphere.

Part of his mind was still on August, and the fact a few doors down, a nurse was currently cleaning and bandaging her hands. The other part was on this mess here, and what they would need to do about it. He would see August shortly, he was sure.

For now, he had to handle this.

Tommaso waved a hand, bringing in his cousins, Cory and Joe, before the four of them headed for the three men waiting at the other side of the room. That was the thing about the boss, and his men. They didn't go to *anyone*. Not even if those men were their sons—they had to go to the boss.

Respect, and all.

"What happened?" Tommas asked his son.

Tommaso hitched a shoulder. "The gang shot up the front of the club while we were inside. The Easties."

"How do you know it was the east side gang?"

Theo DeLuca asked the question that time.

Damian stayed quiet—then again, Beni barely ever remembered the man saying much whenever he was in his presence. It could be disconcerting, but Joe and Cory always said that was just their dad, unless, of course, he was in a family situation. Then, Damian was far more likely to open up, and seemed less like a block of ice.

Beni didn't know if that was true.

"Because," Tommaso continued, "word has already made the rounds."

"And," Cory added to Tom's left, "someone outside reported to the cops that when the windows in the car rolled down before the shooting started, they saw some tattoos."

Damian grunted under his breath, cold eyes turning to his youngest son when he asked, "*Gang* tattoos?"

"They described them accurately, so yeah."

"I told you a club on the east end was not a good idea, Joe."

Joe's jaw tightened at his father's comment. "Listen, we put word out on the street that we were going to be around tonight. It's been *only* the east side crew that's had a problem with the gang. They've never struck out against anyone outside of the crew. We didn't have reason to believe tonight would be the night they—"

"You put word out that Outfit people were going to be at the club?" Beni asked.

All eyes turned on him.

He might have cared that he spoke out of turn on another night, but not this one.

"It was a precaution," Tommaso said.

Beni nodded. "And actually, all you did was invite *trouble*."

"Beni—"

"Nah, Tom, that's what you did. You basically put us on a silver platter, and went, *here you go, fuckers, take what you want.*"

Tommaso turned his entire body to angle it in Beni's direction as though the two of them were going to go head to head in two-point-three seconds if one of them moved. He was willing to accept the challenge from his cousin, though, considering the mood he was currently feeling.

"You think *that's* what we did?" Tommaso asked.

"Unintentionally, maybe. Who the fuck puts word out on the streets that Outfit people are going to be at a club, anyway?"

"We do," Joe snapped, "because it's always worked in the past. We control this city, not the other way around. And we intend to keep it that way, so yeah, when we fucking speak, people tend to listen."

Beni scoffed hard. "Except the Easties have been getting more and more violent toward a specific Outfit crew, and here we are, *in* their territory. Like feeding chickens to wolves."

"Hey, hey," Theo murmured, stepping forward just enough to move in between the men. "That's quite enough of that—made men don't do this, but certainly not in public. Back up, and take a breath."

Tommaso arched a brow at his cousin over Theo's shoulder. A silent question of *well?*

Beni still wasn't made. He appreciated they treated him like he was, however. Swallowing back the pride thickening his throat, he muttered, "Apologies, Tom."

"*And?*" Joe snapped.

"Jury's still out for you."

"Fucking—"

"Quite enough of that," the boss said firmly.

All eyes swung back to him.

Tommas sighed, eyeing Beni. "And where is your brother? Because when your father called, I only had news to give him on you. He was not pleased."

"Don't know."

"Excuse me?"

Beni shrugged. "He fucked off somewhere. Probably to a hotel for the night. He's in a mood."

"He isn't the only one, no?"

Yeah, well …

It was only the presence of Camilla behind the boss and his men that stopped Beni from replying to his uncle. She gave him a nod, and waved her hand.

"Excuse me," he said to the group.

They didn't question it, simply stepped aside to let him go. Their conversation about the shooting, and what the plan was from there on out continued behind him, but he was more interested in what Camilla had to tell him.

"She's all done, asked if you were still around," Cam said.

Beni smirked. "Of course, I am."

"Mmhmm." Her sly grin said she knew *exactly* what was going on between Beni and August. Or rather, what he was hoping to continue once he got that beautiful woman out of this hospital, as long as she was still feeling up to it. "I *will* be calling her in the morning, Beni."

"Good."

"Just to check in."

"I bet she needs someone to watch her back."

"Not really—she'd feed your balls to snakes, if she thought you deserved it. She doesn't need my help to take care of herself."

Damn.

"Just know," Cam continued, "that if, I call tomorrow morning and she doesn't pick up my call, or she does and she's … in any way unhappy, I will use your blood to paint my husband's office that red color he asked for. We clear?"

Beni chuckled, and then cleared his throat when Camilla's severe gaze met his. These women—clearly best friends in every sense of the word—were not meant to be messed with. Certainly not separately, and definitely not when together. "Yeah, Cam, crystal clear."

"Good. Third room on the left."

Cam left him to head back toward the waiting room where her husband was standing with the rest of the gathered men. It took Beni no time at all to find the triage room the nurse had used to clean and bandage August.

Sitting on the edge of a hospital bed, August dug through her small purse in search of something. Although, the second he knocked on the door with two knuckles, she forgot all about her search, and looked up to see him with a wide smile.

"Hey," she said.

Beni stuffed his hands in his pockets, and leaned against the doorjamb. "Hey, yourself. How're those hands of yours, huh?"

She flipped her palms up, showcasing cleaned scrapes, and despite what he thought … *no* bandages. It really wasn't that bad.

"Maybe I overreacted in having you come in," he said.

"Maybe?"

"Better safe than sorry."

August's smile softened. "Yeah, I guess. So, hey …"

"Hmm?"

Her cheeks flushed again.

Beni grinned.

He knew what was coming.

Better for this woman to just *ask* for it. Or demand it, whatever.

He was up for both.

"Is your place still up for—"

"Absolutely," he said, "as long as you're up to it, August."

She peeked up again through those dark, thick lashes of hers. At some point, she must have removed the band from her braids keeping them back in a pony, because now they hung loosely down her back, nearly reaching the bed.

She really was something else.

So fucking beautiful.

"Well, I am free to go anytime," she said.

Beni laughed. "Don't need to tell me twice, baby."

Beni barely remembered entering his apartment. He couldn't even recall how he managed to get August down the hall to his bedroom without hitting a wall, or shit, *falling*. He was too focused on her, how she kissed him, and the way she sounded when he bit that racing pulse point on her throat.

Her lily and sugar scent felt like a perfect mix of her—sensuality, and sweetness. A dichotomy, if there ever was one, but damn him, if it didn't fit her amazingly. He took the chance to admire the soft lines of her delicate shoulders, and the peek of her collarbones under the silk cami when she pulled the leather jacket down her arms, and tossed it to the chair in the corner across from his bed.

She needed to be appreciated.

Admired.

Even when dressed.

Because *look at her*.

God, look at her.

"What are you doing?" she asked.

Beni tipped his head to the side, taking in the slope of

the anticipation he could see in her inviting smile. "Memorizing you."

"Why?"

"Beautiful things deserve admiration, that's all."

"Is it?"

"Hmm?"

"Is that *all*?"

Beni lifted one shoulder. "No, I also like to take my time. *Learn*, if you will. All the things that'll make you crazy, get you screaming. So, one thing at a time, August."

"One thing at a time," she echoed.

He stepped forward, closing the distance between them, letting his hands slide up her arms while he tasted the spot beneath her ear with his kiss.

"Because that's how I'm going to fuck you, August," he murmured in her ear, "so damn soft at first, letting you get a taste of me, feeling how I can fill you and stretch you out, and how *good* it's going to be. Then it's going to come a little faster, so I can get your thighs shaking around me, and that pretty skin of yours heated when I touch it. And so you're ready to beg for it then, see, so it's going to feel amazing when I fuck you harder to make you come just for *me*."

His dark laughter spilled against her cheek before his teeth were grazing her jawline. "Because that's what really gets me off—watching *you* get off."

"*God*, yes. Do *exactly* that, please."

Beni's chuckles burst along the seam of her lips before he kissed her, his fingers cupping her cheeks as he pulled her down to his king-size bed. They were all legs and arms, then, tangled together as his hands rushed under her shirt to explore with his palms, and she grinded herself against the erection beneath his slacks.

All her sweet little sounds fell into his mouth. She was already so fucking responsive like this, before he'd even stripped her of her clothes, and that made his fucking mouth water. She was delicious, this woman … from the taste of her mouth, to that salt on her skin, and as he moved lower, he swore *sinful* became something he could taste.

And August knew what she wanted, head tipping up so her gaze could meet his as he hooked his hands into the front of her jeans. "Are you going to eat me, too?"

"Fucking, *yeah*."

Her dark eyes flashed. "Don't forget to give me a taste, too."

Goddamn.

Some-fucking-how, his dick became harder just like that. Painfully so, really. He loved a woman that could give as good as she got in bed—there was nothing like finding a partner in sex that could match your energy.

That shit was *gold*.

And he found it.

In her.

Beni yanked the button on her pants apart, uncaring how roughly he pulled apart the zipper, before tugging the item down her thighs. He found nude cotton trimmed with lace detail covering the apex of her thighs. The fabric soft under his fingertips as he ran the digits along her hip bones. Her hot little gasp filled his ears when he bunched his fingers in the material to get a handful, ready to pull them down, too.

He didn't, though.

Only for a second.

Just long enough to say, "And make sure I hear *every* sound I get you to make. Yeah?"

August nodded quickly. "Yeah, Beni."

He dragged those cotton panties down her thighs, peeling them away from the part of her that he wanted to see the most. A patch of trimmed, dark hair led to heaven between her legs. And without shame, she spread her legs for him when he pulled the panties away from her completely. He wasn't even sure where they landed on the floor, honestly.

Because he was too busy getting down to where he wanted to be the most. At her pussy, getting a taste of that sliver of wetness he could see at her slit. August's hands slid around the under sides of her thighs, her manicured nails grazing over her pussy before she spread herself a little more for him.

"*Fuck*," he groaned. "Look at that pussy of yours, baby. It's fucking *beautiful*. And begging for me to eat it, huh?"

"*Please*."

He didn't make her wait a second longer. First, of course, he got that taste of her he wanted. His tongue working her slit while the tartness of her slick pussy flooded his mouth. *That taste*—his dick was back to wanting to punch a hole through his fucking jeans. He could happily have sat there and licked off the taste of her for hours, her flavor *that* arousing to him, but he wanted to hear the sounds she made when he—

"Holy *shit*," August breathed when his tongue found her clit.

Yeah, that's what she liked.

His tongue beat a fast rhythm against her pulsing clit while his fingers slid between her thighs to play with her pussy. That slick heat of hers hugged his fingers tight, and her hips jerked up against his mouth when he curled the digits against her G-spot.

"*Beni!*"

God, yeah, he found all of this woman's buttons.

Just like that.

Beni's gaze lifted up to find August watching him with a wild, *almost-there* gleam in her eye. The way her chest heaved with fast breaths before her head tipped back, and he felt her pussy milk his fingers while her clit swelled under his tongue with *heat.*

"Oh, my God," she mumbled.

Every inch of her shook through that orgasm, and Beni soaked it up. Each fucking second of watching her body tense, her face lax with bliss, and free falling because of *him* … yeah, he took that in like the happy fucker he was.

His hands slid up the backs of her thighs as he pulled back from her, moving up to his knees again, so he could watch her better while she trembled her way through the aftershocks of that orgasm. She reached for him, then, her hands fast and rough against him as they shed what remained of his clothes between them.

He pulled back after kicking off his pants and making sure to grab a condom from his bedside table, only to enjoy the sight of her laying back for him on the bed again. Her nude bralette, a lacy fabric that matched the trim of those panties he took off her earlier, a beautiful contrast against her skin.

Her hand brushed over her breast pulling back the lace, so she could tweak her nipple. He came back to climb between her thighs again when she looked up at him looming over her. Tossing that condom beside her so he could admire her for a second, he grinned lazily.

"I knew it," she said, her voice airless.

"Hmm?"

"That you'd look damn good looming over me naked."

Beni laughed a dark sound. "That so?"

"*Yep.*"

This woman …

She made him want to think and do crazy things.

"How do you want to be fucked, huh?" His hands trailed over her thighs again, his hard cock jutting out to tell her just how bad he fucking wanted her. She reached for his length, still playing with her breast with the other hand. Her fingers wrapped around him *tight*, and she stroked him as he said gruffly, "Tell me what *you* want."

"So good," August whispered back, her grip tightening on the head of his cock. "I want you to fuck me so good."

"Oh, it's going to be *that*."

He snatched the condom up from the blanket, and shifted to his knees between her legs so that he could open the foil packet. She let his cock go long enough for him to roll the latex down his length before she was palming him again. He let her, but he still moved over her, hands keeping him steady on either side of her body, while he kissed her.

She worked him between her thighs, rubbing the tip of his cock at her slit while rolling her hips into him *teasingly*.

"Keep doing that," he warned, "and see what it gets you."

"Maybe that's what I want."

She rolled her hips up once more, and let the head of his cock stretch out the entrance of her pussy. "And you know how I want it—exactly like you said."

He did just that.

Filled her slow at first, with short thrusts that ensured she felt every inch of his cock stretching her open for him. And damn, she was wet for him, pussy eager and *greedy*. It was only when she shivered at the feeling of his hands pinning her hips to the bed as he filled her full, that he stilled for a moment.

Just to stare between them, see only the root of his cock flush against her sex, and the way her body rocked into him to get just a bit of that friction.

"Look at *you*," he rasped, gaze tearing up her body to meet hers. "You're a fucking *angel*."

August simpered him with a smile. "Definitely *not* that."

Sure felt like it.

"*Fuck me*," she demanded.

He did, giving her the second bit he'd promised—started a fast pace between them that had her reaching for purchase against his back. Those fingernails of hers raked stinging lines in the ridges of his shoulders as he fucked her harder.

Her taste was in his mouth.

The scent of sex clung to the air.

All her sounds, they *filled* him. The high, broken gasps and moans burrowing deeper into his skin with heat and *need*. That want, it was so vicious, and *hungry*. He couldn't explain it, but he had never wanted anything more than he wanted to watch this woman come for him while his cock was buried nine inches in her pussy.

"Come on, baby," he urged between thrusts, "show me what you fucking got. Give me what I want—fucking *come*."

She whined through clenched teeth.

He just had to kiss her again.

There was something sexy about the way her lips trembled against his when they moved in tandem with his kiss. Something *hot* in her whimper when her body tensed before a thick cry of his name burst from her mouth.

Her brown gaze flew wide.

Locked on him.

He fucked her through that orgasm, too. A ball of tension grew in his spine, but it wasn't uncomfortable. Quite the opposite—it felt like release was coming, and it just made him fuck her harder.

Chase that high.

Get *off.*

"*Come on,*" he heard her whisper in his ear, "*you* give it to *me.*"

Fuck.

He came *savagely*.

It deafened him.

His heart stuttered.

And August sighed, *pleased*, against the grunt of her name that fell from his lips.

"Mmmm," she hummed along his cheekbone. "*That* was fucking good."

Beni laughed, entirely out of air. "I sincerely hope you're not planning to leave tonight."

She tipped her head back, those glittering eyes of hers on only him. "Why is that?"

"Because it's going to be awfully hard to repeat that by myself in the morning."

Her sexy smirk had him winking.

"Good point."

"So that's a yes? You'll stay the night?"

"If you get my wrap from my bag, then yes."

"Your wrap?"

"In my bag," she said, her fingertips coming to drift along the slope of his nose. "It's silk."

Beni didn't question her—not what the wrap was for, what difference it made if she had it, or why she wanted it to sleep in his bed. He simply pulled away from her, feeling the loss of her heat envelope his cock, and reached for the boxer-briefs he'd discarded earlier. He made quick work of tossing the condom to the trash next to his bedside table, and pulled on the underwear before leaving the bedroom, and the sexy woman giggling on his bed, behind.

He found her bag.

And the rather *large* silk wrap—which looked more like a three-by-three-foot square of silk with a teal and pink wave pattern across both sides—that had been folded up neatly inside the purse. August brightened with a smile at the sight of him coming into the bedroom, wrap in hand.

"This?"

"That," she agreed with a nod.

He fell beside her on the bed after handing it over, and

then thoroughly enthralled at the way she gathered her braids at the nape of her neck, was surprised to see her use the silk fabric to wrap her hair into a bun at the same spot, and then proceeded to use the rest of the square to wrap the top of her head as well.

"Cotton pillows are *really* hard on my hair," she said.

"You look beautiful."

And she did.

Her teeth dragged along her bottom lip. "Oh?"

"Yeah, and even better because you're in my bed."

That wasn't a lie.

August shook her head, and laughed that sweet, sexy sound. "Boy, you got a lot of charm on you, huh?"

"They say it's a *Guzzi* thing. All Guzzi men are the same, at the end of the day. Not sure that's true, but we are a prideful bunch."

"What's that?"

"Guzzi?"

"Mmhmm."

"My family name."

"It sounds important."

"Powerful," he returned.

She considered that.

He let her.

"Like Rossi powerful?"

Smart woman.

Asking about his connections or affiliations without outright saying *mafia* or *mob*.

Beni nodded. "Exactly that."

August fell back in the bed beside him and quirked a brow. "Well, *lucky me.*"

Nah.

Didn't she know?

"Tonight, it's lucky *me,*" he said.

CHAPTER

6

It was the constant buzzing behind August's head that had her sleepy eyes blinking open to an unfamiliar room. Her hand stretched across the empty space next to her in the comfortable bed, meeting air where a warm body should be. She couldn't be mad at Beni's lack of presence, not when she could smell something *delicious* cooking outside of the bedroom, daring her to make her way out of bed to find what it was.

Oh, and the memories from the night before.

Yeah.

She definitely couldn't forget those.

A pleased, small smile pulled at her lips while she rolled to her back, and stretched in the bed. With white stucco staring back at her, she tried to figure out what that buzzing which woke her up had been, but the room was silent.

That was okay, too.

It smelled like *him*.

And now, just a touch of her on the bedsheets.

Hookups didn't usually last this long for her, and more often than not, she preferred to have it happen at *her* place. Then, she knew all the places where she had something hidden to protect herself, if need be, and she decided when someone left.

Yet, this hadn't bothered her at all.

She was feeling good.

So fine.

That grin curved her lips as she flipped over in the bed to find her bag that Beni brought into the room, and set on the bedside table before they fell asleep the night before. The tenderness between her thighs—the ache—reminded her of what it felt like to have a hard fucking, and she would be lying if she said she wasn't ready for round two.

And she wasn't a liar.

A buzz vibrated her purse, and all at once, August knew *exactly* what had woken her up. *Shit.* She reached for the device in the bag, fumbling through the disorganization that was her life shoved into her purse, until she found the phone she had set to *vibrate only.* Without bothering to check the caller ID, she didn't need to anyway, she answered the call with a tired, "August here."

"Oh, my *God.* Do you not know how to pick up your phone?"

She couldn't help but laugh at Camilla's exasperation. "How many times have you called?"

"Three."

"That's three times too many for …" August pulled the phone away to squint at the screen until the time came into focus. "Seven in the damn morning, Cam, come on."

"*Well …*"

"What?"

"That was always our thing, you know? It's been a while since one of us left with someone from a club and all, but I still figured I should call, make sure you were good, and whatnot."

August hummed under her breath. "I am *very* good this morning."

A knowing giggle answered her back.

"And safe," August added, knowing that's what her friend wanted to hear the most. "All is good, no worries, girl."

"Yeah?"

"Mmhmm."

"Well, good. Not that you wouldn't have kicked his ass, if he tried anything stupid with you, but I wanted to make sure."

God knows it, she thought.

August had been able to take care of herself for as long as she remembered. She *had* to. Life hadn't given her another choice, really. Some people saw her as an easy target, and she had to learn how to handle herself in *many* unpleasant situations. Men didn't scare her. They were just ... typical assholes, normally.

Well, some.

Not Beni, it seemed.

"And thanks for watching my back."

"Always," Camilla said quietly. "Do you want to meet up later?"

"How about lunch?"

Because she had a feeling that delicious scent wafting in from the opened bedroom doorway was Beni cooking *her* breakfast—or that's what she was hoping, anyhow. She wasn't about to cut that short, not if it meant she had the opportunity to get in a round two with that man before she left his place.

"Lunch is good. I'll text you the address to a place I like in the city. Okay?"

"You got it. Later, babe."

"See you later, Aug."

Click.

August rolled to her side again, grabbing the bag from the bedside table, and dropped her phone inside. She also grabbed her small *kit*, as she liked to call it, which was really just a small makeup bag with a few trial-sized hygiene items, a clean pair of panties, and extra cash as a *just in case*. She always kept it in her purse, whether she got stuck in an airport, or she had a night like the one before.

It was good to be prepared.

Or, that's what her ma liked to say.

Ada.

Yeah, she had to call her *mom*, too. She promised to keep her updated on how she was doing in Chicago, otherwise her mother would get worked into a panic. With a mental note in her mind to do exactly that when she had time later in the day, she forced herself out of that comfortable bed as her bladder was making itself known, used the sheet on the bed to wrap around herself, and picked up the clothes that were now in a neat pile on the chair in the corner.

Had Beni done that?

He really *was* sweet.

August made quick work of using the bathroom, noting how the vanity held a side for each man that lived in the apartment. She had to blink at the way their things had been set up on the counter—identical on each side, and all items in the same location.

By the time she was done pulling on her clothes—including a clean pair of panties—splashing her face with water, brushing her teeth, and fixing the wrap in her hair as it was better to just keep it on for now, she heard the sizzling pop of bacon in a frying pan when she came out of the bathroom. She followed the aromas guiding her down the hallway until she came to stop in the entryway of the small apartment kitchen.

The man at the stove with his back to her, and black boxer-briefs riding low on his hips had her clearing her throat, and grinning a bit when he tensed at the stove. *Ha*. She had managed to sneak up on him.

Well, at first she was amused.

Then, he turned around.

Cocking a brow at her, a man who *looked* like Beni with a spatula in his hand didn't bother to hide the slow perusal of her standing in the doorway. It really *was* uncanny how much the twins looked alike. Clearly, they were identical, but she had met other twins before in her lifetime. Not all twins mirrored each other perfectly in everything from looks, to behavior. Sometimes, it was just an inch or two of height. Sometimes the color of the eyes would be slightly different. Or even the way their features rested in a neutral state.

These twins, though?

A woman could easily mistake one for the other, and not realize it.

Except her, apparently.

"Morning to you," he said, the corner of his mouth quirking up in a smirk. "Wondered when you were going to crawl out of bed."

Not *my* bed, she noticed.

How long would he pretend?

Not for long, she decided.

"Bene," August greeted, not unkindly.

His grin deepened, and while it didn't feel *mean* … she also thought it felt like this man didn't like her, or perhaps, didn't appreciate that she was here. A part of her doubted that the twins were unaccustomed to each other bringing women home for a night, so it couldn't possibly be that. So, what was the problem?

"How did you know it was me?" he asked.

August pointed at the leather band.

On his *right* wrist.

"Someone let me know the secret."

He barked out a laugh. "Of course, they did."

A throat cleared behind August.

And then a firm, "*Bene.*"

She swung around so fast, the white walls, dark-stained

cupboards, and stainless-steel appliances were nothing more than a blur. Behind her, she found Beni standing fully dressed, with a cupholder full of coffee in his hand. Yet, those weren't the things that she noticed first.

No, it was his *stare*.

So hard, and cold as he leveled it on his brother.

"Yeah?" Bene asked, not turning away from the stove again.

"Thanks for watching the stove while I ran down the block. You got a minute?"

"Beni—"

His gaze cut to her, and in a blink, his features softened before he gave her a quick smile. "Sorry I didn't wake you up."

"It's okay."

He nodded, but quickly went back to his brother. "*Now*, Bene."

"Fine, *fuck*." Bene tossed the spatula to the counter, turned off the stove, and removed the pan of bacon to a burner in the back. "It's finished, anyway. *You're welcome*—I basically cooked your piece of as—"

"*Bene!*"

The twin that *clearly* had some issues walked past August in the entryway, who suddenly felt a lot colder than she had a few minutes ago, with his hands held high in the air. Beni gave her another smile, although it felt less true than his first, before following his twin.

Well …

She was eating.

Their shit?

They could handle that.

She needed food.

Not that it made a difference because while she found a plate, and began to fill it with the eggs and bacon from the two frying pans on the stove, the twins' argument filtered down the hall. Loud, and proud, it sounded like. They had to know she could hear.

You like it, I love it, she thought.

Worked for this, too.

If they didn't want her to hear it, they would shut their mouths.

Right?

"What is your fucking *problem*?" Beni snapped.

She only knew it was *Beni* because she remembered that growl of his, and what it felt like between her thighs.

Except now, he was not enjoying it.

Yeah.

August took a seat at the small table and dug into her food while eyeing the entryway. She wasn't a snooper, and she didn't care to eavesdrop. That wasn't her thing, she wasn't nosy. They also weren't trying to hide it, so ...

"*My* problem?" Bene scoffed.

"That's what I said. And what the hell was that? Were you *trying* to make her think you were me, or—"

"Might have worked, too. Better to know, right?"

"*Know* what?"

"You know what," Bene snapped.

"It ain't like *that*, Bene. Jesus Christ. We're not eighteen now—we don't do that kind of shit anymore, you hear me?"

"Yeah, yeah, whatever."

She heard the receding sound of footsteps before Beni barked, "And are you going to tell me why you decided to run back to fucking Toronto without even letting me know about it first? I know that's why you were in your mood last night, too."

"It doesn't matter."

"*It does*!"

"Nah, you showed me it didn't."

"Bene!"

More footsteps.

A door slamming.

It went quiet for a while, and then it was loud again before August watched the two twins pass the entryway to the kitchen without as much as a look inside to her. Just as quickly, those footsteps faded away before the apartment door opened, and slammed shut with a *bang*. Even she tensed in the kitchen chair.

Not twenty seconds later, a very *annoyed* Beni joined her at the table. Although, he didn't get himself a plate, or food.

"This is good," she said, trying to help the awkwardness.

His grin came back out to play.

Yes.

She did love that.

"I'd say thank Bene—because I didn't get the chance to cook it when I had to run out for coffee that I forgot when I grabbed shit to cook this morning, but …"

August frowned. "What's all that about, anyway? Me? I could have been gone before—"

"Not you," he said quickly, leaning closer to her so that he could press a kiss to the line of her silk wrap, and her temple. Her eyes fluttered closed, and she grinned around the piece of bacon she'd just popped in her mouth. "We're just … having a moment. We don't have a lot of those, so when we do, it's *bad*."

"How bad?"

He leaned back in his chair, giving her a nice view of the white T-shirt that stretched across his broad, defined chest from the movement. "We're not used to being apart."

"I heard he's going back to Toronto—that's where you're from?"

"Canadian through and through … well, Ma comes from Chicago. A Rossi, married a Guzzi."

Oh, wow.

Okay, that made more sense about his last name the night before.

Huh.

She thought about the different things she had noticed between the twins. From their similar styles, the matching haircuts, even their *bathroom* ... "You know, it's normal to be two *individuals*, Beni."

He gave her a look.

August shrugged. "I don't know if anyone's told you that or not, but there's nothing wrong with being you, and him being ... *him.*"

Beni's brow knotted.

"What?" she asked.

"We're more like an ... *us.*"

Yeah, but maybe that was part of the problem?

August opted not to say anything.

It wasn't her place.

And her ma would have told her right then and there, *you let others figure out their business, because it's not yours, honey.*

"How long are you planning on being in the city?" he asked.

August smiled. "A bit."

"And that is ...?"

"Three weeks, maybe. My vacation is for another two, but I had a week extra added on for an assignment I'm working on for Bared Brands magazine."

"A journalist?"

She thought about that for a second ...

"Trying to be," she admitted. "That's what I wanted, but something focused on media, and culture, and the effect it has on society. I had a focus, but for the last three years, I've not gone anywhere."

"I don't believe that."

"Well, not for much longer."

All at once, Beni leaned his whole body toward her, filling up her space with his intoxicating presence and scent. He really was *all* man, and she felt it. Every single part of her. He kissed the corner of her mouth, making August let out a pleased hum, in response. She turned her head to the side just enough to catch his lips with her own kiss, and *damn* … it hit her all over as he reminded her just what he could do with nothing more than his mouth and tongue.

Even when it warred with hers.

Too bad it didn't last longer.

"But if you're going to be around," he said, his words whispering over her cheek as she smiled, "then I would *really* like to see you again."

"Me, too."

"Yeah?"

August nodded. "Give me your phone?"

"To plug your number in?"

"Yep. I'm going to be busy for the next week with some locations I want to document, but I'll see what I can do for you after that."

Beni placed a hand over his heart, brown eyes darkening with his amusement. "*Ouch*, I take second to work, that hurts."

August shrugged. "A girl has got to have priorities, that's all."

He didn't even look offended.

"You're absolutely right."

Then, he fished out his phone from his pocket, and handed it over. *Telling* her the passcode to get inside. Now, that was some trust.

August appreciated it.

～

"*So*," Cam drawled as August kneeled on the ground, her Nikon at the ready to capture the *perfect* angle of the mural covering a good portion of the underside of a bridge. "Are we finally going to talk about last weekend, or …?"

August shook her head. "You're doing too much. Trying *too* hard."

Cam laughed. "I mean, come on … you spent the night with a gorgeous man, and you don't even want to tell me about it?"

She got the shot in the frame that she wanted, and held down the shutter of the camera, taking a burst of shots in a spread of seconds. Standing up, and brushing the dirt from her knees, she turned to face her friend.

"You're married now, so do you really want details about my sex life?"

"Um, *yeah*."

August grinned. "You know, I am surprised you lasted this long. I thought when we met up for lunch last weekend, you would mow me over to find out every last thing you could."

"I was trying to let *you* come to me."

Right.

"It was … good."

"*Just* good?"

The slyness to Cam's tone couldn't be missed. August came out from under the bridge, taking note of the towering apartment buildings in the urban neighborhood around them. An area popular in Chicago for the rap scene, and the artists that had come out of it, she knew—without a doubt —this was one of the places she needed to come to and soak in during her trip. Not just for the spread she was working on for the magazine, but also for herself.

There was so much to absorb.

And she wanted it all.

Like the mural—painted by fans of a famous rapper who had grown up just down the street, and got his big break in the nineties during a rap battle that took place in a now-demolished warehouse three blocks away.

The rapper died seven years ago … an undetected heart condition. He was revered by his fans, not just for his music, but also for the legacy he left behind. A *good* man, and his community work had always been a top priority.

His legacy lived on beyond the music people still streamed so much; his tracks regularly made it into the Top 100 lists. Like the murals that continued to pop-up all around Chicago. The city would just remove one, only for another one to be painted overnight in the rapper's honor. *That* was respect.

August wanted to document at least one of the murals during her time in Chicago before it too was gone, like the others. Maybe, if the city stopped removing them, then people would quit defacing property just to prove a point.

But what did she know?

"Well?" Cam asked. "About *Beni*, I mean."

The way her friend dragged out Beni's name like it was dangling a treat for August had her laughing. Camilla was damn *shameless*, but she loved that about her.

"*Really* good," August said.

"Yeah?"

The two shared a knowing grin.

"I told him we could meet up again while I'm here, you know, if I get around to it."

"*Get around to it*, she says," Cam guffawed, "look at that man, Aug."

"I did. *A lot*."

"And you stayed the whole night …"

"Lord," August muttered, peeking up at the sky. "You know I did."

"How was the next morning?"

"I mean, after the other twin had his tantrum and left … not too bad for round two on the kitchen table."

Camilla whistled low. "*Yes*, that's what I wanted to hear."

"I had fun."

"Good. And the twin thing, huh?"

August sighed, packing her camera away. She had an interview a couple of blocks away with the man who had designed the logo for another famous artist's brand, also now passed on, and his legacy a bit murkier. Not that it mattered because the *brand* was what August wanted to focus on, and in Chicago, the music industry and hip hop had been a driving force in the city's culture.

"They've got some issues," she said.

"Really?" Camilla pulled a face. "Because they always seem so … *together*."

"I think that's part of the issue."

"Huh."

The two women were quiet as August finished packing up her things, and then they headed out of the ravine that led them under the bridge. She loved that Camilla was willing to come with her for the work she had to do when she had a day off, as it helped August find her way around a city that she wasn't very familiar with.

"Hey, how much time do you have before you need to meet up with the designer?"

August checked the watch on her wrist. "About an hour, or so."

"Oh, we have time."

"For what?"

"To check out the center Tommaso's aunt opened with Evelina DeLuca for youth in this area. It's part of Manic

Media's Urban Initiative in the city, you know? Gives the kids a safe place to go after school for activities, or tutoring. Whatever they need. Some get signed up by their parents, and some just come with friends. They're not turned away, regardless of how they come."

August passed her friend a look, making a noise under her breath. "Or is this your way of trying to get me to see Alessa again so that she can make me another job offer to work here for Manic Media?"

Not that she was going to tell her friend, but she had already set up a meeting with Alessa. She made it clear it was just to discuss different things, and what she *could* do here, if that's what she decided to step into. However, she didn't want Cam to know about the meeting, or the fact that Alessa's job offer with Manic Media was still very much on the table.

If only because Camilla's excitement and desire to have August live in Chicago would overwhelm her understanding that this would be a huge life change. And not just moving, but her career … *everything*. Alessa, thankfully, agreed to keep the meeting just between them for now, so that August could make rational, smart decisions about her life, and what she wanted to do with it. That wasn't asking for much, right?

She didn't think so.

"No, I just thought … well, you'd appreciate what they're trying to do with the center," Camilla said, "and you know how kids are—they're *way* more in tune with what's happening in media, and with their icons. The center even let some of the popular graffiti artists come in to paint murals on the outside wall, which *did not* please the city, but there wasn't much they could do about it. Private property, all the permits were in place. The kids got to help."

August *did* love that.

"Okay, that's pretty cool."

Camilla nodded. "Right? So yeah, I just thought you

might like to see it. And since we're in the area, you know
…"

"Fine, wear me down."

"Except I didn't really have to wear you down, huh?"

Yeah, not at all.

No shame.

"And if it does make you want to ask Alessa if that job
offer is still on the table for Manic Media," Camilla said,
staring *anywhere* but at August, "then I am just going to
consider that a win, and go on with my happy little life."

Smartass.

"You're lucky I love you."

Cam smiled brightly. "You're right, I am."

Despite the fact that August's mind was now on visiting
the center, and her upcoming interview … her thoughts still
drifted back to Beni, and what he might be up to currently.
He hadn't called or texted her throughout the week, but to be
fair, she didn't mind.

After all, she told him *she* would call.

The two reached Camilla's car parked at the top of the
ravine when August decided to pull out her phone—she
might be busy today, and tomorrow was set for her secret
meeting with Alessa that she needed to get done under Cam's
radar … but after?

Possibilities.

"Who are you texting?" Camilla asked as she pulled open
the driver's door.

"Who do you think?"

"*Ohhhh.*"

"You are literally the worst."

Camilla wagged her eyebrows. "I'm just saying … it
makes me very happy to see you enjoying your time in
Chicago, that's all. Don't judge me."

"Oh, I judge you. *Often.*"

Her friend stuck out her tongue before getting into the car. August stayed *outside* of the vehicle, so that she could at least send the text off to Beni without Cam cooing over her shoulder while she did it. *God*, she loved her friend.

Truly.

Do you have Sunday free? I was thinking we could meet up, maybe.

That was all August typed out.

Beni's response was almost instant, like he had been waiting for her text. Again, she wasn't a liar, so she wouldn't pretend like that didn't appeal to her *a lot*.

Name the time and place, he wrote back.

I'll let you know.

Perfect, bella.

He really was charming.

Amongst *many* other things, too.

CHAPTER

7

"I sincerely hope you're not playing on your phone when we're supposed to be having a meeting here, Beni."

Snickers echoed from the fucking peanut gallery, but Beni took his time looking up from the screen to meet his boss's gaze across the room, before he shut the phone off, and slipped it into his pocket. He could continue his conversation with August later, even if he would much rather be talking to her than doing this meeting.

Everybody's got to make sacrifices.

Next to him, Bene didn't even react to his twin being chastised. A little unusual but considering the tension between the two of them over the last week ... not really.

"Good, now back to the discussion," Tommas said, giving Beni a look before he gestured Damian's way, so they could go over the *new* rules for the east side. "Continue, cousin."

"No major events on the east side," Damian droned on, "no announcements of our presence until we have culled or calmed the issue with the gang and the crew."

The conversation continued, but Beni wasn't that interested. He knew the rules they were setting in place, and the reasons for them. He didn't need to go over them *again*. Besides, he was working on the east side whether or not these rules were followed. His job with the crew wasn't going to change because of this. If anything, it became more important now than ever for him to figure out what in the hell was going on.

"How's that going, anyway?"

The voice behind him—Cory Rossi—had Beni sighing.

"The crew is made up of a bunch of pricks and—"

"Nah, dude, the *chick*. August, right?"

Fuck.

Cory chuckled low enough that the rest of the room couldn't hear him. "Yeah, saw the text over your shoulder. You two were *getting it* at the club, huh?"

Beside him, his twin stiffened.

Beni ignored that.

He didn't know what the fuck was wrong with Bene—or how it tied to August, because it wasn't like this was the first woman Beni messed around with—but his brother needed to get over it. And if he couldn't, then he needed to fuck off and handle his shit elsewhere.

That was his opinion.

"How about you mind your business?"

He swore he could *feel* Cory's smirk when the man murmured, "Got your dick tied in a knot over her already, huh?"

"Knock it off," he warned.

"Have you seen her again?"

Beni was going to punch him in the throat. "No, I let her text me when she wanted to instead of messaging her."

Because he would have texted her the next damn day, but August didn't seem like the type of woman who would appreciate a man asserting his presence onto her just because *he* wanted to. Some chicks liked that, and for others, it made them run.

He figured, better for her to tell him what she wanted.

He could work with that.

"Shouldn't do that," Cory said, "because women are

smart, you know? You can't keep their attention, and they quickly find something else to entertain them, man."

A hot ball of *something* burned in Beni's gut. Not that the emotion made any sense, and he really wasn't interested in indulging the jealousy he suddenly felt. He didn't have a claim on August, and he wasn't about to make a fool out of himself by trying to prove differently.

"Drop it," he said.

"But—"

A throat cleared across the room, thankfully ending Cory's questioning, but bringing Beni's attention to the *other* men who showed up for this meeting. Well, two men, and a woman, even if she was currently downstairs having tea with Abriella Rossi.

His mother, father, and oldest brother, Marcus.

Beni was not expecting to wake up that morning to find his parents, and oldest brother, knocking on his apartment door. Bene, on the other hand, didn't seem at all surprised by their presence, which told him at least one of them knew they were coming.

His father and brother, for the meeting.

His mother because she missed them.

Gian gave Beni a look, raising his eyebrows in a silent comment to *knock it off*. He didn't need to be told twice, because frankly, he had no desire to discuss his situation with August. Not with Cory Rossi, or anybody else, either.

That was for him to handle.

Simple as that.

"Beni," Tommas said, bringing his attention back to the boss, "how has the last week gone on the east side?"

"I've just integrated as a new man for the crew, so no one is really talking … and it's been quiet on the gang side of things. Like maybe they're just trying to let the club incident blow over, or whatever. Wait it out, I guess."

Tommas nodded. "Likely right. Gian, you wanted to discuss … the twins?"

"Mmm." His father folded his arms over his chest where he stood next to Tommas's large desk, but his attention was only on the twins across the room. "Given the situation here and your mother's *concern* … if you would both like to come home to Toronto, at least until the problems here have blown over, in Beni's case—because I don't know if you plan to continue working here for Tommas—then I would understand why."

"And no one would blame either of you," Marcus added, "if you wanted to step away."

Beni didn't even have to think about it. "I'm staying in Chicago."

Again, his twin stiffened.

He continued ignoring the odd behavior, and the heaviness that seemed to be constantly resting on his shoulders and heart lately. He knew that wasn't *his* emotions—it felt different, a bit foreign in his body and mind, if that made sense. It was how he knew whatever his twin was feeling, it projected into Beni.

So that heaviness?

Whatever that was?

Bene was feeling it.

Beni was just getting the tendrils from it.

"I told the boss I would help to figure out what was going on with the crew, and I intend to do that," Beni said.

"And to get your dick wet."

Beni's head snapped to the side so fast, the fucking room *spun*. His gaze nailed to the side of his twin's head, and if it were possible for someone to die from a glare alone, Bene would be on the floor with a still heart.

"What did you just fucking say?"

Bene chewed on the piece of gum in his mouth, staring

at his father, unaffected. "I'm going home like the original plan."

Gian nodded. "All right."

Beni didn't give a fuck. "Seriously, what is your problem, Bene?"

"Hey," Marcus was quick to say.

He ignored his older brother.

"What, you won't look at me, or …?"

"Let's end this meeting here," Tommas said, "and Gian, I will let you handle … *that*."

"Yes, what is that?" Gian asked. "Because that is not normal for them, not at all."

"I don't know. Ask them."

Great.

Beni forced his gaze away from his twin.

The problem?

Now *everyone* was looking their way.

Including his father.

Perfect.

"What in the hell was *that*?" Gian demanded, slamming the door to what seemed to be a spare bedroom behind him after he entered. When neither of the twins opened their mouths fast enough to answer their father, he snapped, "Someone better start talking—*now*."

Marcus cleared his throat, finding a chair in the corner of the room to sit in while Beni and Bene did their best to avoid staring at each other. That heaviness on Beni's shoulders, the projection from his twin, and turned into something else. Something sharper, and *warmer*. He knew exactly what that was—*rage*.

Beni felt it, too.

Except that was his own.

He was ready to snap.

"Ask *him*," Beni muttered, pointing a finger to his right. "Because I'm just as fucking lost as you are, and he's making a problem out of something I don't even understand. All right? Ask him."

Bene scoffed, shaking his head.

"Tell me I'm wrong, then!"

His twin glared his way, replying, "What you are is a fucking—"

"*That is enough.*"

Gian's order silenced the bedroom. Even Marcus stopped fiddling with the button on his suit in the corner chair, and glanced with concern writing heavy lines on his brow. It was not often their father lost his patience, but especially not with his children. And here they were—fucking *adults*, twenty-one-year-old men—and at least one of their parents were still stepping in when they had problems.

Jesus Christ.

"Now, someone," Gian uttered, his jaw tensing with every word, "had better explain why my sons are acting like foolish *boys* in front of another organization when I know they are aware of how to behave. Speak."

"I told you," Beni started to say.

"You didn't even *look* for me," Bene snapped.

Beni's head whipped to the side, his gaze locking onto the mirrored stare of his twin. "*What?*"

"The club—that damn *night*, Beni."

"Are you talking about the shoot—"

Bene turned his entire body in Beni's direction, his finger pointed at his twin like a gun ready to blow as he took one step forward, closing a bit of distance between the two of them. There was *pain* in his features, and rage, too.

God, he was so mad.

Beni *felt* that.

Like an echo in his chest.

He felt it.

"I was looking for *you*," Bene snarled. "I called for fucking *you*, Beni. I was on my feet, hearing the shots, looking for you because that's what *we* do. And where the fuck were you, huh? What were *you* doing, yeah? Because you sure as *fuck* weren't trying to help me like I was doing for you."

No.

Because he'd been on the floor.

Protecting August.

"Didn't give a fuck about me, right," Bene said, his voice rising as he came close enough to shove his brother back a step, "because you were too busy fucking with someone else."

He shoved him again.

Beni came right back for more.

"Hey, hey, *hey*," Gian was quick to yell, crossing the space to step in between the boys. One hand to Beni's chest, and the other on Bene's. Their father, and even their mother, had *never* been afraid to step in when something physical went down with their sons. Maybe it came with the territory— boys fighting, that was—but they weren't scared of it. "Stop it, this is *shameful*, you two. Look at yourselves, huh?"

Marcus was up out of his seat, too, that concern still as clear as day in his stare. "Come on, Bene, we'll go—"

"Fuck off," Bene muttered Marcus's way, and then to Beni, he pointed a finger and uttered, "Fuck *you*, too. You know what you did, Beni."

Just like that, his brother backed away from the altercation, and his father's hand on his chest.

"Two days," Gian told Bene, "be packed and ready to leave with Marcus, all right?"

Bene nodded. "Fine."

Just like that, he was done with it all. Spinning on his heel, he left the room, slamming the door behind him, and leaving Beni with his father and oldest brother. He said nothing, instead absorbing what had just happened, and what it meant.

All at once, this past week of hell with his twin made a hell of a lot more sense. The silence in the room, and in Beni's mind, was deafening. It might seem petty or silly—Bene's problem, that was—but he knew better.

Jealousy was a monster.

And they weren't good with it.

Neither of them.

Jealousy had followed him and his twin for their entire lives. A friend that just got *too* friendly. Someone they spent more time with than their twin. A girl that took up too much of one of their attention.

It wasn't *just* Bene.

Beni had been that way, too.

The difference was, he had grown out of it as they got older, or it seemed like it. Jealousy wasn't something that reared its ugly head with his brother, not as often as it used to, anyway. Apparently, Bene *had not* gotten past that like he had.

"*Figlio*," Gian murmured.

He glanced at his father, saying, "Sorry, I know better than to behave like—"

"It's not about that right now."

Beni swallowed the ache in his throat. "What is it about, then?"

"It's okay to learn how to be two different people, and not just extensions of the same soul, Beni." His father lowered his hand from Beni's chest, too, and fixed the button that had come undone on his jacket in his haste to get in between his feuding sons. "Don't feel badly that you are at a different place than Bene right now, that you have moved into a new space in your life. That's what happens to people. It's normal. *You are not the same men.*"

"Aren't we?"

Gian looked to Marcus.

Marcus only shrugged, openly frowning.

"Beni, you are not the same people. You only look the same. Let him figure it out, too."

Right.

Yeah.

But how?

∾

Yeah.

The following two days were about as uncomfortable and awkward as Beni suspected they would be. It was made worse by the fact that once his mother learned the twins were fighting, Cara decided she was going to stay in Chicago with Marcus to help Bene pack his things, and at the same time, *try* to get the twins to talk.

Wasn't happening.

"Beni?"

"Yeah, Ma?"

Standing at the end of the hallway, his mother bent down to pick up her Hermès bag from the floor, giving him a soft smile. "I wish you two would just *talk* … at least before we leave."

His brother's bags littered the hallway. A good portion of shit had already been shipped out the day before, through a company that would deliver it to the penthouse in Toronto for Bene. He hadn't even bothered lifting a finger to move his twin's shit out.

If that's what Bene wanted, then he could do it.

Alone.

He got that his twin was going through some shit, but it wasn't something Beni could fix, even if he had been the cause of it. That much was *painfully* clear.

Cara sighed, and gave Beni a look. "Well, when are you planning to come home for a visit?"

"Soon," he promised.

"*When?*"

He laughed under his breath.

This was his ma in a nutshell. Her boys were the loves of her life, next to their father, and she was their greatest supporter, and defender. She hated being away from them for any length of time, and already, he had been here for six, going on seven, months now. Sure, he went home for a weekend occasionally, but he knew it wasn't enough for his ma.

"Or … do you like it here?" Cara asked.

Beni had to think about that one. "It's easier, Ma."

"What is?"

"*Business.*"

Cara tipped her chin up, her gaze widening. It wasn't like the *mafia* was hidden in their family, but there were a few unspoken rules that they all tried to follow. Like *not* talking about the business with women, unless it couldn't be avoided. Their ma included.

"How so?"

Beni shrugged. "Marcus … Chris, and even Corrado, though he's not in the business like we are because he does his own shit, they never had the problem I did."

"Which was …?"

"I couldn't separate him in my mind. I couldn't … differentiate, Ma."

"Your father, you mean."

Beni nodded once. "I couldn't switch back and forth with

him—my dad, my *boss*. It was fucking me up, but here, it's easier."

"But do you *like* Chicago?"

"I do."

Cara gave him a soft smile. "Well, then I suppose that's what's most important. I want you to be happy, Beni. You know that, don't you? No matter what you have to do to be happy, that's all I want for you."

"Yeah, I know, Ma."

She came down the hall, then, arms already outstretched to take her son in her embrace. He let her, soaking in the familiar warmth and smell of his mother, even as her arms squeezed tightly enough around his neck that he thought she might take away what remained of his air.

"I love you," his mother said.

Beni kissed her forehead. "Love you, too, Ma."

It was at that moment Bene and Marcus decided to come around the corner, a bag in each of their hands. The last bit of shit that Bene had left in his bedroom. Cara stepped away from her son with another smile, turning to her other boys with a nod.

"I will be in the car, then," she said.

"We'll be right down, Ma," Marcus replied.

Bene cleared his throat, passing a look back at his twin at the end of the hallway. "Actually, I think I'll walk down with you."

"You should have a minute with—"

"I'm good."

"*Bene.*"

Beni said nothing, simply arched his brow at his twin, and waited Bene out. One way or the other, his twin was going to have to work this shit out, and if he was going to do it alone, then so fucking be it.

Coldness stared back.

Shocker.

"Later," Bene murmured.

Beni nodded. "Drive safe."

Without another word, Bene snagged up a handful of bags in his empty hand, and stepped out of the opened apartment door with their mother leading the way. That just left Marcus, the one bag he held, and the three others left sitting on the floor which he easily managed to lift.

"You all right?" his brother asked.

Beni folded his arms over his chest. "Why wouldn't I be?"

"Change is hard."

"I wouldn't know."

Marcus gave him a look.

Beni's expression didn't falter.

His older brother gave one last look at the apartment hallway before saying, "Be safe here, huh? Don't make me come back here just to collect your fucking remains. I wouldn't forgive you for that, Beni. Ma, either."

"Don't worry about me. I'm fine."

Always would be, too.

Marcus exhaled long, and slow. "Think you're going to be bored here without Bene?"

August flashed in his mind. Her sweet, but sly smile, and the way it darkened her brown eyes even more when it turned sexy in a blink. Pretty skin flushed for him, or *because* of him. *And* their date to meetup that afternoon.

"You know what," Beni replied, "I think I'll be okay."

"Right." Marcus headed for the door. "You need something, you call me, okay?"

"I will."

Without a doubt, he could always count on Marcus for that. It was everything else that was currently up in the air. Strange how that worked sometimes.

CHAPTER

8

"What can I get for you, Miss?"

"I can't believe you just got up this morning and left before I was even awake."

August smiled at the girl behind the cash at the café while also rolling her eyes at her friend on the phone. "Just a coffee—two sugars, and cream."

"Sure."

"August?"

She stepped to the side, giving the guy waiting in line behind her a nod at his patience in waiting for her to move before going forward. Off to the left of the counter, waiting for her order, she could finally give her attention to the *very* impatient Camilla on the phone.

"First of all," August said, "it's almost noon, Cam. You act like I woke up at six and snuck out of the house before the ass crack of dawn."

"*Well* …"

"Seriously, I can't sleep in like you do."

"Couldn't you have woken me up?"

August figured that, since her time in Chicago was about halfway finished, Camilla was starting to show it. She had called in sick to work *twice*, to follow her around while she finished up some things for the magazine spread. On more than one occasion, she demanded August stay at her place, even though she had a perfectly fine hotel room in the city.

And, she outright asked her to stay.

Here.

In Chicago.

A part of her wanted to agree to that in a heartbeat. Being here with Cam reminded August exactly how much she had missed her friend since the last time they had been together. Not to mention, whenever they got together, it was like time and distance just didn't matter. They were still just August and Camilla, best friends 'til the end.

It would be *easy* to say yes.

And also hard.

"I just needed to get out of the house, go for a walk, *think*," August said. "There's nothing wrong with that, right?"

That was mostly the truth …

She didn't bother to mention how she had agreed to meet up with Beni at this café, or the meeting she had later in the afternoon with Alessa Conti for Manic Media. Those were the real reasons August left that morning, but she didn't want to share them.

At least, not yet.

Camilla sighed dramatically. "Yes, *without me*."

"*Lord*."

Her friend's familiar laugh filtered through the phone speakers. "I mean, you know I'm kidding. If you want to get up and go for a day, then you can do that. But be safe, okay? Stuff in the city is a little … iffy right now."

"I'm sure I'll be fine."

"Aug—"

"I'll be safe."

She wasn't part of the Outfit. Her life wasn't the *mob* life. She was barely even associated to the business that happened here on the illegal side of things, and her only real attachment to it was Camilla, and … well, Beni, in a way.

Yeah, she figured that out.

Between what he told her, and some questions she asked Camilla about him, and his family, it was pretty clear. August didn't know how she felt about that, to be honest. She tried not to judge people based on surface things—life taught her to go deeper than that.

Although, truth be told, she was *slightly* worried about the current drama and dangers facing the Outfit. Not for her, really, but for the people she cared about.

At that moment, the girl behind the counter slid August's order of coffee over with a wide smile. August snatched the to-go cup up, the warmth heating her hand instantly. "Here you are."

"Thank you." To her friend on the phone, she added, "Okay, I will be back ... soonish. And don't you have to work today, anyway?"

Camilla made a noise under her breath. "I guess so."

"Come on, you know you love your job."

"*Fine*, but I love you, too. Maybe more."

"Only *maybe*?"

"Well, now you're just asking for too much considering you're the same person who wouldn't wake me up to go out to breakfast with you."

Jesus.

"You're lucky I love you," August said through her laughter.

She swore she could *see* Camilla's grin in her mind when her friend replied, "I am easy to love, and we both know it."

"Right, that's what it is. Anyway, meet up later?"

"Sure, Aug. And please, be careful."

"I will."

August ended the call with a shake of her head and a smile. Even if she was keeping things from her friend—just until she figured stuff out for herself, because that was fair, right?—she knew, no matter what, she would always have

Cam to count on. Forever watching her back, ride or die. Everybody needed a friend like Camilla.

"So, do we consider this a *second* date?"

That smile of hers grew wider at the voice behind her. That tone, unmistakably his with the dark tenor, and teasing nature seemed to caress her skin, and even had the fine hairs on the back of her neck standing up on end. The same way the heart in her chest picked up beats, hearing something it very much liked and wanted, and willing to race right out of her ribcage to get to it.

Strange, really.

And yet, she liked it.

Spinning around while taking a sip of the hot coffee, August came face to face with a smirking Beni. *Damn*, he looked good today. Gone were the dark wash jeans, leather jacket, and the Converse shoes. Oh, sure, she liked him in that, too, but today he had settled on something a bit more … *classic*, and fancy.

Black slacks, and a white button down that was rolled up to the elbows. A blazer hung over his arm, forgotten, likely because of the current summer heat sweeping through Chicago. No tie, she noticed, but that was okay because he'd left the top two buttons of his shirt undone, giving her a peek at the golden skin of his throat, a couple days' worth of facial hair covering his jawline, and the way his Adam's apple bobbed when he looked her over, and swallowed.

So good looking.

Did he know how he looked?

Because *Jesus* …

At least, August didn't feel underdressed standing in front of him, considering she had thrown on a black dress with elbow-length sleeves, a scoop neck, and a pencil skirt that fell to her knees. Black pumps matched the dress, and she went for a simple, rose gold necklace and matching earrings to draw attention to her little makeup, and the braids she had piled high on her head in a spiraling bun.

She *did* have a meeting today—one that involved talks about a possible job. She had to look professional, didn't she?

"No work today?" she asked.

Beni flashed her another one of his sinful smiles. "Nah, I had better things to do."

Was she one of those things?

He *was* here.

So … *yep*.

August liked that.

Too much.

There was something about a man that made a woman his priority that did it for her. Beyond sex, a man that cared enough to put in effort … it was all about the fucking *effort* with a woman like her.

She appreciated it.

"And you didn't answer me," he said. "Is this the second date?"

She gave him a look. "We didn't really have a first."

"Well—"

"That was *not* a first date."

Beni chuckled, shoving his hands into his pockets as he looked her over from head to toe. There was something about his slow perusal that had her heating up from the inside out, butterflies beating hard in her stomach all the while.

What was he doing to her?

"So, we consider *this* a first date, then?"

August nodded. "And depending on how it goes, well, we'll see about another one."

His dark, husky laughter coated her in something sinful and wicked as he stepped alongside her to wrap a strong arm around her waist. He pulled her into his side for a one-armed hug, his mouth coming down to press a quick kiss to her soft line of baby hair along her forehead.

"Never stop doing that," he told her.

August tipped her head back so that she could stare up at him. "Do what?"

"*That*—keeping me on my toes. Nobody ever does that anymore, and I like it."

Noted.

"So, what did you have in mind for today?" he asked.

"I only have a couple of hours—something to do later—but I thought we could take a walk somewhere, maybe."

"Did you drive here?"

"Called an Uber. Easier, you know."

"I know a place, and I did drive. I hope you like fast cars."

At her questioning stare, Beni nodded toward the line of windows showcasing the city street outside the café. There, parked alongside the street was a sleek, black Porsche.

"That's yours?"

"Yeah, but I only take it out on special occasions. I bought it for myself as a twenty-first birthday gift, but it's not as fun when I drive it all the time."

"And I'm a special occasion, huh?"

Beni winked. "*Very* special."

Beni's hand tightened around August's as they came to a stop on the middle of a small bridge that connected the walkways over a creek in Jackson Park. The green water bubbling beneath the bridge danced over smooth rocks, and lead into a larger pond down the way.

Their walk through the park had been mostly silent, with Beni occasionally pointing out facts about the place, and the design of it. Like the fact that the south side park sat on over five-hundred acres of land, and they were only seeing a very small portion of what it offered.

Shame, that.

She was loving it.

All the green on a beautiful summer day.

"What are your plans later?" She let him tug her into his chest, and he quirked a brow when she grinned. "And could I possibly convince you to change them for me?"

God.

Right now, she wished.

But … "Probably not."

"Why not?"

Since there was no one else walking up to the bridge, she didn't care that they were standing right on the middle of it, blocking the path. Her arms snaked around his waist, and she breathed in that heady cedar and smoke cologne he seemed to prefer.

"It's for a possible job, actually."

Beni's brow lifted high. "Oh? *Here?*"

"Don't say that too loudly. Camilla might hear you, and then I'll have to explain to her why I didn't tell her about it, or that I'm seriously thinking about it."

He quieted for a moment, his hand on her lower back drifting back and forth in a slow, soothing motion. His other slid under her jaw, tipping her head back so their brown gazes locked together, and all she could see in a beautiful park was this incredibly handsome man.

"Why not tell her?"

August shrugged. "Maybe because it's a big change? You know, moving my whole life from New York to Chicago. Or because it means probably starting over in my career, when what I am doing now is the first chance I've been given to move forward at my job in three years. Or because she'll get so excited that she won't let me have a moment to think about it alone without her opinion—I love Cam, but that's just how she is."

"Huh."

"That's all you got for me? Just a *huh*?"

Beni chuckled, and dropped a sweet kiss to the tip of her nose. The action had her closing her eyes and feeling those butterflies again. Not to mention the sparks of heat that traveled all over her body in seconds flat.

How he managed it, she would never know.

"What's the job offer?"

"A position with Manic Media."

"Alessa's company."

"You know her?"

"My mother grew up in the Chicago Outfit—I know everybody who is anybody here, and my ma is friends with Alessa, too."

"Oh."

"Manic Media is a good company, though. They do *a lot* of good work for the communities, and the youth of Chicago."

"I know. That's one of the draws."

"And the holdout is …?"

Because, of course, there was one.

"The move. The change. I'm an only child, so I would be leaving my parents behind. It also feels like starting over, in a way, when with my current company, I have finally just started getting what I wanted. I don't know … I just haven't given it *enough* thought, if that makes sense."

Beni's arms wrapped her tightly, his embrace a safe place, she found. "I get it, actually. Well, not the only child part, but—"

"You have four brothers, right?"

"How do you know that?"

August's cheeks flushed.

Shit.

"And what's *that* for?" he asked, waving a finger at the red color in her cheeks. "But *damn*, I do like it when you blush, *bella*."

Well, she might as well just admit it, right?

"I might have asked around about you, that's all."

She tried to play it off.

Be *cool.*

It wasn't a big deal.

Beni grinned like it was.

Cocky man.

And yet, she liked that, too.

"Did you?" he asked.

August sighed. "You're going to make that into a thing, are you?"

"Maybe I just like that you asked about me. What did you find out?"

"Nothing *too bad*. Seems everyone likes you, and you're a decent guy, if not a little wild spirited."

"They're not telling lies."

August giggled, and glanced away. "I guess, I just wanted to know who that man was who looked at me from across a club, and made me think *wow*. So yeah, I asked some questions. None of them had bad answers."

"Good to know."

He stepped a little closer to her, his hand coming back under her jaw to turn her face toward his once more. Her tongue peeked out to wet her lips when that intense gaze of his locked on her mouth like he was considering kissing her.

She couldn't get over that.

How he *stared.*

She felt it all over.

"Your mouth is … *perfect*," he murmured.

She dragged her teeth over her full bottom lip. "Is it?"

"It's what I want the most whenever you're near. It taunts me in the best way."

"Does it?"

"*Constantly.*"

Yeah.

Wow.

How any woman could be near this man without falling head over heels for him after a conversation, August would never know. And that was dangerous, too, she knew. How his charming, confident nature drew her in like a fluttering moth to a dancing flame.

Never had a man seemed so enthralling.

This man did.

August wasn't sure if she could afford to change something else in her life when she was already going through enough as it was. How would she dare to hand over her heart, when she didn't even have the rest figured out, too?

Instead of getting in her feelings, August decided to change the subject. In a *very* good way. Tipping her chin up just enough to catch Beni's lips with her own, she kissed him on that bridge until the sounds of the birds and bubbling water drifted away, and she felt numb from the electricity singing through her bloodstream.

He held her tighter.

Kissed her *deeper.*

Like he couldn't get enough of her mouth, her taste, or … *her.* God knew she understood that, because she couldn't get enough of him, either.

Her lungs burned when he pulled away, her bottom lip trembling as he dotted the seam of her mouth with soft, sweet kisses.

"*When* can we do this again?" he asked.

"Are you asking for a second date?"

His eyes flashed with darkness and sin. "Absolutely."

"You might have to work around my best friend. She's getting a little possessive about my time."

Beni laughed, sexy and deep. "Not a problem. I have an inside source."

"Oh?"

"Her husband is a very good friend."

Right.

August kissed him again, quicker that time, although she still felt it everywhere. "Then, that's a yes. This time, *you* decide what we do."

Beni's handsome features turned boyish in a blink, and she almost laughed. "So, something *fun*?"

"What's your type of fun?"

"You'll see."

"At least two a month?"

Across the desk, Alessa Conti nodded, her smile soft. "Two articles monthly for the online publication, and that guarantees your pay. One will be a project *you* choose to work on—one will be promotional for the company that will be a team effort. However, I'm sure you don't need me to tell you that Manic Media's reach spans far wider in the grander scheme. From working with Fortune 500 companies to perfect their brand in the media, to work in our communities to provide better opportunities to those who need it … we are constantly expanding and growing. There are *many* options for you here, August, and I would hate to see you pass them up."

The woman leaned forward a bit, her messy chignon a perfect style to showcase the rope of pearls around her throat, as she added, "And I know you want your focus to be on journalism, which is why I offered the online publication—still paid—until you figure out where else you might like to work in this company. I read your article, the one that went viral a couple years back, on the distinction between a brand becoming a household name, and a brand that becomes part of a cultural movement. It's the perfect example of not only can you *write*, but you see things in a perspective that others do not. It's that kind of mindset that gives you a seat at the table, if you want it."

God.

She did want it.

Badly.

And at the same time … things were not simple.

At Manic Media's home office, set dead center in the middle of the city, it only became far more apparent to August how much she would fit into the place. Diverse, with a work environment that supported and encouraged *everyone* to not only do their best, but feel their best, it was a dream. At the home office alone, the ratio of women to men were five to one. Practically unheard of anywhere, but women were the face and driving force of the company.

All kinds of women.

August wanted to be a part of that.

She had every good reason to take this job.

"There's a very good chance that when I go back home, I might have a place on the editor's team at Bared Brands. I've worked three years—"

"Blood, sweat, tears, and all the rest, right?" Alessa asked.

"Basically."

"And for what?"

August dragged in a breath. "Recognition. Respect. Working my way up."

"Or driving their traffic by spilling yourself to their

pages, but without anything to show for it on your side of things. They mine your talent for a payoff you never see."

Hit me where it hurts, August thought.

Didn't the truth always hurt?

"I know it feels like starting over," Alessa said, "but in the end, it's about what *you* want for your career. Is your goal to work for a company that has only given you something in return after they've taken everything else you had to give them, or is your goal tied into what *you* really want for your career and person?"

She didn't miss how Alessa didn't offer that choice with Manic Media at the forefront. Instead, she posed it as a choice August had to make based on what would be best for her, something she wanted and would do her good, or another thing that had yet to prove fruitful and worth it for her.

"The choice seems simple, doesn't it?" Alessa asked.

"And yet," August replied, letting it hang between them. "When is it ever?"

"What holds you back? How about we start there?"

She listed off the usual things.

Uprooting her life.

The *change*.

But this time, she added, "I do feel like I owe Bared Brands something, in a way. I got the internship because of my father's friendship with the CEO, for starters. The editor allowed me to work with her *while* attending college. Not everyone has had that chance. I know the opportunities they've given me haven't amounted to a lot, but they mean something to me. It's the respect of the matter, and I promised to deliver them something for it. I'm trying to do that."

"And you're providing it while you're here, are you not? The spread you mentioned—although, with something like that, we would have incorporated ways for the article to help the community that it was born from, where as they plan to …?"

August glanced away. "Not much, I imagine."

In fact, she doubted Bared Brands would even allow her to use some of the photographs and information from the urban neighborhoods she visited for her article and spread. The parts of Chicago that wouldn't be *pleasing* to a certain eye, so to speak.

Alessa nodded. "I see. "

"I do want to take this job."

"But?"

"First, I have to finish what I started."

"Then, you should do that. And know, I like you more because of it. That you're willing to see something through, no matter what. That it's tied to your morals and ethics as a person—it shows who you are, August, and that's a good thing."

Was it?

"Now, how are you getting back after you leave here—are you staying at your hotel, or Cam's place?"

"Cam's."

"I'll call a man to drive you."

August shook her head, already standing from the chair. "No, I'm fine to call an Uber."

Alessa gave her a look. "The city is dangerous right now. Even for people associated to us. Let me call a man to drive you back."

She didn't bother to argue.

Other things were on her mind.

CHAPTER

9

"*Ciao*, Marcus here."

Beni checked the watch on his wrist, brow furrowing at the time staring back at him. It wasn't so much the time as it was the fact that Marcus sounded like he had been … *sleeping*? At nine in the morning? That was entirely unusual for his older brother, who, was always awake, dressed, and ready to start his day by six-thirty sharp. No excuses.

"Were you sleeping?"

Marcus cleared his throat. "Yeah, why?"

"It's … a weekday, Marcus."

"Obviously."

"Since when do you sleep—"

"It's been a long week," his brother interjected, his tone clear that he wasn't going to explain further. "What can I do for you, Beni?"

He did want to press for more information, though. Was something happening back home that he should know about?

"Is there—"

"What do you need?"

All right.

Marcus was no-nonsense today.

"To tell you happy birthday, actually, but if you're going to catch a fucking attitude, I take it back."

Chuckles echoed over the phone. "It is, huh?"

"Pardon?"

"My birthday."

Beni arched a brow, nearing the side entrance to the warehouse. He met up with the Capo of the east side crew privately once a week to fill the guy in on what he had learned or seen over the week that might be of any interest to him, or the boss. Not that he had learned anything so far.

The crew was … difficult.

Yeah, that was as good of a word as anyway.

"Twenty-six today," Beni returned.

Marcus cleared his throat. "I guess, I forgot."

"How do you forget your birthday, dude?"

"You become more concerned with taking care of everyone else than yourself, Beni."

His steps halted two feet from the door he used to enter the warehouse without being seen by anyone on the street, or any crew members lingering nearby. He certainly didn't need to get caught seeming friendly with the Capo by members of crew he was trying to infiltrate as *one of them*. That wouldn't do him any favors, when so far, he hadn't even managed to make a goddamn friend here.

Still, he stayed in the alleyway.

Something more important just came up.

Family was *always* more important.

"You okay?" he asked Marcus.

"Why wouldn't I be?"

"I just … well, what you said a moment ago," Beni returned, glancing over his shoulder quickly to see if anyone was standing there; it was empty, thankfully. "About taking care of everyone, Marcus. You know we're all adult men, right? We can handle our own shit, and you don't need to bend over backwards to look after us anymore."

"Not really how it works for me."

"You're not *Dad*—you don't have to be, either."

"Not about Dad," Marcus replied tiredly, "it's about *me*, and what I want to do. It's fine, Beni, really."

"But—"

"I don't mind letting my brothers be selfish, and do their thing while I do mine. It just so happens that mine is looking after you all, that's all."

Huh.

It was kind of funny how a perspective could change with nothing more than a conversation. In a way, Beni had always seen his older brother as ... a stick in the mud. Stuck the fuck up. Too busy trying to follow their father's footsteps than to make his own.

It was possible none of that was true.

"I gotta go," Marcus mumbled, "I'm going to hear it that I'm late today."

"Yeah, sure, sorry. But hey, happy birthday."

"Thanks. And be careful there, yeah? The body bag thing still applies."

"Got it, Marcus."

"Love you, bro."

His brother didn't give him the chance to return the sentiment before he hung up the phone with a loud *click*. He wasn't offended and figured he could just revisit the conversation with Marcus another time, if that's what he wanted to do.

Not bothering to linger any longer where he might be seen and knowing the crew would be arriving soon to get their daily tasks around the city, he headed into the warehouse through the side entrance.

The smell of cardboard boxes—probably filled with counterfeit goods that would need to be unpacked and sold on the streets throughout the week—greeted him first. He made a beeline to the back of the large building, bypassing a couple of stolen cars that were covered with tarps, but that he knew were being held until someone could move and chop them up for parts. Weaving in between the steel beams that jutted down from the ceiling, and the wall of boxes of fake goods that had been delivered the night before, he came around the back to see the Capo's office was already open.

Waiting for him.

Beni didn't bother to knock—Jerome, the Capo—wasn't particular with that shit with him. Anyone else, though, and he didn't let them make the mistake of not knocking a second time.

Stepping inside the office, he found Jerome sitting behind his small, worn-down desk. It looked like one of those metal ones that teachers used in high school, except it had a couple of dents on the top, and someone had tried to spray-paint it *green*. And not a nice green either, no like a puke green.

"Couple minutes late, yeah?"

Beni shrugged. "Sorry—traffic."

It was a lie, but Jerome didn't pick up on it. With his boots resting on the top of the desk, and the chair he sat in dangling dangerously on two legs, the Capo wearing his standard three-piece suit, waved a hand for Beni to come in further.

"Hurry up, because we're running short on time today. The guys know it's the day of the week they like—goods to be sold, easy cash, and they'll go home happy tonight. Chances are, they're going to get here early just because."

"Right, right."

Beni closed the door behind him leaving only a crack, so he could hear any movement in the warehouse outside of the office before he turned to the Capo. "How did last night go?"

"Neil didn't have any issues to report," Jerome muttered, sitting up and letting his Italian leather loafers snap to the cement floor. "Said the goods came in fine, and they managed to get it all unloaded without anyone noticing."

Beni nodded. "And when he left with the guys?"

"Same thing."

"But yesterday, the gang did a drive-by on two guys from the crew working in the Heights?"

Jerome tapped the side of his nose before pointing the same finger at Beni. "You're starting to keep up, I see, good job."

Was that an insult, or a ... compliment?

Beni didn't know.

Nor did he care.

"I haven't been able to get close enough to anyone in the crew to see or know anything," Beni admitted. "They've got their own groups within the crew, and they're *not* open to letting someone new into their ranks."

Sure, they worked with him.

Because they were *told* to.

That was it.

Jerome nodded, letting out a sigh. "Give it some time— they're a close knit bunch, and given the fact they know thieving has been happening, they're all looking at each other, wondering which one it is, you know. Gonna make for some paranoia, that's all."

Sure, but ...

"You said the problems with the gang only started *after* you noticed the stealing within the crew, right?"

"What about it?"

Jerome was a big guy—easily two-seventy in weight, well over six feet tall, and while he didn't have time to fuck around with the crew a lot of the time, he also had no problem with coming in to lay down the law when it called for it. The crew knew that, too, it was what kept a lot of them in line. That fear of their Capo, harsh and unforgiving, who looked like a fucking bear coming their way whenever he came out of the back of the warehouse.

Was it possible …?

"It could be a distraction," Beni said.

"What?"

"The gang."

"For what?"

Beni shrugged. "I guess that's what I'm going to have to figure out."

Jerome gave him a look. "Should hurry up on that."

Yeah, right.

He'd get right on it.

As Jerome had said when Tommas first put him into this crew to work, and the boss agreed, Beni was just young enough, and respected because of his name and status within the life, that he might be able to chill the crew out. Weed his way in, gain their trust, and figure out what the fuck was going on here.

Well, it was not working out that way.

Not so easy, after all.

Beni was thinking he might have to approach this situation at an entirely new angle to work through what was happening here. Not that he really had all the time in the fucking world to start over from the ground up, but what else could he do?

The shuttering of metal being lifted had Beni and Jerome passing a look between one another. A quick check of his watch said the man had been right, and the crew was starting to arrive a little earlier than was normal or expected for them. Loud laughter reached their spot at the back of the warehouse from the guys just filtering in through the front. The Capo nodded toward the door, a silent order for him to head out of the office before he was found back here alone.

He was still supposed to be the *new* guy, after all. Even if he was Beni Fucking Guzzi to everybody else. New was still new in a crew.

With a wave over his shoulder, Beni exited the office quickly. The Capo's quiet voice rung out behind him with, "You'll be helping with the goods today."

All right.

That order stayed in the back of his mind as he moved through the warehouse again. Only this time, he stopped at the wall of boxes, as that was where he would be working today, and pulled himself up to sit on a pile of crates while he waited for the rest of the guys to gather. It didn't take them long to start filtering in, really.

Within ten minutes, the warehouse was filled with twenty different guys—all their faces were familiar to Beni in the way that he had worked with them over the last couple of weeks, but some he hadn't even bothered to learn their names.

Kenny, one of the guys who was *slightly* kinder than the rest, joined Beni on the crates. He didn't initiate a conversation while they waited for the day to get started. That didn't bother him, though, as he had other things on his mind. Like scanning the faces of the young men waiting for their orders and wondering which one—or if it was a small group of them—thieving from their Capo, and if they might be, in some way, working with the gang, too.

He had shit to consider.

A lot.

Out of the corner of his eye, Beni watched as Neil—the one guy on the crew who worked closest with the Capo—headed for the back to speak with his boss. He was typically the one who designated the tasks, gave the orders from the Capo, and kept an eye on everybody.

And he was no better or worse than the rest of them, honestly.

He didn't care for any of the guys, or Beni, and they didn't care for him. Of course, that was normal when one was … the favored in a crew.

Kind of like the teacher's pet, so to speak.

"Anybody know what we're selling today?" one of the guys asked.

"Unloaded it last night," Kenny replied beside Beni, "Neil said the usual—counterfeit makeup, purses, shoes … some electronics that were boosted out of a warehouse last week, I guess."

Another whistled low. "Good payday."

"Not that Beni cares about *that*."

Beni tensed at the comment, his gaze traveling to the fool that dared to say it. Sitting on a box in the corner, the crew member with his hair a little too long, curling around the nape of his neck, and dark blue eyes seemingly pensive, glowered at Beni.

"What was that?" Beni asked. "Speak up, and share with the rest of the class, now."

Dillan was his name.

Beni wouldn't soon forget someone who insulted him.

"I'm just saying," Dillan muttered, gaze darting away from Beni's, "we all know a Guzzi doesn't need to be selling fakes on the street to make bank, you know? Bet you were born a fucking millionaire, man. What are you even doing here?"

A millionaire *several* times over, in fact.

Not that it meant shit. Beni still had to work for his respect—he still busted his ass trying to get his *in* to the family business, just like everybody else did. And comments like Dillan's weren't anything new, either.

Beni opened his mouth to tell the guy right where he could shove his opinion, but it was only Neil coming around the side of the wall of boxes that shut him up. Or rather, what the man had to say.

"Beni's here to work," Neil said, "like the rest of you fucking idiots. Stop wasting time—you can see the shit we've got to unpack and distribute. *Get to work.*"

That was all it took for the group of them to move. Including Beni and Kenny, who jumped down from the crates to move for the boxes. Neil stood back for a while, surveying the crew as they worked in a line to open and separate all the fake goods.

Carrying a box of what looked to be a knock-off of a luxury makeup brand to the right side of the warehouse, Beni passed a stone-still Neil. The guy's gaze caught his, and Neil quirked a brow at him.

"You got something to say?" Beni asked.

Neil shrugged. "Just watch your back here, huh? Don't cause a fucking problem."

Right.

Beni realized something, then … he couldn't trust any of them.

Busy?

Beni stared at the screen of his phone with his back to a punching bag that was currently getting the stuffing beat out of it by Tommaso. He was acting as a resistance for it, although he was *supposed* to be facing the bag.

What difference did it make?

Finishing up a piece of this pitch, came the reply.

Beni sighed. He liked that August had goals, for sure. The fact that her job was important, and she made it a priority, was attractive. Women who had places to be, and shit to do that mattered to them at the end of the day was something he respected. Because as a man trying to be *made*, Beni had to constantly be on the grind, too.

Nonstop.

And yet, it also messed him up—or rather, August's work schedule did. Because he didn't know if she would appreciate him outright asking if she would put it away for a night to go out and have a good time with him.

After all, if it was that important to her, then he shouldn't be stepping in on it to ask her to sacrifice time for him.

Right?

Fuck.

He was getting too deep here.

This was too deep.

A hard punch landed to the bag, making it snap away and then bump into Beni. It took his attention away from the screen of the phone. Cussing, he turned to shoot Tommaso a glare that he hoped voiced his displeasure at being interrupted without having to say anything at all.

Tommaso wasn't bothered.

He stared right back.

"Wasn't it *you* that asked me to come here and workout with you four times a fucking week?" Tommaso asked.

Beni scowled. "*Well—*"

"Yes, it was. Get off your phone and help me here."

"Starting to regret asking you, now."

Well, not really, but he wasn't going to tell Tom that. Mostly, he hated working out alone. He needed a bit of competition to keep it fresh and give him the motivation to get through particularly rough workout days. It used to be his twin, but with Bene gone, he was on his fucking own, it seemed.

And just *that* … a brief thought of his twin, had Beni scowling all over again.

Perfect.

Tom lifted a taped hand, pointing at Beni. "What's that mood about right there? A second ago, you were grinning like a fucker at your phone, and now you look like someone pissed on your shoe when your back was turned."

"Nice imagery there."

"I do what I can."

Beni sighed, grabbing onto the bag so that Tommaso could go for another round, if he wanted. The man did, and he spoke while his friend beat the bag.

"Bene hasn't called."

"Oh?"

"Not since he left."

Tommaso's gaze flicked to him, but he kept working the bag all the while. "And that's …"

"Listen, we're going through a thing, that's all. Except, you can't fix the fucking *thing* when he doesn't even bother to call me, you know?"

"Or maybe he needs time."

"We're not *girls*. He doesn't need time away with his *feelings*."

"You sure? Because your attitude sounds like you need some Midol and—"

Beni let go of the bag and took a wide step back when Tom threw a particularly hard punch. Expecting the bag to not move, when it did, he fell into it.

"You deserved that," Beni said.

"And you're an asshole."

"Yeah, well …"

What could he do?

"Besides *Bene*," he added, "I've also got this shit with the crew on my mind lately. I'm not closer to figuring out who is causing the issues, or stealing, than I was when your father first put me in there to work with them. Nothing is going right for me lately."

"What about August? You seemed just fine with that."

Beni frowned. "I don't want to take her away from her work."

"I don't think she would mind."

"Well, *I* don't know that."

"What it sounds like to me," Tommaso said, "is that you need to get your mind off the shit that's bothering you with something—or *someone*—that does the opposite."

Someone like August.

He heard what his friend didn't say. It wasn't that Beni didn't agree, but more that he wasn't even sure what in the hell this was between him and August. Were they just having fun with one another, or was it something else?

Because he leaned toward *something else*, more than just fun. And that wasn't *at all* his usual style. He wasn't a hit it and quit it type, but he had never had time to fuck around with a chick more than once, either. Yet, he found he wanted to do exactly that with August Rivera, and all it took was meeting her in a club, getting her in his bed, and taking a walk around a goddamn park.

There was just something about her.

He liked it a lot.

But where was her mind?

Like his, or was she just having fun?

Beni didn't know if he wanted the answer.

Tommaso shrugged, pulling the tape from his hands as he added, "And a little bird—my wife, you know, because she gossips all the fucking time—told me that she and August were meeting up today after her shift was over. And since Camilla is *very* invested in whatever this thing is between you and August, although I told her to mind her business ..."

Beni chuckled. "Oh, is she? And what does she think is going to happen?"

"Listen, I'm not giving details. I'm just trying to tell you that Camilla would do *anything*, even give up her dinner and movie with her best friend, if it meant August was going to go out with you."

Huh.

"And what time are they meeting up?"

Tommaso grinned. "See, *that's* what you needed to be asking from the start."

Fucker.

CHAPTER 10

The Uber dropped August off at Camilla's home a little earlier than expected. About ten minutes before she was supposed to get home from work, so it wasn't a big deal. She used the key her friend had given her years ago to get inside, and wait.

Maybe it was the fact that during this trip to Chicago, more so than any of her previous visits, she had been reminded time and time again about the *mafia* side of her friend's life. About the dangers they faced, and the risks they took to be who they were … the only thing they had ever known. August was on the outside of that bubble, just close enough to see inside—so not entirely naive—but also far enough away that she wasn't touched by it.

Except she couldn't ignore it this time. Not when it had been placed in front of her face time and time again. It showed her how protected and sheltered her friend's life actually was … in a sense that she never got to feel *normal*.

It made her understand how much trust Camilla and Tommaso must have felt for August, to give her a key to their home. Their *haven*.

She was still mulling that over, and the fact that she had never realized it before, when a rumbling began outside of the house. A deep growl that had her heading to the front door to peek outside, and see what was causing the noise.

Holy sweet Jesus.

August found the source in the sight of Beni pulling a racer style motorcycle helmet from his head as he stepped off a Ducati SuperBike. The matte black of his leather jacket matched the bike's paint job. And even the silver detailing of the bike was mirrored in the buttons and clasps of Beni's leather jacket.

He looked like living, breathing *sin*. Black jeans molded to his defined thighs—and the denim looked even better on that damn fine ass of his—when he turned a bit to place the helmet to the handlebars of the bike. August liked to think of herself as a strong, *smart* woman—proud, but not so much that she couldn't admit to her own faults; firm in her wants and beliefs, but still soft in her heart and soul. And yet that man right there could turn her into a blinking, breathless mess with nothing more than the sight of him shifting from foot to foot and grinning toward the house.

His fingers drifted to the hair that had fallen over his eyes, pushing it back with the rest of his high fade as his gaze drifted over the yard with a flash of familiarity. As though he had looked at the place a hundred times before. It made her realize just how long she and him might have passed each other by throughout the years.

How long had he been friends with Tom?

He *had* said his mother was from Chicago.

Before August even understood what she was doing, because she was still a bit stuck on the sight of him out there, she pushed the door open enough to say, "It should be illegal to look like you do right now."

She was *shameless* with him.

He did that to her, too.

Beni's laugh carried to her as he quickly crossed the paved driveway and reached for the smooth railing of the steps. "Is that so?"

"*Yes.*"

"And what if I could sweeten the deal, too?"

August arched a brow as he reached the top step. "How so? That a challenge?"

"You," he said, crossing the porch in two strides, "tell *me*."

She pulled the door open wider as he came to stand on the threshold, so close she could smell his unique scent, and new leather. *That jacket.* "Sweeten it, Beni."

He leaned down just enough that their lips were a whisper apart as his husky voice murmured, "*Ma chérie ... sei bella, sempre.*"

August blinked.

Shocker.

It took her a couple of seconds, and with each passing one, Beni's grin grew into something *far* more sinful and sexy.

"Is that ... French *and* Italian?"

"It is." He winked, adding quickly, "But my French is *far* more limited than my Italian. I know enough to carry a *very* simple conversation. Italian was a ... must for my father, and mother's side of the family. No excuses—I *had* to learn. French was a choice, although I just never picked up on it as well."

"Huh."

Why was her mouth dry?

Beni's tongue peeked out to wet the line of his lower lip before he said, "It worked though, didn't it?"

Her gaze snapped up to his. "What did?"

His laughter washed over her senses in the best way before his form filled the doorway entirely, pressing against her body with one movement, and then he was kissing her. A kiss so hungry, and brutal, and yet now familiar and addicting to her. Every stroke of his tongue against hers took away what little sense she seemed to have left. Supple leather smoothed against her fingertips, and his three-day stubble sharpened her senses as it dragged along her sensitive skin with every sweep of his lips.

Though it felt like the last thing he wanted to do, if the look in his stare was any indication, Beni pulled back a bit to say, "*Definitely* sweetened that deal."

August swallowed hard, nodding. "I guess so."

"*Perfetto.*"

That reminds me …

"And what did you say, huh?"

"Before?"

August nodded. "Yeah, what was it?"

Beni cleared his throat, long lashes fanning downward when he lowered his gaze. Was that … *shyness?*

Oh, my God.

This man was killing her.

"It was …" he said low, "My darling, you are beautiful, *always.*"

Lord.

Of course, that was what he said. Because *that* just made her heart feel like it was going to beat right out of her chest.

"You are something else," she told him quietly.

Beni tipped his head down like he might kiss her. "And you are *perfect.*"

August sucked in a breath. "Are you trying to make me fall—"

A throat clearing behind Beni had the two of them breaking apart, even if it was only a couple of inches. August wished she could be surprised to see Camilla grinning like the cat who found the cream on the top of her steps, but she wasn't.

"How long were you standing there?" August asked.

"Long enough."

"You are *terrible.*"

Camilla shrugged. "*Wonderful*, I think, is the word you're looking for. Now, if you'll let me get inside my house, I can hunker down for the night in my robe with my reruns and wine, and you two can get a start on your date."

August's brow furrowed. "What date?"

"Tom said," Camilla drawled, stepping beyond the two of them when they moved out of her home's doorway, "that Beni here was coming over to take you out for the night. And while I might want to bitch and moan because you're my best friend and I want all your time, I should shut up because I might get other things I want. So, that is what I am going to do."

Beni gaped. "What did you just ramble on about?"

August pressed her lips together, entirely amused, because she understood just fine what her friend had *pointedly*, albeit still crazily, said without directly saying it. "Seriously, Cam?"

Camilla shrugged. "Just let it happen, that's all I'm saying."

Her friend *really* thought that.

Believed it to be true.

She thought August was going to—if she had not already—fall in love with Beni, which might give her yet another reason to want to be here. *Closer* to Camilla. A win-win, she imagined, for her friend. And yet all August could do was shake her head.

"Anyway," Camilla said, closing the door behind her as she entered the house, "I'm totally cool with missing that dinner and movie, Aug, so you're fine to go with Beni on this date he has planned for you tonight ... you know, according to Tom."

"You are something else. You are ... trying *too* hard, Camilla."

Her friend winked. "But am I, *really*?"

The door closed with an audible *snap*.

Beni still just looked entirely fucking confused. It was sort of … a little bit, though she would never tell him … *cute*. "What just happened?"

August pressed her lips together to stop from laughing. "You know what, I guess we're going on a date."

∿

"So yeah, Tom must have called her as soon as I left him at the gym and filled her in on what I had planned," Beni said.

August shook her head. "Figures. Although, this is nice, too."

"*Just* nice?"

She gave him a teasing wink before popping a fluffy bit of blue cotton candy into her grinning mouth. He only laughed, and then dragged her in closer to his side as they continued their stroll through the carnival.

"I still can't convince you to get on another ride with me, huh?"

August shook her head. "Not after that first one."

"*Come on*," Beni groaned, "that was fucking awesome."

"Yes, being whisked fifty feet in the air, and then rolling forward mid-air so that we feel like we're about to fall to our deaths is exactly what I call fun, too!"

He eyed her from the side. "I can hear the sarcasm."

She beamed. "That was the point."

"There are other—"

"Listen, I have what is known as *self-preservation*. It means when something screams *this looks like it might kill you*, I make smart decisions and stay away."

"Funny," Beni murmured, "when something feels dangerous to me, I tend to like it more."

"That sounds like something you should work on."

"Thanks for that."

Their laughter drifted through the line of food concessions. He pulled her closer to his side, an arm wrapping tight around her waist as the lights from the stands and rides lit up the sky. Young teens darted past them after grabbing their bags of popcorn from a concession stand, while the noise from the carnival kept the place awake and alive, despite the sky being inky with night.

"No rides, then," he said, his words murmuring along her hairline, "so does that mean we can play a game?"

"Think you can win me something?"

"Is that a *challenge*?"

Her mind drifted back to that challenge in her friend's doorway, and she spoke before she could think better of it. "Absolutely."

Beni's hand found hers before he was tugging her through a crowd, and on the other side, through a line of concession stands filled with games. She was sure most of them were probably rigged to the carnival's benefit, but she was going to have fun watching Beni try to win something.

"That one," he said, pointing at a specific game.

August arched a brow at him. "*Darts*?"

Well, specifically, he needed to hit very *small* balloons with darts.

"Darts," he agreed.

They passed a game with pellet guns, and a similar task. And another shooting game, although that one was water, and one needed to get the stream of water into the mouth of a strange looking clown to blow their balloon head up to the max.

"Not a shooting game?" August half-teased. "I thought … you know—"

"What, that because I'm connected to the mob, I'd want to shoot something?"

Her cheeks pinked.

Beni laughed.

"Well, I wasn't going to say it like *that*."

Beni shrugged as the two of them came to stand at the dart game, the man behind the stand already holding a hand out to take money. A twenty-dollar bill was handed over—enough for five shots.

"Nope," Beni said, flipping one dart between his fingertips, and surveying the back end of it. "See, the sights on those guns are *shit,* and the way I was taught to handle a weapon was with respect. They're not toys, we don't play with them, and actually, I rarely have one on me unless I know I'm going to need one."

"Really?"

His stare jumped her way quickly, before he raised his hand back, glanced at the target across the stand, and let the dart fly from his fingertips.

Pop.

August didn't even look to see which balloon he'd popped. She was too busy still staring at him. And now, his attention was back on her where she clearly liked it to be the very most.

"And who taught you to play darts?"

"My brother's boyfriend—Alessio."

"Boyfriend?"

Beni laughed. "They've got a chick with them now, too. Ginevra."

"Wait, what?"

"You know, they're like an all-in-one thing the three of them."

"How does that work?"

Beni shrugged, and let the second dart fly. *Pop.* "You tell me."

Well …

"Does it work for them?"

"I guess so."

"That's what counts," August replied.

"And she's pregnant, too."

"Are your parents—"

"Crazy happy. Couldn't be fucking happier, if I'm honest. Mostly because Corrado, that's my brother, walked around like an idiot for a few years with Alessio pretending like they weren't a thing ... we all knew what they were doing. Anyway, Ginevra came into the picture, and that shit was done right then and there. It works."

Huh.

That seemed like a situation where a family might be wary, really. If only because it wasn't the *norm*. Yet, his family, including Beni, offered the information like it was totally normal to him. That, she found, was kind of amazing.

"Corrado's an identical twin, too," Beni added, letting his third dart fly, "him and Chris."

Pop.

"So, there's *two* sets in your family?"

"Three, if you include my ma, but her twin passed on a long time ago. She was killed ... here. In Chicago, I mean, when they were younger."

August frowned. "Sorry."

"A long time ago, that's all."

Pop.

Pop.

The stand lit up with lights and a whirring noise wailed from the speakers, a robotic voice congratulating Beni for winning.

"Third level prize," the guy behind the stand said, waving a hand at the line of large stuffies hanging from the top. "Feel free to pick whichever one you want, little lady."

Ugh.

Little lady.

Beni grinned her way, making that annoyance drift away instantly. August just shook her head, not surprised in the least at the sight of his cockiness. The man couldn't help it, and frankly, she liked it too damn much to tell him to stop.

None of the prizes overhead really caught her eye. Instead, one hanging from the right wall did. A dark brown bear wearing a black leather jacket. He wasn't nearly as big as the other stuffed animals—maybe only a foot long to their three and four feet.

"That one," she said, pointing at it.

Beni laughed.

The guy behind the stand shook his head. "Second level prize. You have to pick—"

Before he could even finish his statement, Beni dropped down another twenty-dollar bill, picked up five darts, glanced at the rules plastered on the side of the stand, and immediately threw the darts one right after the other.

Pop, pop, pop, pop.

For the fifth dart, he tossed it down on the stand with an, "Ow, hand cramp."

It was the fakest hand cramp she had ever seen, but he proved his point.

August pressed her lips together, looking at the man with an annoyed expression behind the stand. "I'll take the bear, please."

She got her bear with the leather jacket.

Beni pulled a bigger one, a purple elephant, down from the top for his first prize, too, but he handed it off to a tired looking girl who couldn't be more than eight as they were leaving the carnival.

"That was sweet," she told him.

He shrugged as he backed her against his Ducati bike. "It's a little thing, that's all."

Hugging her bear between them, she peered up at him.

His head tipped down, lips hovering above hers with the promise of a kiss, but not quite giving her what she wanted just yet. A shuddering breath escaped her chest because *damn* … what was it about this man that just made her feel so high?

"Thank you for tonight," she said. "I haven't had this much fun in way too long."

"That so?"

"Yeah."

He sighed. "Me either. Best way I spent a night in a while."

Despite his sexy grin, she still heard a lingering sadness in his words.

"How's your brother?"

"Which one?"

August gave him a look. "Your *twin*?"

Beni pulled a face. "Not good."

"No?"

"Haven't heard from him in a while, and I don't want to think about it right now."

"Point taken."

"Where do we go from here?" he asked. "It's all on you, August."

"Oh, you're coming back to my hotel."

"Am I?"

"Definitely."

August was trying to remember how they ended up like *this*. With Beni naked and on his back on her hotel bed. With her knees pressed into the bed, her hands using the mattress to keep her steady, as she rode his cock at her own leisure and pace.

"You like that? Tell me how that cock feels, yeah?"

"So good," she breathed.

Whined was more like it.

Reverse cowgirl took a bit of work, and a lot of fucking energy. But like this? *So much easier*, and God, she could ride him forever.

And still, she wondered how they had gotten here.

It started with a kiss in the elevator.

His words in her ear.

Can't wait to fucking eat you.

A hand slipping down her pants as he backed her into the corner as soon as they had gotten inside her hotel. More dark promises to make her wet before he could even really get started.

Are you going to let me fuck this pussy, August?

He stripped her down first. Removing each article of her clothing one at a time, slow enough that every drag of his fingertips to her overheated skin had her feeling like she was going to come the very second he started touching her pussy.

She wasn't entirely wrong.

And once he got his fill of her that way, they found the bed. Ended up … *like this*.

Jesus, was it *good*.

"*Oh, my God, yeah*," Beni groaned behind her, his hand coming down to spank her ass against before grabbing tight to the same spot. "Such a pretty fucking *pink*, August. Your ass gets so damn pink from me spanking it. And you just *love* that, don't you?"

She kept her rhythm up riding him, although how, she didn't know. Her legs trembled so much with the promise of that oncoming orgasm that she could keep herself steady on the bed. And every lungful of air that she dragged in wasn't nearly enough.

So fucking hot.

So *high*.

She loved it.

"Fuck yeah, you gonna come?" he asked. "Get my dick dripping with you?"

All she could do was nod.

She needed just a little bit more, and her pace came a little faster, hands pushing into the mattress firmer as her shaking knees dug in, too. Backing into his cock harder, trying to take him impossibly deeper to *get off*. She was almost there.

"*Almost ... almost,*" she mumbled.

That seemed to be all he needed to hear. One more slap to her ass had her skin flaring with a delicious heat, right along with the familiar bite of his fingertips grasping to her flesh. And then his hand slid across the curve of her ass, his thumb playing at the bottom of her pussy, driving over his cock, and her sensitive tissues, taking the slickness of her arousal up to her ass with his thumb. He didn't stick the digit inside her, but rather, massaged the pad of his thumb against the tight ring of muscles.

That did it.

Her pussy clenched, milking his cock as she came down on his length one more time to sit with him deep inside her, as her orgasm raged on. Sparks lit up over her skin, heating her from head to toe *instantly*.

She could breathe.

And she couldn't.

She could cry his name.

And yet she couldn't hear a sound.

Before August had even finished trembling through that orgasm, he was lifting from his back. His hands ran up her spine, kisses following the same path as he pushed forward so that she was on all fours. A palm found her throat, a hot mouth at the top of her spine as he pounded into her from behind.

Harder and harder and harder.

"Christ, you take me so good," she heard him praise. "You're gonna fuck me up so much, woman. Do you know that? Is that what you wanted—to *ruin me*?"

Thick pleasure curled through her.

And then he was coming, too. Hands tightening to her body, dark grunts falling against her skin, his weight pressing hers into the bed as their bodies fell to the mattress, and his thrusts stilled all at once.

"*Fuck*, August."

He hummed against her back.

She smiled against the sheets.

"Did I?" she asked in the darkness of the room.

Beni swallowed audibly. "What?"

"Ruin you?"

"Sure fucking feels like it."

Then, why did he sound like he liked it?

Then quieter, he said, "You should take that job here. Manic Media, I mean."

August stilled. "Why?"

"How else are we going to figure this out? Seems easier if you're here."

"Nothing is *that* easy, Beni."

"Why not?"

Yeah, right.

Why the fuck not?

The answer was easy.

He just wouldn't like it.

Nothing was that easy.

CHAPTER
11

There was nothing Beni hated more than to be woken up by the sound of a phone ringing—it almost always meant someone was going to drag his ass out of bed before he was ready. And yet, he found he didn't mind at all as he rolled over in an unfamiliar bed to grab his phone where he had left it sitting on the bedside table the night before. If only because his thoughts were still filled with memories of the night before.

Of *her.*

August.

Her taste on his tongue.

The scent of her and *sex.*

Good dreams, you know.

His mind drifted back to the shower they'd shared before falling back into bed as he picked up the call without bothering to check the ID first. "Yeah," he mumbled, running a palm down his unshaven jaw—someone was going to start bitching about that soon, he was sure of it. Made men and their rules, after all. "Beni here."

"Just waking up?"

Beni cleared his throat at the sound of his twin's voice greeting him first thing in the morning. The hard-on he had been sporting was gone in an instant, and he blinked away what sleepiness remained in his vision so that he could focus on the call.

"Yeah, getting up and around."

Bene *huh'd* under his breath before saying, "Thought I should call, you know."

"Oh, did you?"

Because it had been … a while.

A fight or argument was certainly not the first thing Beni wanted to have with his brother after going a week without speaking. In fact, he couldn't remember another time when they had gone this long without speaking or seeing one another.

It felt strange.

"Was thinking we should talk," Bene said.

"All right, so talk."

"Can't even ease me into it, huh?"

"What's the point in that?"

Bene sighed, the air crackling through the speakers. He gave his brother the second he needed to gather his thoughts, and at the same time, glanced at the empty space next to him in the bed. August's blankets had been tossed to the side, and her pillow was left with nothing more than the indent of where her head had been laying.

You know, when it wasn't on his chest.

He liked being her pillow better.

"I just … are you making a trip home anytime soon?" Bene asked.

"Hard to say. I've got shit going on here, you know that."

"Right, right. Uh, you know me leaving wasn't really about *you*, don't you?"

"I don't know fuck all, Bene." He shifted in the bed, raising up so that his back laid against the plush headboard, and he could stare at the empty doorway a few feet away from the foot of the bed. Where had August gone to, anyway? It wasn't like the hotel room was *that* big, unless she had jumped in the shower again right after waking up. But why bother when they'd had one the night before? He shook off those thoughts and went back to the conversation with his brother for the moment. "All I know is that it kind of felt like you went behind my back to talk to Dad about going home, and then when I found out, *you* had the nerve to be pissed off at me when I said you should have told me. And then you got in a whole fucking mood about August like—"

"It wasn't *her*. It was—"

"You acted like a full-on asshole."

"Jesus Christ, would you let me speak?"

"Doesn't negate the fact you were a prick. I like this girl, Bene. *A lot*, okay? And if I get my way, she's going to be around for a while. So, whatever your fucking issue is with that, I need you to get over it."

"Listen, I—"

"Everything okay?"

Beni's attention had drifted away from the doorway to focus on the red detailing of the comforter covering the bed, thus missing August coming to stand there. His grin stretched his cheeks as his gaze landed on her, and despite the worry in her stare, she still smiled back.

"Just a minute, yeah?" he asked.

August nodded. "Sure."

On the phone, however, his brother had gone silent.

"Bene?"

"You're busy, huh?" Bene muttered.

Beni *tried* not to get irritated that his brother seemed pissed just from hearing August in the background, but that was impossible. "That again?"

"No, I'm just—"

"Listen, give me a call when you're ready to grow the fuck up."

"You know what, fuck you, Beni."

That was all he got before his twin hung up the phone on

him. He wished he could be surprised, and maybe he should have let Bene get out whatever feelings he had about *whatever*—because God knew he didn't understand it—but it was too late now.

"So, that's a *no* on everything being okay, I guess."

Beni turned his stare on August again as he discarded the phone to the bedside table. It didn't matter what he was currently feeling about his brother, or that eventually, he was going to have to deal with that little issue, and *soon*. How could it matter to him when he had a beautiful view of this amazing woman standing in the doorway wearing his T-shirt from the night before, showing off her sexy legs, and part of her thighs that he *loved* having wrapped around his head.

It was impossible.

And his erection was back.

Shocker.

"Don't mind that," he told her.

August sighed. "Kind of feels like I should, though. Like maybe he's pissed because of me, you know?"

"Nah, Bene's got some issues he needs to work through. And before he can do that, he likes to blame everyone else around him first. He never wants to look in the mirror."

"Oh, is that how it goes?"

"Usually. Besides, you don't owe him fuck all. You got me?"

"I don't like that you're fighting with him because of me, though," she said, quickly adding when he gave her a look, "even if you say this is just him ... being a prick before he looks at his own problems."

"That's enough of that. *Come here.*"

"For what?"

"Because I want to *touch* you—maybe fuck you again. Who knows, August? And you won't know either, if you're going to stay over there when I am *here*."

"I ordered us food, and you want to drag me back to bed?"

His tongue peeked out to wet his upper lip, grinning suggestively. "Are you saying you don't like what happens in this bed?"

Her cheeks pinked.

God, he loved that flush.

"You know I do."

"Then, *come here*."

She didn't hesitate to give him what he wanted. Quick and steady, she crawled into the bed at the foot, coming to him on all fours with the sexiest grin that he had ever seen. She tugged at the sheets that had pooled at his waist, letting his already hard cock free to the slightly cooler air of the bedroom. Not that it mattered how cold the bedroom was because she fixed that problem of his in a blink.

Her mouth found his cock, wet and fucking warm. She sucked him at first, eyes locked on his, so he could watch his cock fill her mouth while she moaned around his shaft. He had no problem keeping his hands to himself because *damn* … she knew exactly what she was doing, and how to suck his cock just fine. She didn't need him giving her any direction.

Her tongue teased at the head of his dick, the tip playing at the slit before she licked him right down to the base. Over his balls, drawing a hiss out of his tightening chest, before she went right back up his shaft again.

"Holy fuck, your mouth is something else," he breathed, the best he could do for words, really. Because that's what she did—she made him speechless. Time and time again. In bed, and out of it. "Love the way you suck my dick."

"Do you?"

Her words whispered against the head of his cock.

Beni groaned.

"Jesus Christ, *August*."

"Tell me again."

He swallowed hard. "Love the way you suck my fucking *cock*."

Once more, he was in her mouth.

Getting that *heat*.

Feeling her tongue, and cheeks hollowing, lips wrapping his shaft as she sucked and sucked and *fuck* ...

Beni did reach for her, then, about to blow his load as his hands slipped along the column of her throat, making her gaze dart upward to meet his. Although, that's exactly what she seemed determined to make him do, too. He just wanted to have her *look* at him again while she made him come. Then, maybe she could see what she was doing to him.

Maybe she would understand.

Because he sure as hell didn't.

But he liked it.

"You know," Beni said, letting August use his hand to steady herself as she climbed off the back of his Ducati, "for someone who has such a high sense of self-preservation, you don't seem to mind riding on the back of my bike."

She pulled the extra helmet off her head, giving him a look. He'd flipped his visor up on his own helmet, so she had the perfect view of his teasing smirk.

"Or maybe it's the man on the bike that makes me forget how much I value my life. Ever consider *that*?"

Beni laughed. "Well ... as long as you know you're safe with me."

August's stance softened. "I do know that."

She went to hand the helmet back to him so that he could strap it onto the rear of the seat like he had done before, but Beni shook his head. Nobody else got on the back of his bike—*ever*. No one except her, now.

"Keep it," he said. "You'll probably need it again."

She gave him a look.

"What?"

"What are we doing, Beni? *This*, I mean. You and me. What is it?"

She wasn't the only one wondering about that. He glanced over the front yard of his friend's home—she wanted to come back to Camilla's place, as she said she at least owed her friend breakfast after flaking on her the night before. He had to head out to the goddamn warehouse across the city after getting called in.

A break in, or something.

The crew.

Again.

Because of course.

He would have much rather spent his day in bed with this woman, or shit ... even following her around with Camilla, if she would let him do that, but here they were. Adults, and all that good shit, with real responsibilities they had to handle.

Fun.

Beni tugged his helmet off, wanting to speak to her face to face, and not with that thing on his head. Setting it to the handlebars of the bike, he leaned against the helmet and locked gazes with her. That way, there was no chance of her looking away when he said what he wanted to say.

"I think the better question," he started, "is what *you* want here, August."

"Or that's your way of getting out of a tough conversation."

"Not at all." Beni sat up straight, leaning back a bit on his bike because this woman had *no* idea. None at all what she had done to him in their time together. "I know exactly what I want when it comes to you. I want *everything*. Whatever you want to give me, that's what I want to take, okay. But here's the thing—that's hard to do when you're not here because you're somewhere else. And how are we supposed to figure out what we're doing when one of us isn't going to be here to do that?"

She swallowed hard. "You're asking me to stay in Chicago … *again*."

"I didn't say that."

"Suggestion is enough, Beni."

"You asked what I wanted from this, though. Why ask if you don't want a truthful answer?"

"My life is in New—"

"And mine was in Toronto, but shit changes. That's life."

"I have a job there. My *parents*. You and Camilla … you both think that it should be easy for someone to just uproot *everything* at the drop of a hat because something feels like it might be great, but that's the thing. I don't know that anything here will work out. The job … *you*. None of it, and I am not the kind of woman who risks a sure thing on *something*."

Ouch.

She hit him where it hurt.

A part of him respected it.

Another part wanted to grab that woman, drag her to him, and kiss her until she understood that nothing was ever going to feel right or good in his life again until he could see and speak to her every single day of his life. It didn't have to be normal or make sense. It just *was*.

She made him crazy.

He *liked* that just fine.

And yet, Beni didn't argue with her. He wasn't going to push August into something she wasn't ready for just because he was at a completely different place than she was. That wasn't fair to her, and he wasn't that type of asshole.

Maybe not today, or tomorrow ... but *someday*, if he did that, and forced her into a choice that she hadn't willingly made because she wanted it too, then she would resent him. It wouldn't be any different for Camilla, if her friend did the same.

He didn't want that at all.

"For the record," he said, "so it can be known it was said and all, I want you to stay here. I want you to take that job. I want you to be *mine*—my fucking girl, okay? But I want it to be what you want, too, and that's what matters more."

"Killing me here," she murmured.

Beni shrugged. "Fair is fair, woman. You killed me from the jump."

From *second one*.

First glance.

She had him caught.

Every step, each word after was just ... *bonus*. A lure drawing him in closer while she reeled and reeled until she had him caught in her snare.

What was he supposed to do now?

Wait her out.

August glanced back at the house before coming back to him just as fast. "It's not a *no*, okay? It's just a ... *I need time.* I have things to take care of back at home when my time here is done, and then I can seriously give this a shot."

Beni nodded once. "Okay."

He could deal with that.

"*Just* okay?"

"Whatever you want, woman. I am game."

Her sweet laughter colored the driveway before she darted forward. He caught her in his embrace, their kiss a fuel to an already raging inferno. He surely didn't need to go to work this morning with a hard-on while also thinking about the fact that all too soon, this woman was going to be even further out of his reach.

And yet, that's exactly what he did.

~

August still clung heavily to the back of Beni's mind even as he arrived at the warehouse. After parking the Ducati on the street next to the side of the place, he headed for the door he always used to enter the building to the find it was already opened.

He surveyed the broken lock on the side of the door-jamb. *Shit*, someone must have used a power tool to grind out the fucking lock. And given the security on the building basically boiled down to an alarm that engaged twenty seconds after someone entered the place … well, if they knew where the panel was, and how to shut it off, no one would even know they had broken in. Not to mention, there weren't any goddamn cameras in the place.

A made man's paranoia, and all.

No one wanted to catch their *own* crimes on tape.

"Well, fuck," Beni muttered.

"Fuck is *right*."

He glanced up, standing straight to see the Capo coming his way. Jerome wore a scowl that could rival the devil's on a bad day. Looking far more disheveled than he had ever seen the man, the Capo even had his tie loosened around his neck, had lost his standard suit jacket, and his white dress shirt was rolled up to the elbows. That was *before* the man's messy hair, and the dirt smeared to the knee of his pants like he had been kneeling on the ground, or something.

"Think it's related to the gang and the—"

"Yes," Jerome snapped. "Because they lifted a bunch of

shit out of the warehouse. And of course, because I don't have cameras, well … I got nothing."

Beni nodded. "Yeah, that's rough. What does it look like inside the place?"

Jerome sighed harshly and glanced over his shoulder. "You know what, look for yourself. I am going to run down the street, grab myself something to drink at that fucking Irish pub that stays open all hours of the day, and think about what I'm going to do next here. This is getting out of control."

To say the least …

He didn't say that out loud.

"We'll get it figured out," Beni said, shrugging. "The fact that whoever it is, especially if we believe it's someone *inside* the crew, is getting this blatant speaks of … well, desperation. And we all know what happens when fuckers get desperate, right?"

"They make mistakes."

"Exactly. It's a matter of time."

"Or I could just shut down the whole crew—clean house and be done with it."

"Is that what you want to do?"

Jerome grunted under his breath, stepping out onto the side street with a shake of his head. "No because that crew … I have been building it for years. Never had a problem until recently. They're a *good* group of guys who know what the fuck they're supposed to be doing. And to rebuild a crew like that from the ground up? *Impossible*."

"And a lot of money lost in the process."

"Losing fucking money *now*."

Point taken.

"And it's hard on them," the Capo added quieter, "knowing someone in their ranks is fucking them over—making it harder to work and causing me to be distrustful of them all. To make a crew work, a man needs two things. Rapport with their people, and a common reason that keeps them all wanting to work together. This is ruining what I worked for with these guys. That's breeding a whole other problem for me here. I need this to be fixed, and *soon*."

The man's threat was clear.

"It will be," Beni assured.

Although how, he didn't know.

"I could clean house," Jerome muttered, "or start picking them off one by one until I find the right fucker. But what does that do? Makes them *scared* of me, makes them bitter, and vengeful. Because they're all friends, or some of them. And when you start fucking with one, you fuck with them all. They might not come back on me right now, but *eventually* … and I can't afford that risk. I know how this works. I need to find the one without hurting the others, or else they'll make me pay for it."

Huh.

All Beni's life, his goal with the family business had been the position this man right here held. A *Capo*. He'd never looked at the boss's seat like it was good for him, because he didn't fit the mold of what a boss needed to be, and he wasn't so arrogant that he couldn't admit it. But a Capo? That felt right, and he wanted it.

It was only now that Beni realized just how complex and intricate the job of a Capo running a crew on the streets could be. They were as dependent on their men as they were on themselves, and *la famiglia*. To punish one, meant to screw with the others. And when one chip started to fall, the rest would soon follow.

Beni absorbed that.

He wouldn't soon forget it.

Once the Capo had disappeared down the street, and out of sight, Beni headed inside the warehouse. Sure enough, it was a mess. Boxes overturned from the recent shipment of fake goods that would need to be sold on the street. Some shit had been broken, a lot of it was just missing entirely.

The one car left to be chopped up, that had yet to be touched, now had dents beaten into the roof, hood, and doors. Glass from the windows sprinkled the cement floor, and slashes had been cut into the leather seats of the Benz.

Damn.

Someone had taken cans of spray paint, and went to work on the floors, walls, metal beams, and everything else they could fucking touch, by the looks of it. Gang signs had been painted on whatever they could find—ruining *more* shit that would need to be replaced.

Definitely connected to the rest of it, then.

Except ... this kind of confirmed it to Beni, he thought, as he lingered in the doorway of a now trashed office that belonged to the Capo. Stuffing his hands into his pockets, he had zero doubt now that whoever was stealing and fucking around *within* the crew was working with the gang to cause the crew and Capo problems, too.

Simply because of the alarm system.

Whoever came inside here last night *knew* about the alarm, and likely where the panel was to shut it off, not to mention, how to shut the fucking thing down. So, someone had to have given that information to the gang or were here to do it for them.

Unless, of course, the person wanted them to believe it was the gang who did this. Beni seriously doubted that ... if only because soon enough, if it had been the gang, they would send out word about that they did. Prideful fuckers that they were wouldn't pass up an opportunity to brag about how they fucked over a mafia Capo.

It was the *whys* that tripped Beni up.

Why work with a gang?

If all the fucker in the crew wanted to do was steal, and make some extra cash on the side, if that was the case … why make it *this* blatant?

Because now, it meant trouble.

Now, they were looking for them.

Now, they were certain to die.

It reeked of desperation.

Again.

So, why?

What was the cause?

Beni turned to leave the doorway of the office and head further back into the warehouse to possibly begin cleaning up. Except he just made it far enough to see a bat swinging in his direction. And then all he saw was blackness.

CHAPTER
12

"And then after this morning, he brought me back to your place."

Across the table, Camilla raised her brows and wagged them suggestively, all the while, keeping her to-go cup of coffee high to her lips to hide her grin. August didn't need to see it to *know*—her best friend would never change, and that was a promise.

"Oh, so you just *woke up* and he brought you home? That's all?"

August laughed. "*Well …*"

"I knew it!"

Camilla's crow brought the attention of several people in the café their way. The bustling business had great sandwiches, according to her friend, but they were still waiting for their order to show up on their table, so August was holding off on making any rash statements like they were the *best*. Some people forgot that spices and flavoring was needed and depended on only salt and pepper to do the job.

Right.

"Details, details." Cam smacked the table with the palm of her hand. "I need them *now*."

"You really are the absolute worst."

Camilla preened. "And yet, you're still going to give me all the details."

Obviously.

"He certainly made my morning worth while," August admitted, "a couple of times over."

Camilla pressed her lips together and squealed under her breath like they were two teenage girls talking about their first time fumbling around with a boy. All she could do was shake her head and laugh along with her friend's antics.

"You know, I honestly didn't think someone like Beni was your type," Camilla noted.

"What's that supposed to mean?"

"Connected. Affiliated. You do know his father is a major crime boss in Canada, right? *Gian Guzzi*—has controlled Canada for years. And his mother? Sister to Tom's father, so he comes from … well, I mean he's a *principe*, by all standards. A mafia *prince*. I just didn't think you would go for a mob guy."

Oh.

That was not what August thought her friend meant at all.

"I guess I just never thought about it."

Camilla's brow dipped. "Or was it that you chose to ignore it? Because even though you like to act as though you don't know about this life, you *know* … you really do, August."

"That's fair. And maybe, yeah. It did cross my mind, but …"

"What?"

"I was more interested in the man than the details. He makes that really easy."

Too easy, maybe.

"So, what you're saying is that you *like* him, right?"

That question was *so* fucking easy to answer that it was sickening. *Yes*, she liked Beni. Far more than she probably should, if she were being an honest woman about it all. There was something about that man drawing her in, and the more time she spent with him, the harder his invisible hold became around her heart.

He *gave a shit*.

He didn't push.

He was just the right amount of confidence mixed with sensitivity and *good fucking genes*. Like an all-in-one package of the perfect man. They weren't even supposed to exist, but August was pretty sure she found one in Beni.

Her curiosity about the people who raised him, and where he came from had grown tenfold simply because she wondered … were they the reason he was like he was? Was his family as accepting and kind as him, and yet still as enigmatic and charming, too?

He was supposed to be *fun*.

Something to do while she was here.

And yet, there August was, thinking about if she might someday meet his family, and if she could get in one more chance to see him before she left to go back to New York.

So, yes.

The answer was easy.

She didn't just *like* that man—it was more than that. More complicated than that. A complex wrapped around a *yes* she was scared to say.

"Aug?"

She glanced up to meet Camilla's stare, finding her friend looking less *amused* and more … caring. "Yeah?"

"You didn't answer me. Do you like him?"

"I do."

"Why did it take so long to say it?"

"Because it's not simple."

Camilla nodded, but said nothing. August appreciated that. It was one of the things about her friend that she didn't think a lot of people realized, honestly. Yes, Cam was a little over the top, and could be a bit much to handle at times.

And then there were moments like these when her friend just knew to … back off. No questions asked.

"I uh, didn't tell him that my flight leaves in two days," August added quieter.

Air hissed through Camilla's teeth. "No?"

"Couldn't bring myself to say it."

"You would rather him find out when he realized you weren't here anymore, then?"

"*No.*"

"Well, that's what will happen."

God, she knew.

She did.

Camilla shrugged, setting her cup down to the table at the same time. "Look at it like this … if it's something that will go somewhere, or he's a man worth keeping—and you know I never believed in *that* before Tom—then he's going to wait, or he will figure it out. *You both* will figure out something, or a way to make it work, no matter what. If it's real, if he knows what he wants and so do you, then what's meant to be will be."

"Cheesy."

"And?"

Yeah.

August just sighed.

The two fell into a comfortable silence as their food was finally brought to their tables. Sub sandwiches and freshly sliced fruit. A refill on their coffees, and they dug into the food. August was grateful for the lack of conversation because she wasn't willing to face the fact that she had yet to make a *real* decision on Beni, Chicago … and well, everything else, too. Maybe because she was just scared of what it would mean, but that didn't matter.

Right?

August had no clue.

"Cam, August, what are my chances to find you two here?"

August didn't mean to stiffen at the sound of Alessa Conti's voice behind her, and yet she still did. She still hadn't told Camilla about the meeting she had with Alessa to talk about taking a job with Manic Media in Chicago, and didn't think *now* would be the best time for her to figure out.

And yet, it seemed like she wasn't going to be given a choice.

"August," Alessa said as she came to stand next to their table, "have you given any thought to what we talked about? I hear you're leaving soon, so I was curious."

"What did you talk about?"

August glanced between Camilla on the other side of the table, and Alessa's warm smile. It wasn't anyone's fault for this but her own, and yet … *damn.*

"Uh, I have and I haven't," August replied.

Alessa gave her a nod. "Still trying to figure out how to justify and balance what you think you owe to what you want and know is best, hmm?"

"That, and more."

"That's okay. Just know that whenever you are ready, there is a job at Manic Media waiting for you."

"Thanks, Alessa. I really appreciate it."

"You talked to Alessa while you were here about a job?"

Ouch.

Why did Camilla's tone sound almost accusatory?

"It was just a meeting to *discuss* the possibility," August said quietly.

Camilla's brow furrowed. "Why didn't you tell me? I would have been … over the fucking moon, Aug."

"Well—"

"Sorry to interrupt, ladies."

Their attention swung to the familiar man approaching

the table. He came to stand beside Alessa with a severe expression, and a stare locked on Camilla—his *job*. August didn't even know the man's name, honestly, but he always followed her friend around. She asked about it once, Camilla shrugged, and explained he was her enforcer.

A bodyguard, basically.

Rarely did he show himself.

If he did …

August knew that meant bad things.

"What's wrong?" Camilla asked.

"Something's happened, Cam," he said quickly, "an attack on the east side, and to be safe, Tommaso asked that I take you home. Tom will be there to meet you."

They didn't question the man, quickly gathering their things to leave. Alessa said her goodbyes, with another reminder to August that the job was there when, or if, she wanted it. At the same time, Camilla shot August a look that spoke volumes without ever saying a word.

We're talking about this later.

Yeah, she didn't doubt it.

As the enforcer promised at the café, Tommaso was home to meet his wife when they arrived back at their place. However, Camilla seemed less interested in her husband and his conversation on the phone in the living room, and more focused on throwing question after question at August.

"When did you have a meeting with Alessa about the job in Chicago?"

"Shortly after I arrived," August replied, although she wasn't entirely in the conversation. Camilla might not have been interested in listening to the conversation Tommaso was having, but she heard him say a name that had *all* of her attention at once.

"And Beni is okay?" Tom asked in the next room.

Oh, God.

Beni.

It was *Beni*.

Or was it?

She didn't know, but she intended to find—

"And you didn't think to tell me at all about it?" Camilla demanded.

August let out a hard breath, turning to face her friend. "Do you tell me every single little detail about your life?"

"I at least *try*! You purposely kept this from me, August. Like fine, I get it … maybe you don't want to be in Chicago, or whatever. But you could have just told me you had the meeting with Alessa. You didn't have to keep it a secret, you know?"

That's what she thought?

Honestly?

"You think it was just about me keeping a secret and not the fact that maybe this is a *huge* choice for me to make, and I might have wanted to do it alone without yours, or someone else's, input, Cam?"

"I don't know what you thought because you didn't tell me!"

"A concussion, and some bruises?" she heard Tommaso ask. "Good, good, then he'll come back from that after a couple of days of rest, no worries. Get someone on Beni, make sure he's got an enforcer posted at his door, so he can do exactly that … no, I'll call my father, and let him know. He'll deal with the rest how he wants to … yeah, later."

It *was* Beni.

He had been hurt.

Attacked.

August's entire heart felt like it fell right out of her chest, and shattered to a million and one pieces on the floor. She turned on her heel, not bothering to explain to Camilla what she was doing or why she wanted to end their conversation, before heading to the living room where she found Tommaso slipping his phone into the pocket of his slacks.

"Is Beni okay?" she asked.

Tommaso nodded her way. "Yeah, looks like he's going to be fine. Although, we don't know who in the hell attacked him. Mostly superficial shit, but—"

"Where is he?"

The man's gaze drifted behind August before coming back to her just as fast. "According to my man, he's been released from the hospital, and should be getting back home anytime. If he follows my orders, that's where he'll stay for a couple of days until he's feeling like his usual self."

That should make her feel better.

She should breathe easier.

And yet …

Nope.

All it served to do was make her feel worse because all she had was third-party information, and she hadn't actually seen Beni for herself. That was not going to work for her at all in this situation.

"Can you get someone to drive me over to his place?"

"Yeah, absolutely. Just let me call—"

"Are we not going to finish our conversation, then?" Camilla asked.

"We'll talk about it later, okay?" she asked, slipping past Camilla in the entryway to grab the things she'd left in the hallway. "It's not a big deal."

"Or are you just trying to avoid it the way you didn't even bother to tell me in the first place?"

August swung around on her friend, *knowing* and understanding damn well why she was mad, and that she had a right to be. At the same time … "Cam, I love you."

"I know."

"But I am also allowed to make my own decisions. And sometimes, that means doing things alone. Making decisions *by myself.* Especially when it is something as big and important as changing careers, or moving to an entirely new state away from the only family I really have. And no, you don't get to be mad at me because I want to take the time to decide whether or not that is the right decision for me. It's not about *you*, or us being friends since forever, okay? It's about me, and what I need."

Camilla snapped straight, the annoyance in her features drifting away. "I … know that."

"Do you?"

"*Yes.*"

"Then, act like it!"

"*August.*"

Jesus.

The very last thing she wanted to do was fight with her *best* friend. The girl who had her back all through high school. The first person she told when she kissed a boy, and the night she lost her virginity. The woman who, without question, would be there for her at the drop of a hat simply because she said she needed her.

She didn't want to fight with Camilla *ever.*

And yet, she couldn't stay here like this, either. She sighed, the panicked need in her chest growing and thumping deeper in her bloodstream with each beat of her heart—the desire to go see Beni because he had been hurt taking over everything, including her desire to continue this conversation.

"I know, Cam," she said. "You're mad—because we *always* talk about everything. I *know*. And this time, I didn't tell you. I just needed to make the decision alone, that's all."

"I'm sorry."

Her friend was still mad, though.

August understood why.

"I'll tell you what Alessa offered me, and what I'm thinking about it, *later*. Okay? Right now, I just really want to go see Beni."

Camilla nodded quickly. "Yeah, sure. I understand."

But did she?

God.

August hoped so.

"Oh, my *God*, look at you," August whispered when Beni pulled open the apartment door. A *massive* bruise colored the side of his face right up to his temple. It continued into his hairline. Other than the discoloration and the obvious bump left on the side of his face from whatever hit him, the rest of his face was left untouched. "That looks like it hurts."

"Apparently," he drawled, "one hit was enough. Whoever it was just wanted to knock me out. Probably because they hadn't been expecting me to be in there, or whatever."

The guy posted at Beni's apartment door—the enforcer Tommaso mentioned earlier—cleared his throat. "Didn't think you would mind me letting her in."

"Of course, not. Thanks."

"Are you going to make me stand in the hallway, or …?"

Beni laughed tiredly, but shrugged as he moved back, and opened the door wider. She stepped in behind him, giving the man at the door a smile before closing it to leave him in the hallway alone. Not that he looked like he minded.

His job, and all.

"What happened?" she asked.

"Work," Beni replied, turning around to head deeper into the apartment, while giving her a great view of his muscular, defined back at the same time. "I got called in for something that had happened, and someone hit me when I came out of the office. But hey, at least they didn't hit me when my back was turned."

August frowned, following him until they reached the living room, and Beni fell into the corner of the couch. She didn't sit, though. "Was that supposed to be a *joke* about this?"

"Woman, if I don't find something to fucking smile about right now, someone might die."

Well, then.

Okay.

She came around the front of the couch, folding her arms over her chest as she surveyed his injury again. It really *did* look terrible, and she bet it was mighty sore. Her fingers itched to reach out and graze the bruise just to see if it was warm under her touch, and if she might be able to soothe whatever pain he was feeling.

Her stare did not go unnoticed.

"It's not as bad as it looks," Beni murmured, his hand coming out to rest overtop the denim covering her hip. "A concussion, and some bruising. That's it."

"Yeah, *this time.*"

His gaze darted up to hers.

August just shrugged.

"Cam's really mad at me," she said, tone dropping lower.

"Why?"

"She found out that I had a meeting with Alessa for the job offer."

"Shouldn't that make her—"

"And that I still didn't tell her about it until she found out by accident."

Beni sighed. "Ah, yeah. I mean, that might rub somebody wrong, I guess."

Somewhere in the apartment, a phone rang. She recognized the tune as his cell phone, but he didn't look the least bit interested in getting up to answer the call. In fact, he brushed it off with a roll of his eyes.

"Fucking thing won't shut up, and if I didn't feel like the room was spinning every time I stand up, I would find it and turn it off," he muttered.

August smiled a little. "I'll find it for you after, and shut it off."

"Oh, does that mean you're staying?"

Why did that question sound like *more* than just him asking for her to stay the night with him? She pushed the thought out of her mind, unsure if that was his intention, or just her subconscious making its desires known.

That hand of his stroked up and down her hip, but his gaze focused on her face. "Don't move too much, okay? Makes me dizzy."

"Jesus Christ, Beni."

"Yeah, concussions *blow*."

She shook her head. "You know, all this showed me was that even more of my life would change, if I decided to move here permanently."

His brow furrowed.

So fucking cute, too.

She pushed that thought away.

"How so?" he asked.

"At home, I don't face this kind of thing. The *mafia*. All the business, and issues. And since I've come to visit, it feels like that's all I've seen. It kind of makes me think that it would be yet another change for me to handle, and that's … well, it terrifies me."

"August?"

"Hmm?"

"*I'm fine.*"

She reached out to let her fingertips graze his bruised temple. She had been right, too, as the injury felt warm to the touch, and that only concerned her more. This was *scary*. That he was involved in something that could end his life. That her best friend married the same kind of man. She had chosen to see the man Beni showed her, instead of the details of his life that promised sleepless nights filled with worry, and days like today.

And *still* …

She wanted him.

There were just other things she had to handle first. Her thoughts, and feelings. A job back home that she hadn't loved in a long time. Her parents … all of it. And she wasn't going to explain or apologize to anyone for wanting to make sure that *this*—Chicago—was the right choice for her. Even if that meant going back home for a while to figure it out alone.

August leaned down, and pressed a soft kiss to Beni's lips, and reveled in the feeling of his smile growing against her own. "I'm still allowed to be worried."

Beni nodded. "You are, and is that a yes on staying the night?"

"Who the hell else is going to make sure you stay awake for twelve or more hours?"

CHAPTER

13

"Are you seriously telling me," August teased, pointing a confectioner's sugar-dusted finger at the pile of fluffy pancakes she had let him make for her, "that this is only the *second* time you've cooked pancakes?"

Beni nodded, and tried to tamper down the urge to lean forward just enough that he might be able to suck on the tips of her sweetened fingers. It was a *strong* fucking urge though, and he really wasn't in the mood to ignore it. After the night he had before, the *few* hours of sleep he was finally allowed to have, and the sex he couldn't have because this woman was *sure* it wasn't okay with a concussion ... he was ready to just *get what he wanted.*

Which was August.

On his dick.

That sounded like a *really* great way to begin a day like today after a shitfest like yesterday. That's all he was saying.

"*Really?*' August demanded again. "And just lick my damn fingers if that's what you want to do—I can see that, you know?"

Beni laughed deeply, adoring this woman even more for that. Leaning against the counter like he was beside her, it allowed him to be able to look up at her, and he winked. "Listen, *yes*, much to my mother's displeasure, I never wanted to learn to cook. Someone else was always willing to do it for me. My brother and I ... well, we mostly just ordered in or got easy shit anyone could cook with directions on the box. Apparently, you give me *Google* and a how-to video, and I can cook just about anything."

She arched her brow. "So, what you meant to say is you were spoiled."

Well …

"Basically," he said, shrugging. "We're the babies of the family. Probably a little too wild for our own good, and we got away with *a lot* of shit our brothers never would have been allowed to do just because we were the youngest. It was just these last few months, being here in Chicago, that I chilled out a bit."

August *huh'd* under her breath before asking, "And why did you just all of the sudden decide to start cooking?"

Beni glanced away from her, an unusual emotion heating his cheeks.

"*Oh, my God,*" August said, a laugh coloring her words, "is that *the* Beni Guzzi *embarrassed?*"

Fuck, this woman.

She was going to kill him.

In the best way.

Swallowing his pride just to admit she was right and let her in on another secret that she had probably already figured out, he said, "I thought … fuck, you were the first woman I let stay the entire night—*ever.* I figured if I was gonna do that again—because I *was* going to do that again—then I should know how to make you something to eat in the morning … or you know, whenever you needed to eat while you were here."

August just … *stared* at him.

Still, and smiling softly.

Beni grinned, remembering the *other* part of this conversation that he had been trying to have before they got into this one. "And come here …"

His hand darted out, his fingers circling her delicate wrist, so he could pull her to him. He brought those still-sugar dusted fingers of hers to his lips, kissing the soft sweetness on the tips before he enclosed them in his mouth.

And *yes*, sugar on this woman's skin was *perfect*.

Like her.

He locked eyes with her as his tongue slid along the side of her fingers, making sure to take every last bit of it that he could find. There was something primal at the swell of satisfaction in his blood at the sight of her moaning for nothing more than his mouth on her fingers.

"Fuck, you better do something with that mouth of yours, Beni. *Somewhere else.*"

He let go of her fingers with a dark laugh—thick, and pleased. In one fell swoop, he had her picked up at the waist, and sat down on the small island in the moderately sized kitchen. It was the biggest room in the whole damn apartment, for whatever reason.

Unashamed, she widened her legs for him. That T-shirt of his that she'd worn to bed riding up around her hips to give him a beautiful view of her bare pussy spread out for him to *feast* on. Because that was the thing—when he ate pussy, he wanted to *drown* in it. And there was something about the taste of August that just got his dick rock-hard at nothing more than the thought of it alone.

It kind of drove him crazier that after she jumped out of the shower that morning, she put on his clothes for bed. The shirt that still smelled like him, but looked so fucking good on her. And she didn't even put her panties back on.

He knew why, too.

He wasn't the only one wanting his dick to get wet.

"Give me your mouth," she said, voice hot with anticipation.

His hands curved to her inner thighs, pushing those legs

of hers open even more as he leaned in for his first taste. A full stroke of his tongue from the slit of her pussy to her shuddering clit. The cry that fell from her lips was *heavenly*.

A new song for him to learn.

Beni went back down to her slit, feasting on that taste of her just long enough that her legs started to shake under his hands. Then, he was right back at her clit with a fast, hard beat that'd he learned she liked. He kept that pace up until she was digging her fingers against his scalp and threading into his hair, hips rolling into his mouth, and his name on her lips like a fucking *prayer*.

Her orgasm came on hard.

Broken cries.

Flushed skin.

And the taste of salt and sex against his tongue.

He watched her fall apart above him, hotter than fucking ever with his dick feeling like it was about to punch a hole through the pants he'd thrown on earlier to be respectably decent. He dotted kisses up her pelvis, across the expanse of her stomach, letting his tongue pick up the distinct taste of her as he went.

Then, he kissed under her heaving breasts, and up the valley between them, stopping to let his teeth find her collarbones as her whispers came out needy and fast.

"I fucking want you so bad."

"Do you?" he asked, mouth grazing hers.

"*Yes.*"

"Say it, then. *Fuck me, Beni.* Tell me what you want, August."

She didn't even hesitate.

And *God*, that was even better.

"Fuck me, Beni."

"*Yeah*, that's what I wanted to hear."

He kissed her mouth, hard and deep, their lips parting

instantly for a taste of each other. He felt her reaching for the bag she'd thrown to the counter earlier with one hand, while her other worked between them, rubbing over his hard cock through the fabric of his pants before moving higher to tug at the waistband.

She found the condom she was looking for in the bag, and he managed to get his pants down ... even if it wasn't as fast as what he would have liked for it to happen. He let her roll that latex down his cock, the feeling of her fingers tightening on him with fast strokes as she finished was damn near enough to bring him to his knees.

What was even better was slipping inside that tight, wet heat of hers. So fucking *slick*—she welcomed his thrusts with tightening inner muscles and low moans that said she *loved* the way his cock stretched her out.

Shit.

So did he.

That brutal, frantic pace of theirs was familiar to him now. The knowledge that he wouldn't be able to get enough of her urging him on faster, and harder. Right along with the demands of *more, more, more* from August, too.

He bunched that shirt of his she wore in a fist, pulling it taut so her naked skin was flush against him. His other found the underside of her throat, so he could tilt her head back and stare into her face as he fucked her harder. Like this, he could feel all those shivers wracking her body, and the sounds rumbling from within before she even let them loose.

And he could *see* her.

See that pleasure.

See his name come out of her mouth.

See her.

That alone was enough to get him off. There was something about the way she looked like this, and how *privileged* he felt to have her give it to him. To trust him enough to let him do it at all.

He'd never thought about sex that way before.

Not *that* deep.

And that's when he realized this was more.

"*Beni*," she breathed.

He knew already.

"You gonna come for me?"

Her high whine answered him back.

"Fucking give it to me, then."

She did.

And that was beautiful, too.

He enjoyed the sight of her coming apart like that just long enough for her to catch her breath before she was demanding the same of him.

To come.

To *please, come in me.*

His control was gone.

He saw stars when he came.

Goddamn.

Beni licked the remaining powdered sugar from the tips of August's fingers as she shivered, a pleased sigh falling from her plush lips that had him wanting to kiss her again. *Hell*, he could and would spend the rest of his life *happily* doing exactly that.

Kissing this woman.

Touching her.

Being with her.

All of it.

He wanted it.

The words that Beni had refused to really say because he wanted August to make her choices about him and Chicago without his influence started to bubble up from his chest. They were going to spill out, irrevocably changing this agreement between them, if he didn't get a hold on it, and *fast.*

"Now *that*," August murmured, still trembling in his hold, "was a *great* way to make breakfast, even if it's probably cold now."

"Microwave," he said, "and it'll heat up just fine."

"Mmm, maybe."

"Except right now, I'm wondering how much convincing it would take for you to let me take you back to bed instead of—"

A knock echoed throughout the apartment, cockblocking Beni in the *worst* possible fucking way. August laughed at the deep scowl that settled into his expression, but it quickly melted away when she leaned forward to press a kiss to the underside of his jaw.

"Someone checking up on you, probably. Don't be mad people care."

"Right, right." He stepped back from her, although it was the very last thing he wanted to do. "Better get dressed, but just know … the clothes won't stay on you for long. As soon as I can get whoever the fuck that is gone, they'll be going. And me and you will be—"

"Go answer your door," she said, tossing a dishrag at him.

Damn her.

He loved it.

Loved her.

Beni blinked as the words drifted through his mind fast and yet, not at all fleeting. They couldn't be something he just *thought* and then they went away when it felt like an echo chamber in his brain, the words coming back again and again to reverberate through his entire soul.

Love her, love her, love her …

You love her.

God.

It was so fucking obvious.

Once the words were there, he couldn't forget them. Once he allowed himself to think them, there was no taking them back. His mind made good and sure of *that*.

"Yeah," he said gruffly, stepping back to tuck himself away, and do up his pants quickly. Annoying, considering he hadn't even discarded that fucking condom, but he would do it soon enough. "But get dressed."

"Okay."

She was oblivious, though.

Didn't have a clue that a simple thought had just changed his whole life. To be frank, *she* had been the one to change his life from that first meeting, but it was only now that he was truly realizing what it meant, and that he had no fucking idea how to deal with it.

Strange how that worked.

The knocking continued, annoying the hell out of him further. Beni left the kitchen, shouting toward the apartment door, "Just a second—relax, fuck. I need a minute to get decent in here."

The knocking stopped.

Thankfully.

Beni made a beeline for the bathroom, quickly discarding the condom and washing his hands. He grabbed a semi-clean shirt that he'd left sitting on the vanity counter the day before, and punched his arms through the sleeves as he headed for the door. He didn't even bother to check the peephole before swinging the door open.

"Do you realize what fucking time it is?" he snarled.

And immediately regretted it.

Because there stood Bene.

Except his twin looked two seconds away from a total, and complete meltdown. The dark circles under his twin's eyes spoke of *no sleep*. The slight trembling in his hands told him something was wrong.

Very wrong.

Bene was a mess.

His clothes rumpled.

Hair wild.

Panicked stare.

"Bene?"

Bene's gaze darted to the bruise that was still ugly looking on the side of Beni's head. "I called. *A lot*, Beni."

Shit.

His phone hadn't stopped ringing.

August turned it off for him.

"The phone was shut off so I could—"

"I felt that," Bene said, pointing a finger at his brother's head. "*That right there*—I fucking felt it."

Yeah, damn.

Beni hadn't even given his twin a second thought the day before when the attack happened. Although, he figured his excuse was justifiable considering the whack he took to the head, and the concussion he suffered because of it. Not that any of those excuses would make his twin feel any better about the situation.

"I figured Tommaso would get someone to call Ma and Dad, and that they would let you know what was going on. I should have picked up the phone, and let you know shit was okay. Did you drive all the way here, or catch a late flight?"

"Drove."

Yikes.

That was a good sixteen hours or more.

Depending on traffic, and other shit.

"You couldn't call me back this morning or something?" Bene asked.

"I haven't even turned my phone back on. We were just cooking, and—"

"*We?*"

"Everything okay?"

Fucking hell.

Beni was able to watch the way his brother's features morphed from worry and panic to something else entirely. That understanding washed over Bene's face, replacing his pain and fear with anger and disbelief.

Bene didn't even look past Beni to see August standing down the hall. Instead, he just glared at his brother. Like he blamed *him* for this. Like it was Beni's fault this had happened. And shit, maybe it was, but he still didn't have the first clue what was going on with his brother, never mind how to help him through it.

If he even could …

"Oh, now I fucking get it," Bene muttered, nodding as he took a wide step backward. "Now I get why you were too busy to call me, yeah."

"Beni—"

Bene held up a hand, except really, it was just a single finger. The *middle one.* "No, it's all right. I got it, Beni, no worries. You've made it really clear where you and I stand here."

"Would you knock that off?"

"What, the fact that you'd rather bury yourself in new pussy instead of—"

"Watch your fucking *mouth.*"

He didn't know why the suggestion that August was *just* pussy to him—something to fuck, and keep himself distracted—bothered him so much, and so *quickly.* Violently, even. Oh, sure, he'd had moments with his twin over the years where the two of them went to blows over something fucking stupid. That was typical *boy* nonsense. Average for brothers. And yet, he'd never wanted to really hurt Bene before, but he felt like he might right then.

And that scared him.

It was also a lie.

He knew exactly why Bene's words bothered him. It reminded him of something his father had once told him about men and women, and it was a lesson he refused to forget. *A woman's worth should never be based on her behavior in the bedroom, but a man's should always be determined by the way he treats her outside of it.*

There had never been an *act like a slut, be treated like a slut* rule in the talks he had with his father and brothers as he grew up. Things like that, his father made clear, were just a way for men to shame women for the same shit men did all the time without consequence or thought to their own morals. Men didn't get to expect more from women than they demanded from themselves. It was something that stuck with Beni.

It made sense.

He wasn't an angel, God knew it, but he also didn't speak with negative connotations toward women like his brother just did, either. But neither did *Bene*. That was the thing— his brother would never have done that before.

He took one step out of the apartment, but Bene stayed firm in his place. "Don't you *ever* say something like that about her again, unless you want to bleed an apology for it. Do you fucking hear me?"

Bene flinched at Beni's sharp warning. "It's not *her*."

"What?"

His twin's gaze darted behind Beni, past the doorway to the beautiful woman who was likely still standing down the hallway, watching them. "Her—I swear this isn't about her … I don't even know her, but it's an easy way to hurt you.

She's an easy way to hurt you, and that's what I'm doing. I'm sorry it's fucked me up. *I'm sorry*, Beni."

Too little, too late.

That was all.

"Go home," Beni snapped, stepping back into his apartment, and grabbing the door in his grip. "And figure your shit out because I'm not doing this with you anymore. I can't do this with you."

Not without hating you.

And he didn't want to do that at all.

He got it now—what his uncle and father meant about the two of them really needing to spend some time apart, and figure out who they were without the other constantly at their side. His whole life had been defined by his brother. He didn't feel like *Beni* without Bene. He used his twin as a way to distinguish who he was as in individual, and that wasn't *normal*, or healthy.

Because he couldn't be his own person when he depended on someone else to define who he was. It was only now … *now*, when he found a woman that he loved, who wanted him, and defined him as *just* him that it was becoming very clear his twin was still at that old place.

That *them* place.

Bene wasn't him without Beni, but his twin had already figured out who he wanted to be without him at his side.

"Just work your shit out," Beni muttered thickly, "*please*."

Bene nodded. "Yeah, I hear you. I will."

"Good."

Beni slammed the door, but he didn't move away from it. Behind him, August cleared her throat, and he swore he could *feel* the change in her mood and demeanor without even needing to see the expression on her face in that moment.

"Sorry," he said quietly.

"It's all right. I just …"

"What?"

"I think now's a good time to let you know. My flight leaves tomorrow, so I'll be heading out of the city. It's clear I've got some things to figure out, and I think you do, too."

"Is that what you want to call it—*figuring things out*?"

"What would you call it?"

Beni turned around to face her. "I don't know."

"Yeah, me either."

"It's fine," he lied, "I get it—you have to do what's right for you."

"Beni—"

"No worries, August."

She sighed. "I should get going … Camilla is probably worried about me, and whatnot."

Right.

Because five minutes ago, before Bene and this fucking conversation, she had been perfectly fine to stay there with him. He didn't bother to mention the food she hadn't even eaten that was now cold in the kitchen.

He walked past her in the hallway.

She wouldn't meet his gaze.

It kind of felt like heartbreak.

That was the thing about life, though. It kept moving even when his came to a standstill. The universe didn't revolve around him and what he needed, and so he was going to keep on keeping on, so to speak. Whether he was fucking happy to do it, or not.

"I'll see you later," he murmured.

August dragged in a shaky breath. "Yeah, I hope so."

CHAPTER
14

"You don't have to walk in with me to check in," August said.

Outside of departures at the O'Hare airport, one could tell the place was busy. There was barely any room, and even Camilla said they might as well just take a cab over because she wouldn't be able to park her car for long enough to say goodbye. Not without getting ticketed, or told to move the fuck out of the way.

August could see why.

"I won't, if you don't want me to," Camilla replied.

August sighed. "Are you still mad?"

"No."

"*Really?*"

Cam's familiar smile curved her lips upward at the edges as she met her friend's gaze. "You were right, even if I didn't want to admit it. Had you told me about Alessa and the meeting … I probably would have gone a little overboard trying to make you stay."

"I want to, you know?"

"Hmm?"

"Stay," August clarified. "I want to be the kind of person that can just leave everything at the drop of a hat—someone who can take that kind of risk, but I'm not."

"You always were a planner."

Facts.

"And maybe I should have told you, anyway," she added,

shifting the bag hanging off her shoulder to ease the weight of her laptop, and couple of books inside. "But I didn't want to tell you that, Cam, and have to turn right back around and say I didn't want to be here."

"Except you do."

"Now, yeah. Things changed since that meeting."

Camilla arched a brow. "Or did *someone* change your mind?"

Well …

"Beni helped," August admitted, "but I don't know what's going on with that now, either. He's not very happy I'm heading back to New York—I get why."

"Because neither are you."

God.

Life was not simple.

Or easy.

August wished her heart didn't feel so heavy standing there. It only grew heavier as she watched the people flood in and out of the automatic glass doors. Maybe that should have been her first clue that this really wasn't what she wanted to do, and her heart was trying to be louder than the rational side of her brain.

That side screamed *be responsible, make the right choices,* and *don't make decisions based your feelings.* The other side, and her heart, whispered *stay, stay, stay.* That was it. Just one fucking word.

Stay.

It was almost heartbreaking how the part of her asking that she stay was quieter than the rest, and yet she still heard it loud and clear simply because of how strong the feeling was for her. And yet, the disconnect between her wants, and her rational side was a bright contrast … leaving her confused, and lonely.

Surprise, surprise.

"So, I didn't miss sending you off, then?"

That voice.

August didn't even need to turn around to confirm it was him. The goddamn *smirk* on Camilla's face was more than enough for her to know it was Beni. Like her friend was a cat that had just caught the mouse, and was proud of herself for it, too.

"A little bird might have told him what time to be here," Camilla said.

August gave her a look. "Why?"

"Because even though I'm not mad, I still want you to stay. I will pull *all the punches*, even last minute."

Lord.

Camilla winked.

August laughed.

What else could she do?

Reaching for her friend, the two hugged tightly. She wasn't ready to let Camilla go, either—that was the thing, it wasn't just *Beni*. Or the job. It wasn't even the fact that the longer August stayed in the city, the more she found that she liked it.

It was *Cam*, too.

She loved her friend.

Missed her already.

"I'll let you two have a minute before you have to go in," Camilla said, stepping out of August's embrace with a smile, but watery eyes. "Love you and miss you—call me as soon as you land, okay?"

"I will."

August turned to watch Camilla head for the line of cabs down the way, but her attention was drawn in by something else. Or rather, *someone* else.

Damn him.

Beni came dressed in black leather, and dark wash jeans.

He'd found those Converse shoes of his again, only these ones had been designed similar to the jacket she wore the first night they met. Clearly marked with Frankie Zombie's custom graffiti. He looked like her wildest, wettest dream standing there.

All she wanted.

"You didn't have to come," she said.

Beni stuck his hands in his jacket pockets and shrugged. "I kind of wanted to. Figured I should apologize in case I seemed like an asshole yesterday. I knew you were going back home soon, but I didn't realize it was ... today. That took me off guard."

"Huh."

"Because if you haven't figured it out yet, August, I don't want you to leave."

She nodded. "Yeah, me either."

"But I get why you have to. You should do whatever you need and want to do, and please don't think I'm going to sway you one way or the other. This is all about you."

Right.

Except he already had done that.

Sway her.

Even if he didn't know it.

"But that doesn't change the fact," he continued, "that it kind of feels like you and me have unfinished business here, you know?"

"Yeah, I do."

"And I'd like to figure this out. Whatever it is."

"Me, too."

Beni grinned a sexy sight.

That alone could make her stay.

"Good," he said, pulling an item from his pocket. A piece of paper, except the logo and time stamps that she could see looked like ... flights? "Someone told me you have a long weekend coming up in a couple of weeks or so, and so I thought you might want to come back for that."

She blinked.

"You bought me a flight back?"

He nodded. "*If* you want to take it, it's open. It's yours."

Damn.

"Was that *someone* Cam?"

"It absolutely was."

He didn't even try to hide it.

August laughed.

"She is shameless."

"She loves you," he said softer.

August swore she could hear the lingering words that he left unspoken between them. It almost felt like he was going to say, *and so do I.* Except he didn't, and so she tried not to get too caught up in the way that made her feel.

"And you know," he added, shrugging one leather-clad shoulder, "if you decide you want to say fuck Chicago, then the ticket is changeable. It'll take you anywhere you want to go in the states—I hear LA is nice this time of year."

August grinned. "I got it."

Beni's smile dropped slightly. "I'm really going to miss you."

She dragged in a heavy breath. "Yeah, me too."

In a blink, he had closed the space between them. The hug came *hard*—his arms locking around her so tight, letting her breathe in the scent of him, and leather. She buried her face into the crook of his neck, wanting the rest of the world to just disappear for those few seconds.

All her doubts.

The worries.

Anything.

And everything.

She wanted it to *go.*

From the jump, things had seemed so easy with Beni. All of it, really. From leaving with him that first night, to walking through a park in heels far too high to be walking *anywhere*. Every single bit of it was easy.

This was the hard part, now.

"Call me," she heard him murmur.

August nodded. "I will."

"And let me know that you land safely, okay?"

She leaned back a bit to look up at him. Beni smiled back, but she didn't think it reached his eyes like it usually did. Her handsome man just seemed … *sad*. And that broke her heart a little.

"See you soon, August."

Tipping her head up, she pressed a kiss to his lips that quickly turned into something else entirely. Something that burned hotter, and reached parts of her soul that she hadn't known existed until right in that moment.

Funny how that worked.

"See you soon," she whispered against his kiss.

That was a promise.

August was not at all surprised to find her mother *and* father waiting to greet her when she landed in New York. They didn't even need to wave for her gaze to find them in the crowd waiting at arrivals. There was just something about her parents—their impressive height, stunning beauty, and their matching auras—that shot out into the atmosphere around them.

They didn't *create* attention.

They did, however, draw it.

She took most after her mother in features with just a dash of her father in the shape of her eyes, and the set of her lips when she smiled. And whenever she was in their presence, it always felt like coming home.

Cameron came forward first, although he didn't let go of her mother, Ada's, hand as he reached for August. In his three-piece suit, a staple for her father, while her tall, statuesque mother preferred long dresses and silk wraps tied up in her hair, he smelled of that familiar cologne he preferred.

It was comforting.

Familiar.

She hadn't realized just how much she missed her parents until this moment. For the most part, despite being their only child, they allowed August to freely live her life however she wanted. And yet, while they never told her *not* to do something, she often found herself thinking about them before she made choices that would change her life … and as a by-product, theirs, too.

Would that ever change?

It was hard to say.

She loved them so much.

Wrapped in her father's one-armed hug made her forget about the flight that had gone through a thunderstorm, and the ignorant passenger who kept giving her dirty looks whenever the bitch saw what was playing for music on August's iPod. She was starting to think she should really shell out the extra cash for first class when she flew, but that was a big expense to justify just for some peace and quiet.

"You didn't have to come to greet me. I was going to grab a cab, drop my bags off, and come over to see you guys later."

"Of course, we had to come," her mother replied, dark eyes glittering with love. "You've been gone almost an entire *month.*"

She didn't need the reminder.

"Chicago treated you well, then?" her father asked, pulling away just enough to let her mother get in on the action, too. "It better have because I would hate to make a trip, otherwise."

August laughed, taking her mother's tight hug. "It treated me just fine, Daddy."

"No trouble?"

She gave him a look.

He raised a thick eyebrow in response.

She knew better than to try and get smart mouthed with her parents. It didn't matter that she was twenty-two, and out on her own. They would still tell her to check her attitude, regardless of time or place. She loved them for that, too.

"There were some … things happening," she admitted.

Cameron and Ada shared a look.

"But nothing that came near me," August was quick to add.

Her father's gaze came back to her in an instant, and she could tell just by the look in his eye that her assurance was not enough for him. "Well, still, I think it might be better if you stayed away from Chicago until their trouble blows over there. You hear me?"

The flight itinerary from Beni burned a hole in her pocket where she had folded it up, and hid it away for safe keeping. She wasn't sure that she would be able to follow her father's request, but for now … she could *say so*.

That was good enough, right?

"Sure, Daddy."

"*Now*," her mother drawled, throwing an arm around August's shoulders to pull her into another hug from the side. A kiss was pressed to her temple, making her smile. "Let's go get your bags and find somewhere to eat. I am *starved*."

"That sounds great."

"Plane food is trash," her father muttered.

It really was.

"And how did the *work* side of Chicago go?" Ada asked

with a wide smile. "Because I know you probably got most of that done as soon as possible, so you could spend as much time as you could with Camilla."

She shrugged.

No shame.

Her mom was right.

"It went well, and I have everything I need. I'll make a mock-up before I go back to work in a couple of days to present to the editor and her team and see what they think, or if they're willing to expand the idea and let me work on the spread with them."

"I'm sure the team *and* the editor will love it," her father murmured. "And that they'll accept the pitch for the spread."

Right.

Thing was … August didn't even know if she wanted it anymore.

Her parents pulled ahead with a comment to grab her bag. She didn't mind letting them go to the luggage carousel by themselves. It allowed her to hang back and pull her phone from her pocket. She wasn't quite ready to spill *all* the details of her trip—like Beni—to her parents, if only because she still needed to figure out what in the hell she wanted to do with that. Even if the choice seemed clear, that didn't mean it was easy to make.

Not that her parents would be *bothered* by the fact she was interested in a guy—quite the opposite, as they were like every parent with an adult child that they wanted to settle down and give them grandbabies to love. It was more the fact that Beni was in Chicago, and that might concern them.

But who knew?

Things to deal with at another time.

Keeping an eye on her parents, whose backs were still turned to her, she first sent a text to Camilla letting her know that she had landed and would call her later in the evening. Then, she switched contacts, and sent one to Beni, too.

Safe and sound in NY, she had wrote.

Beni's reply was almost instant. *NY is damn lucky.*

"How did the presentation go?" Beni asked.

On the phone, August found that hearing his voice only made her desire to see him even worse. She swore he kept that smooth, dark tenor at the same level whether he was in bed with her or running on his treadmill. And it made her miss him.

Terribly.

"Really well," she said, "they're going to try to work the idea into an upcoming issue after the team goes through it."

"Really?"

"Yeah."

"Congratulations."

August smiled. "And they offered me a new job … with the editor's team."

It was everything she wanted.

The spread pitch had done that.

"Did you accept it?" he asked.

August chewed on her inner cheek. "No. I asked for some time to think about it, actually."

"And have you?"

"Barely."

Might as well be honest.

She was still acting as an assistant to the main editor of the magazine, although she had written an article for Bared Brands online magazine since returning two weeks ago. It had been published the day before, and like her other articles that she wrote for them … hit viral status within hours of going live.

That's how August knew her worth here.

And that they couldn't afford her.

Or she couldn't afford them.

"They're not going to use my voice and platform for a good cause," she said, "and I have to consider if that's what I want, regardless of how much they're willing to pay me. You know what I mean?"

"Sort of," Beni agreed. "It depends on what *you* want, though, not them."

"That's the point."

"I get it."

She pulled in traffic. Her words, and articles, and socials gathered more followers by the day. The stats on her online articles were some of the highest the magazine had ever received. They had a place for her on the team.

And yet, she still knew the truth.

They would make final decisions on her work. They would decide what she could and couldn't write, regardless of her intentions or wants. Her work wouldn't be used to better struggling communities like she had hoped, and she had the distinct feeling her words would soon become a click-bait *mess*. She'd be given assignments to write that had little to do with what she wanted to cover, but more about what would draw in traffic—good or bad—for revenue. She understood this was a business, but that didn't mean it had to skew her morals, too.

Not what she wanted at all.

"You'll get it figured out, I'm sure," Beni said. "You're too driven in what you want to be stuck for too long in one place, overthinking. And if they haven't figured out they should bend over backwards to give you what you want by now, then they are fucking stupid. Sounds like a them problem, and not a *you* problem. You know what I mean?"

She did.

Beyond that, August appreciated the effort Beni put in *not* to pressure her one way or another when it came to her job, the offer in Chicago, or moving. In fact, in all their conversations—a couple a day since she arrived home—he hadn't once brought up any of those things unless she did it first. And even then, he was very careful about letting her know it was always going to be her choice, and he wasn't going to sway her one way or the other.

Not that it mattered.

Everything he did swayed her.

"So, next weekend," he said.

August grinned, knowing exactly what he was hinting at. "What about it?"

"Still catching that flight to see me?"

"I *definitely* am."

Unquestionably.

And while there … August was going to make some choices. She didn't think they would be easy, and yeah, they were going to be a risk.

Was it worth it, though?

She wouldn't know unless she tried.

CHAPTER
15

Beni hung up the phone, effectively ending his conversation with August, although he had waited for her to end it first. Leaning back in the torn booth of a rundown bar, with what he imagined was a stupid fucking smile on his face—because that's just what that woman did to him with nothing more than a *phone call*—as he surveyed his shitty surroundings. The conversation with August was enough to make up for the fact that this building smelled like goddamn mildew.

Well, *almost*.

He still wasn't even sure why he was here.

His companion chuckled across the shoddy booth, bringing Beni's attention to him for the moment. With his booted feet kicked up on the edge of a chipped table, Cory Rossi arched a brow like he was asking a question without saying what it was.

Beni stared back, unaffected. "Problem?"

"Just never thought I would see the day, man, that's all."

He didn't like where this conversation was going, but because he was apparently feeling stupid today, Beni decided to ask.

"What day, Cory?"

"The day where a Guzzi twin would be hung up over a *chick*."

Beni's jaw tensed, flexing with his annoyance. "First, her name is *August*."

Cory nodded. "I know."

"Then use her name."

"I get a better kick out of watching you get pissy when I don't, you know."

"You're an asshole."

"And yet, we still meet up for breakfast every other day."

Speaking of which …

Beni reached for the coffee he had sat down on the booth's table, picking it up for a drink. It helped to rid some of the mildew stench lingering in his lungs. He had less than zero interest in digging into his breakfast sandwich, however.

"Regretting that at the moment," he admitted, "because who the fuck eats in this kind of mess? *Pigs* wouldn't even want to play in this shit."

Maybe that was a bit too far.

Not by much, though.

Cory peered around the rundown place.

What had it once been, anyway?

A bar?

Restaurant?

Both?

Who knew?

"I kind of like it," Cory said, waving an ink-covered hand to gesture at the mess around them, "it's got potential. And now I just need to convince my brother that we can turn it into something, and go from there."

Ah, now it made sense.

Cory, and his older brother, seemed to take pride in turning rundown, old buildings that were better being torn down into something amazing. They had a whole portfolio of different businesses—favoring bars and eateries, but dabbling in other shit, too—between them that they worked on together as partners. People always said not to go into business with your family, but it seemed to work for those two brothers.

"How much *convincing* do you have to do for a place that looks better suited to be burned down?"

Cory shrugged. "Act out."

"What?"

"Yeah, you know … Joe thinks he has to look after me, or I'll find myself in some kind of shit. So, when I want him to do something like this with me, and he's hesitant, I just do something outlandish—cause some shenanigans— and he'll do whatever so I'll fall back in line. See, *easy*."

Beni dead stared his friend. "You're fucking *crazy*."

"Or am I smart?"

No, definitely the other bit.

He didn't say it, however.

"And you know I'm kidding, right?" Cory asked.

Beni shot him a look. "About what?"

"*August*."

Ah.

"Yeah, man, I know you're just fucking with me."

"She's a great girl—you're a lucky fuck, if she sticks around."

Jealousy flared in Beni.

"Just how do you know that?"

Cory laughed, pulling his boots down from the table and shaking his head. "Not for any reason you're thinking. I've just been around a few times when she visits. Besides, girl isn't even my type … she's *in control*, you know? Got her shit figured out, or whatever. Knows what she wants in life. I tend to chase after women who—"

"Are crazy like you?"

It took Cory a second.

Then, two.

"Yeah, that's fair," he murmured, "but they're always fun."

Well, then …

"And how's the east side thing going?" his friend asked.

Beni scowled. "Hard to say."

"What's that supposed to mean?"

"It means exactly what I said. After that attack on me … shit's been really quiet. No obvious thefts from within the crew, no more fighting amongst the guys than usual, and the gang hasn't been causing us problems like they were. Hard to find the person causing this trash when they're not stirring the shit, you know?"

"Huh."

"What?"

Cory shrugged. "You didn't see who it was, right?"

"Little too focused on the bat swinging toward my head, that's all."

At least the bruise was gone.

"Right," his friend muttered, "but what if the person *thought* you did? It could be that everything is quiet because they're waiting shit out. They got too close, too fast. Thought it was over for them, and yeah, took a step back to let it chill out."

"That makes sense."

"See." Cory pointed at his temple and smirked. "I *am* smart."

"Still crazy, too."

"Life's more fun that way."

Whatever his friend wanted to believe, okay.

"Besides," Cory added, "it being quiet is a good thing right now. Theo's got a major shipment of cocaine coming in from Mexico soon, and they always use Jerome's warehouses to store it while they get it ready to sell, you know? Wouldn't want someone fucking around, and getting into that. Be a lot of money lost."

Beni stilled in the booth, a thought popping into his

head without warning. It wasn't at all strange to him that *Cory* knew about the cocaine, and shipment coming in considering Theo was his uncle, and he worked closely with the Outfit's top men to do his job. A lot like his brother.

Sure, Beni hadn't been told about the cocaine, but he had to wonder ...

"What's rolling around in that head of yours? I can practically see your wheels turning."

Beni made a noise under his breath. "How come they didn't tell me about the shipment coming in, you know, considering I'm supposed to be finding *who* is causing the issues within the crew and with the gang?"

"Loose lips sink ships. The less people that know about something like this, the better. It's always been that way. We don't advertise our business and dealings because we don't want other people *in* our business. You know what I mean?"

Yeah, sure ...

But what if the cocaine was the goal?

And everything else ...

Was that just a distraction?

Beni was surprised to find a few guys hanging around the warehouse when he arrived later that day to speak with the Capo. Typically, by this time, the guys were done with their work, and back to whatever holes they crawled out of.

Then again, *nothing* was normal about this crew lately. Honing in on the fact that they were all suspects in the problems happening, he suspected some thought if they worked harder, and showed up more, then the Capo would believe it wasn't them. And for others, they were just so fucking bitter to be caught up in this mess at all that they were constantly in a mood.

Made work fun.

Not.

He wouldn't usually speak with the Capo where someone could see him approach the man privately, especially seeing as how the crew was supposed to think he was just another guy like them … but he didn't have much of a choice today. Here they were, and he had an idea that he wanted to put to work.

About the cocaine, that was.

Who knew when that shipment would arrive?

He didn't have time to wait.

One of the guys sitting on the hood of a car that had to be at least twenty years old, and in serious need of body work, nodded to Beni before he headed inside the warehouse. Figuring it was better to be kind, given the current circumstances, he nodded back.

After all, he hadn't forgotten what the Capo's little favorite—Neil—told him a while back. Nobody here could be trusted, and they were all out for what was best for *them*. They didn't give a shit about Beni at the end of the day.

Words to live by.

Speaking of Neil …

Beni found him standing on the opposite side of Jerome's beat up desk when he entered the back office of the warehouse. Not that he even bothered to pass Beni a glance, let alone a proper fucking greeting.

He didn't care.

"Didn't expect to see you tonight," Jerome muttered, leaning back in his chair. "What's up?"

Beni passed Neil a look before giving his attention the Capo. "Do you have a minute to chat?"

The man waved a hand. "Floor is free, go on ahead."

No.

He wasn't going to do that with Neil right there. To be honest, he wasn't sure exactly how much Neil knew about

Beni's reason for being put on this crew, or if he was aware of the *true* purpose. And he hadn't forgotten what Cory told him earlier, either.

Loose lips sink ships.

His little plan—he was determined to figure out if the cocaine was the goal for the gang, which meant everything else was a distraction—would only work if everything else went according to plan, too. As few people as possible needed to know.

Neil didn't have to be one of those people.

"Alone, if you wouldn't mind," Beni said.

Neil gave him a look over his shoulder, blank and yet still *loaded*. "If you have something to say to the boss, you can do it with me here. Since when have we ever allowed guys on the crew to have an all-access pass to the boss, huh?"

That told Beni a lot.

In just a few words, Neil had basically let Beni know that, in fact, he was not aware of Beni's true purpose on this crew, and the reason why he was here. And if the man's gaze was to be trusted, and that annoyance he found staring back at him, Neil was just a little bit jealous that Beni seemed to have free reign with Jerome here.

Huh.

He tucked that away for later.

"Boss?" Beni asked, not bothering with Neil. "Do you have a minute for me *alone*?"

He didn't need to make a scene to get his point across with the asshole, and frankly ... the Capo would always have the final say when it came to his guys.

"Step out," Jerome said to Neil with a flick of his wrist. "And we'll continue our discussion on your idea later."

"And what idea was that?" he dared to ask after Neil had left, slamming the door behind him. "Because he doesn't seem too happy to leave it hanging. Or hell, maybe it was just *me*."

Jerome chuckled. "Easy, Beni. I like Neil … been looking after him and his brother since they were kids, you know? Friends with their deadbeat father, and all. Their ma is a good woman, but needs help every once in a while to get by."

Interesting.

And yet, he didn't care.

"What did you need?" Jerome asked.

"The incoming shipment of cocaine, actually."

That got the man's attention.

And fast, too.

"What about it?" Jerome cocked a thick brow, an underlying threat coating his words when he added quickly, "And just how the fuck do you know about it, anyway?"

Exactly.

"Have you considered that everything else might have just been a distraction, and the real problem is someone might be coming for that cocaine?"

"What?"

"Think about it," Beni said, "a load of cocaine in the hands of a small, but organized, gang would do them … *wonders*. The money they could make? Insane. Now, imagine they have someone willing to help them out with getting what they need. Or maybe they *made* someone work with them, who is to say? Point is, when your attention is on everything else they're doing, it's very unlikely that it's going to be on that cocaine. You know, where they don't want your attention to be because they're going to steal it right out from under you when you're not looking."

Jerome was quiet.

Beni waited him out.

"That's … an interesting thought," the man finally admitted. "But also not something we know to be true."

"Except, it could be."

"What do you suggest I do?"

"Move the shipment's arrival location, and even the day, if possible. Tell *no one* but those who will have a direct hand in actually handling the cocaine. I don't care if it's another made man you drink with on the weekends, don't tell *anyone*. Unless they have to handle the shipment in some way, then they don't need to know all the details."

"What then?"

Beni shrugged. "Let me look into some things … if this is what I think it is, then it's not going to be hard to find the connection between whoever it is in the crew, and the gang. You just worry about protecting that shipment while I work."

"I can do that."

"Good."

"And keep me informed, Beni."

Yeah, he would.

As long as he had something worth saying.

Loose lips, and all.

"Oh, and say hello to your father for me," the Capo added. "The boss mentioned you were going home for a couple of days to see your family."

Beni nodded. "Will do."

"Bene."

"Beni."

A throat cleared behind Beni, drawing his attention to where his father was currently standing next to his mother by the front doors of the mansion. His twin, on the other hand, sat on the bottom stair of one of two winding staircases leading into the upper levels of the house at the grand entrance.

"Let's go find Marcus," his mother said, "and leave these two … to talk, I suppose."

"Play nice," his father warned.

Beni rolled his eyes.

Bene was still staring at the marble floor, and he didn't even bother to lift his gaze until Beni crossed the foyer, and sat down next to his brother on the stairs. They were quiet for a while, and he took that chance to soak in the familiar space of his parents' large mansion.

His childhood home.

Shit.

"Remember when we used to see if we could get lost in here?" he asked.

Bene chuckled under his breath. "The house seemed *a lot* bigger then."

"Nah, we were just smaller."

"Yeah, you're right."

Leaning back, Beni used his elbows to keep him steady one step higher. He eyed his brother from the side, wondering if Bene had gotten his shit figured out yet, or if he was ready to talk. Sometimes, it was better just to wait it out and see, but that fucking sucked, too.

He loved his brother.

Always would.

"What'd Ma make for dinner?"

"That chicken you like," Bene replied, "and whatever else Dad wanted, probably."

"Nobody makes chicken like Ma."

"I swear it's not *her*, Beni."

He let out a breath, the tension in his chest releasing all at once. It seemed like his brother might be ready to talk, but he still wasn't sure if *he* was. Or rather, if he could do it without being horrible to Bene at the same time.

"Isn't it?" he asked. "All this shit started when she came around, so …"

"It's not her."

"You heard what I said, right? That she's important to me, and—"

"You need me to get in line," Bene said, laughing under his breath. "Yeah, I heard you loud and clear, man."

"If it's not her, then what is it?"

"I don't know."

Well, he didn't believe that.

"I think you do, but you don't want to say it, Bene."

"Maybe you're right."

"So, just *say it*."

Bene sighed, leaning back on the stairs and matching his brother's posture. The two of them stared upward, surveying the large golden and crystal chandelier that hung over the staircase. It matched the one on the other side, too.

Money.

The whole house dripped in it.

Nobody knew how to spend cash like their father.

"I thought you'd follow me," Bene said quietly, never looking away from the chandelier even when Beni glanced his way. "When I made that deal with Dad to come home, I mean … I thought for sure you'd come back with me. Maybe not right away, but *eventually*. That's what we always did, right? We followed each other—did the same shit. Why would that be any different?"

"I like Chicago."

"I *hate* it."

Beni laughed. "Yeah, I know."

Bene shrugged, glancing his twin's way with a faint smile. "And then everything else happened, too. You were pissed at me because I didn't tell you that I was leaving. It all piled up, and every time I tried to explain … she was there, so it messed me up. I'm not used to someone else being between me and you, you know? I didn't mean for it to seem like I was in a mood about her—it's not her."

"No, it's you."

"I guess so." Bene cleared his throat, and quickly sat back up on the stairs. "It feels like I'm losing something here, and I don't know how to deal with it. I don't know how to stop it."

"Nobody is losing—"

"Doesn't make the feeling any less real, Beni."

Right.

"And," his twin added, "I just ... have to figure it out, that's all."

"If you could not be an asshole about August, that would be great."

"You're really on for her, huh?"

"I fucking love the girl."

His brother quieted.

Beni knew that feeling *well.*

"How's Chicago?" Bene asked, changing direction altogether.

Beni didn't mind. "Problematic."

"How so?"

"I think the gang causing issues has connections to someone in the crew. I just don't know who, how, or *why.*"

"Yeah, that's a problem."

Beni grinned over at his brother. "But hey, you know *a lot* of people ... and shit, you know how people like to talk, too."

"What about it?"

"Care to do me a favor, and ask some questions?"

Bene grunted under his breath. "Does that mean I have to go back to Chicago?"

"Only if you need to."

"I'll probably need to. Especially if you want me to be asking around about the gang, and their business. Have to be careful with that, you know."

Beni smirked. "Chicago is really not that bad."

"It's not home."

True.

Or maybe his brother just hadn't found a new home yet. He opted not to point that out.

CHAPTER
16

August went over the letter one last time, figuring that since the offices were mostly quiet, and a good portion of the employees at Bared Brands had already left for the day, that she was safe to do so. Without someone possibly looking over her shoulder, or sneaking up on her, anyway.

At the bottom of the letter, she had signed and dated it as was company policy. Although, if she were being honest, she didn't even need to do *this*. Not write this, or hand it to her boss directly. She was technically *in between* jobs at Bared Brands. No longer an assistant to the editor of the magazine, except she had yet to fill the other position she had been offered.

She didn't need to give them a weeks' worth of notice to quit her job. Well, really, she wasn't even giving them that. She was giving them a letter that told of her resignation, and that she wouldn't return on Tuesday after the long weekend.

The new assistant would start that day to fill her position. August was supposed to start her new position on the team the same day. This letter was simply her being kind, and professional. Maybe someday, she might need the editor here to write her a letter of recommendation at some point or another, and so this would also help with that.

Was it enough notice?

Probably not.

August also didn't care at this point—she had given

several years of her life to Bared Brands and received very little back in return. And what she had finally been given came too little, too late. Starting over somewhere else—if the Manic Media position was still up for grabs, and she suspected it was—terrified her, but so did staying *here*.

Being stuck.

Doing … nothing.

Or, that's what it felt like.

Just as August stood from her desk, tucking that letter into three folds, and then picking up her bag on the floor to sling it over her shoulder, the phone on the desk rang. A little light flashed on the base, telling her it was someone from downstairs. Which was better than the asshole CEO from *upstairs*, she supposed.

She wasn't going to have to deal with him anymore, either.

Winning.

She could have ignored the phone, but habit made her reach for it. "Mrs. Coss's assistant here, how can I help you?"

"Hey, August."

She relaxed at the sound of the girl from the front desk downstairs.

"Hey, Marney. What's up?"

"You have a visitor down here in the lobby. Or … well, he just went outside for a minute. But anyway, he's down here whenever you're ready to leave."

"Who is it?"

She wasn't expecting anyone.

People didn't randomly show up at her job.

"He said it would be a nice surprise, and when I say he is *very* persuasive … anyway, you'll see when you get down here. Later!"

Marney's cheery voice and vagueness was still running through August's mind long after she had left her desk.

Down the hall of glass walls that made up several offices, she came to the largest one at the end. Through the door, which was also clear glass, she could see Michelle Coss, the editor of Bared Brands, sitting behind her desk on the phone. In her usual black pant suit, hair pulled back into a severe bun, and that signature red lipstick that never looked like she had to reapply it, the woman could be ... well, intimidating.

Just a bit.

Sometimes, she used that to her advantage to get shit done, and other times, it was nothing more than a mask to make new people stand a little straighter in her presence. For August, it had always given her a vision of what she wanted to be in this business. Tough as nails, no excuses, and driven to succeed. She was more than grateful for the experience she had been given working as Michelle's assistant here.

Michelle's gaze turned to August, and she smiled before waving a hand to invite her inside. *Okay, here goes nothing ...* She ignored the way her heart thundered in her chest, beating so deep and hard that she could feel it in her throat. Maybe she should have worked her way up into doing this, but here she was now.

"Just a minute, August, I'll be done in a second."

She nodded.

Michelle went back to her conversation on the phone. She could have listened in, but she wasn't that interested, and had never been the type to spy. People who minded their own damn business got a hell of a lot more done than those who didn't.

That was fact.

The phone clicked when it was placed back to the cradle, and Michell's attention turned on August once more. "Ready for your long weekend?"

Yes.

The ticket in her bag for Chicago was burning a hole.

Tomorrow morning, she would be on a flight back to see people she had missed more than she could explain. None of that was important right now, however.

"I am," she said, "but before that ... I have to give you this. And I hope you'll understand when I say that I am so grateful for what you and Bared Brands have done for me— from the internship, to this job. I learned a lot. About this business, about sacrifice, and even myself. I also learned what I did and *didn't* want, which is why I have to make a different choice now."

She waved the folded letter.

Michelle didn't even glance at it. "That's what I think it is, then?"

Her heart wasn't beating as loudly now.

August shrugged. "My resignation, yeah."

"I figured."

"Why was that?"

Michelle sighed, leaning back in her chair, and folding her hands on her lap with grace and poise. "Because I thought you were wasting your time here, too. Except I couldn't say that—not to you, or to the people upstairs."

August stilled on the spot. "What?"

"This company is filled with gatekeepers, and sometimes, getting past them is a career achievement in itself, if you understand what I'm saying. The thing is, you never needed gatekeepers. You needed someone who believed in you and would let you do what you did best. You're not going to find that here ... not with the new job they offered you, or otherwise."

"I figured that out."

"I appreciate the formal notice, though."

"Well, it's really only for the long weekend."

Michelle laughed, and waved a hand. "That is fine for me. My new assistant will be here next week, and while I will miss you, I am sure I can whip her into shape in no time at all. Have you found something—somewhere—else to go?"

"I think I have."

"Then, I wish you all the luck and success in the world, August. You deserve it. You have *earned* it. And I can't wait to see what you produce with the right team behind you."

"Thank you."

August was still thinking about her conversation with Michelle and feeling better about her decision to do what she had done, long after she left the office. Somehow, she had even managed to forget about the fact that *someone* was waiting for her downstairs in the lobby.

She only remembered when she passed a slyly grinning Marney at the front desk, who pointed to the revolving doors of Bared Brand's building, and said, "Can't miss *that* man for a mile, girl."

She found that *someone*.

Beni, actually.

And damn, Marney wasn't lying. Not in the slightest. He looked like sin poured into the mold of a fucking man in black skinny jeans, leather loafers, and a beige cable-knit sweater. She was a little sad that he lost the usual leather jacket, but *hell* … he looked good like this, too.

No lie.

No shame.

Leaning against a sleek, black car that she suspected was a rental, his feet were planted shoulder-width apart, and he'd stuffed his hands into his pockets. With his head turned to the side staring at something down the street, she had a perfect view of the line of his cut jaw, and the way his cheek jumped with each chew of his mouth.

Gum.

He was always chewing on gum when he waited.

August gave Marney a wink before heading for the

revolving doors. As though Beni could feel her coming his way, his attention came back to the entrance, but she couldn't see his eyes behind the aviators on his face. Not that it mattered, because she could absolutely *feel* his stare nailing into her, and that was more than enough.

She came out of those doors in a rush, asking, "What are you doing here?"

Beni grinned widely. "That's your first question?"

She thought about it.

"Yeah, it is."

"Cam helped me out with some details … what time you got off, where you worked, and all. She didn't think you would mind *me* showing up, but threatened if I did some weird shit, that she would pickle my balls for later use."

August *huh'd* under her breath. "Sounds like something Cam would say."

He pushed off the side of the beautiful car—a Benz, by the looks of it—and stepped one foot closer to her. It wasn't nearly close enough, and yet it still had her heart racing out of control. She didn't think this man knew what he did to her, but damn him, because she loved it all the same. *Loved him*, too. For reasons she understood, and many more that she didn't. Soon, she was going to let him know exactly that, too.

"Truth is," Beni said, rocking from foot to foot with his hands still stuffed in his pockets, "I've been thinking about you a hell of a lot more than I should lately."

"Oh?"

"And I couldn't wait to see you. So, if you're busy or whatever, don't feel like you have to entertain my ass, or anything. I'm a grown man, and I can take care of myself. *But* … if you do have some time, I would be happy to do whatever you want for the night."

August grinned. "Hmm."

"Although, about that flight tomorrow …"

"What about it?"

Beni brought his hand out of his pocket to flash a folded piece of paper. "I thought you might like to have someone to fly with, you know."

Damn him.

She loved it.

"You would be right."

His laughter spilled into the air as he crossed the distance between them in three long, confident strides. There was something about the sight of his strong form, made up of beautiful lines and the hardness of a man, coming for her that had a shiver racing through her body. His embrace found her like bars that planned to lock her away from the rest of the world, but she didn't mind *at all*.

And when he was kissing her?

Drinking her up?

Taking the very taste of her right from her mouth?

God.

Life was perfect again.

August had decided not to tell Beni about the job thing, and her decision, until after she had settled things in Chicago. She wasn't even going to tell her parents until she had every single last detail hammered out, so then she could feel like at least they wouldn't think she was crazily jumping into something.

It was still a risk.

She felt way better about taking it, though.

Although, it took all of her willpower not to tell him her little secret as his thumbs stroked her cheekbones while he kissed her like it was the only thing he ever wanted to do. All too soon for her liking, he pulled away, but not too far.

"Do you like fried chicken?" she asked.

"Love it, why?"

"That's what my mom is cooking tonight, and I promised to have dinner with them. I was also going to tell them about my trip to Chicago for the weekend while I was there because I hadn't told them yet."

He arched a brow. "Any reason for that?"

"They're worried."

"Ah."

"I would love it, if you came, too."

Beni flashed her a sexy smile. "I get to meet your parents?"

She poked him in the chest and laughed. "Don't get in your feelings about it, or anything."

"Kind of a big deal."

"Ever done that before?"

"Not once."

"They'll love you."

Of that, she was *most* sure.

∼

August was right.

Of course.

She usually was.

Her parents loved Beni, no questions asked. She bet it was because really, she didn't bring guys home to meet them —*ever*. He was the first man to ever walk over her parents' threshold, holding her hand, with an almost shy smile—*that* was a sight, to be sure—as she introduced him to her mom and dad.

It was enough to say he was important.

Serious.

Something good.

So, her parents fell in line, welcomed him into their home, and tried not to ask *too* many questions. Except a few fell out here and there, like now.

She heard her father's question from the dining room as she helped her mother plate the fried chicken, and gather the potato salad and greens.

"And when did you two meet?" Cameron asked.

Beni didn't miss a beat. "When she came to Chicago."

"Oh, that's where you're from."

"Canada, actually. Toronto, but my mother grew up in Chicago, and I moved there a few months ago for work."

"What kind of work?"

"*Daddy!*"

Ada gave August a look. "*Hush*, you."

"*Ma.*"

Her mother just gave August *that* look again. One that said, *child, you will quiet your mouth.* Everyone's mother had that goddamn look, and while it might vary from woman to woman, the meaning and intention was still the same. It didn't matter at all that she was an adult.

"I do a lot of things," Beni said, clearly careful about choosing his words before he added, "but mostly I answer to Tommas Rossi at the end of the day."

"Do you now?"

"Yes."

"And does that make you connected to the business Tommas has in Chicago?"

God.

"Ma, tell him to knock it *off.*"

Ada shook her head, and took her time pulling sliced cucumbers from the fridge. "I will not. You brought a man home, and didn't think he was going to ask questions? Come on now, I know you to be a smarter girl than that, August."

"But—"

"That's dangerous business," her father said.

Beni cleared his throat. "Only if we let it be, yeah."

"I *trust* that my daughter isn't getting mixed up in any of it, right?"

"On my life," Beni returned.

"I'll hold you to that, young man."

"I would hope so, Mr. Rivera."

"Call me Cameron, Beni. I only like being addressed as *Mr.* in court."

"You got it."

"Good."

Her father chuckled, a *warm* sound, really. It surprised August because she had been so sure that this conversation was going nowhere good. And yet, just like that, it seemed to change entirely without warning.

That was her parents, though.

In a damn nutshell.

Ada passed her daughter a wink, and smile. "*See …* although, this *Chicago* business. Your father is going to worry, whether you like it or not. You know he didn't want you going back there until things calmed down."

Yeah.

So, her dad hadn't been too happy about that.

Win some, lose some.

"I'll be fine," she said, "and you can keep telling him that. It's only for the weekend."

For now, she added silently. She had other plans about when she was going back permanently, and hopefully that would be soon. Until then, she was just going to ease her parents into that idea slowly. Fingers crossed that it worked.

Ada shook her head, nodding her head toward the plated chicken. "Grab a couple plates, and help me serve, please."

"Sure, Ma."

Beni's gaze was already turned on August the second she entered the dining room. He didn't hesitate to get up from his chair, and help her handle the plates with chicken, either.

His hand found the small of her back, helping her into a chair while pressing a quick kiss to the side of her temple and murmuring, "Do they like me, you think?"

She laughed under her breath.

"I think so," she replied at the same level.

Beni nodded.

All the while, August was acutely aware of her parents watching the two of them, but she did her very best to ignore it. More than anything, she wanted Ada and Cameron to *love* Beni ... sure, there were things about him and his lifestyle that were concerning, but it was underneath all of that which counted the most. That was a lesson she had needed to learn over and over again in her own life, and one her parents repeated to her when people judged them without knowing anything about their family and love.

She expected they would offer the same respect to Beni, and so far, they had done exactly that. She appreciated it.

He was a good man.

He treated her well.

And she loved him.

Beni was quick to take the seat next to hers, his hand snaking over to rest upon her thigh as they all started to grab what they wanted for food. It was only after grace had been said that they started eating, though.

"So," her father said, pointing a fork at August, "I expect a phone call while you're in Chicago ... just to be safe, and I expect Beni will keep you out of trouble."

"Absolutely."

She shot the man next to her a look.

He only shrugged.

"Everything will be fine," she told her dad.

Cameron sighed. "And yet, I still worry."

Story of her life ...

"But also," Cameron was quick to add, glancing Beni's

way before winking at August, "I hope you have fun. Seems Chicago keeps calling you back, hmm?"

More than he possibly knew.

"I guess so, Daddy."

He smiled faintly. "Yeah, I know."

Did he?

~

"Did I pass the test, or …?"

August glanced to the side, taking in Beni's grin as they walked the hall to her apartment on the second floor. "What test?"

"The meeting the parents test. Isn't that what all boyfriends have to pass to be *good?*"

"Is that what you are?"

"Hmm?"

"My *boyfriend.*"

Her tone was as playful as his smile. She didn't mean for it to be a serious question at first, but as the seconds passed when they stopped in front of her apartment door, she kind of wanted to know the answer … and she wanted it to be a very specific answer.

"I certainly hope so, but you tell *me.*"

August wet the line of her top lip as she tried to play off his question with a laugh. "Nice trying to deflect it to me, but—"

"Not deflecting. I know where I stand. I haven't even thought about another women since you stepped into my path. Can't be bothered when I have one like you standing in front of me. I'm certainly not *here* doing this with someone else, now am I? Didn't catch a flight just to spend one night with someone else in a city that doesn't feel like mine just to accompany them on a flight that will take off before I even typically roll my ass out of bed on the weekends."

She dragged in a quick breath.

His point was certainly *made*.

And yet, he drove it home with, "And the only person I'd really like to get inside the apartment behind them, so I can get a taste of that pussy I've been thinking about since she jumped on a plane a month ago ... is *you*."

Jesus.

She knew she was wet.

Didn't even need to check.

"Is that *boyfriend* enough for you, or—"

August let her actions do the talking for an answer to that one. Her mouth crashed against his, her palms finding his jaw to drag him in closer as she kissed him. The door snapped against her back when he shoved her against the heavy wood. Frantic and seemingly unaware that they were still standing in that goddamn hallway, his hands drove up under her shirt to find the lacy cups covering her breasts, while hers dropped down to grab at the waistband of his pants.

"Get the door open," he groaned against her mouth, "before someone gets a fucking *show*."

Well, at least one of them hadn't forgotten.

Anticipation curled around and down August's spine as she turned to unlock the door, her hands shaking as she found the keys in her bag. The need only became thicker when Beni's hot mouth found the column of her throat, his tongue striking out to taste her skin before his teeth dragged across the same spot.

Heat.

And *chills*.

She felt them both at the same time.

"Can't wait to *fuck* that pussy," he murmured in her ear

as her trembling fingers slid the key into the lock, "and do you know why?"

She did.

Or she was pretty damn sure.

"Because it's yours," she said when she turned the lock, and the doorknob at the same time.

"Exactly that."

His hand found hers on the knob, flexing to twist it as she did, but with just a little more force. The two of them slipped into the apartment without a look back, the door slamming shut although she wasn't sure if it was by his hand, hers, or *both*.

Her bag hit the floor when her back met the wall. That cable-knit sweater of his went first, exposing hard muscles and the sleek lines of his torso and chest to her palms. He had that lean tone of a runner, with just enough bulk of a boxer, and she fucking loved it.

Once his sweater was gone, though, he didn't let her admire for long before he went to work on shedding August of her clothes one piece at a time. In between each came a kiss from him that burned her from the inside out, promising bliss and wickedness all rolled into one.

As he reached for his back pocket in search of the condom she knew he kept on hand just in case, she pulled open his jeans, fingers dipping below his boxer-briefs while her other shoved the pants down around his hips. He let her roll the condom down after he'd opened the packet, his groan at the way her fingers flex down his length to cover him enough to make her thighs clench.

Anticipation, *again*.

He didn't let her tease him for very long, though. Once he got his hand between her thighs, his deft fingers sweeping across her slit and straight up to her clit, he leaned in for another kiss. The pads of two of his fingers roved circles over her clit while his tongue warred with hers. And then he was crowding her against the wall, hard lines pressing against her soft curves.

His hand left her pussy to find her right thigh as his other found her left. In a fluid motion, he had her up against the wall, letting her grab the base of his cock to slide against her slit as he raised her a little higher.

Fuck.

And then he was filling her.

Stretching her.

The moan that fell from August's lips felt *raw*. She hadn't realized until that moment just how much she missed this man, and the way he fucked her. A lot like the way he touched her, *kissed her*, and more. All of it, really.

His hold kept her steady against the wall while she pulled him in for another kiss. The taste of his mouth—tinged with the mint gum he'd been chewing earlier—saturated her senses as each flex of his hips had his body slamming into hers.

Again and again and again.

The beat was steady.

Sure.

So fucking deep, too, because he pulled her into every thrust, his teeth pulling at her bottom lip to draw out her whines, and pleas. Every push of his body to hers rubbed against her clit, making her desire skyrocket fast enough to make her see stars.

"I'm going to come," she breathed.

"You *better.*"

It was curling in her belly.

Teasing her mind.

His hands squeezed hard to her ass as she finally reached orgasm, and though she felt the lead up … it still felt like a surprise. As though she hadn't been at all ready for it when it crashed through her senses. He fucked her through the orgasm, too, each thrust sending shockwaves of shudders running through her body.

"*Oh, my God.*"

Beni's approval came out in a low groan that vibrated against her mouth. "Fuck, *yeah.*"

"Let me make you come. *Let me.*"

He said nothing, simply lowered to the floor, and she went with him. Like that, she could control the speed, slow at first, until his teeth were clenching, and his breaths came out a little heavier. She sped up, his hands driving up her spine, and then down to grab her ass, too. Gazes locked, she enjoyed the sight of him losing control under her until his head fell back to the wall.

"Fuck, gonna—"

"Give it to me," she whispered.

Never stopping.

Not slowing.

Until his fingers dug into her ass, and he pulled her hard onto his cock, stilling them both as she felt him jerk inside her with his release.

"*Fuck,*" Beni grunted. "Shit, yeah."

A second passed.

Then, two.

It hit her all at once what the two of them would look like in a pile of forgotten clothes in her apartment's entrance hallway. God save the poor soul of the person who might have made the mistake of passing her front door in the last fifteen minutes.

Her laughter coated the hallway in between her breathless pants. Beni's chest heaved as he stared up at her, a mixture of amusement and disbelief lighting up his eyes.

"*Why* are you laughing?"

"We're *still* in the hallway."

"So?"

"On the fucking *floor*, Beni."

"*And?*" His hands flexed against her ass, that sting from his fingertips clenching in mixing in sweetly with the bliss still singing in her blood. "Laughing after fucking a man is *not* good, August."

She heard what he was saying, and managed to sober up just enough to tell him, "I was just thinking … I can't remember a time when I was crazy enough over a guy to fuck him wherever we stood just because I couldn't help myself."

His palms flexed again.

A grin curved his lips. "*Oh?*"

"Just now," she whispered, "just you."

"You know it, baby."

She hoped that didn't change.

Whatever this craziness was between them … she hoped it stayed *exactly* the same.

CHAPTER
17

"You know," Beni said, thoroughly enjoying the feeling of August's fingertips walking up his naked back while he rested on his stomach, and hugged a pillow to the side of his face, "you never did show me that project for the magazine."

Her touches stopped *instantly*.

He felt that hesitation.

"No, I guess I didn't."

"And it got accepted, so ..." He turned his head a bit to the side, eyeing the way she grinned but refused to meet his gaze. The naked slope of her throat led his gaze further down to her chest as she propped herself higher with an elbow to the bed. "I was curious to see it."

"Right *now*?"

He hummed under his breath, leaning over just far enough that he could press his lips against the curve of her shoulder. Kissing the spot, and then quickly darting higher to drop one to her lips when she tipped her head down for him, Beni nodded. "Yeah, why not? How long do we have before the food gets here?"

"Forty-five minutes or so. That's their usual."

She didn't want to cook.

He didn't care as long as they fed themselves.

In a couple of hours, they were going to be rushing to the airport to fight through TSA checks, and get on a damn plane. Right now, he could enjoy being in bed with her, because like this, they didn't have to pretend like the rest of the world existed.

It was just them.

August and Beni.

"I have the digital spreads they made as a mock-up on my phone," she said, "but I won't know how it'll all look and what will make it in for sure until closer to printing time."

"So, show me the digital."

Shaking her head, which caused her headful of corkscrew curls to go wild in every direction, he smiled at the unusual shyness she displayed. He wasn't sure when she had taken her braids out, but those curls of hers looked just as good as her braids.

"Come on," he said, "I want to see what made it in."

She sighed. "That's part of the problem."

"What?"

Without answering, she was fast to jump out of the bed, just barely out of his reach when he tried to smack her ass. *Almost.* Her light laughter followed her out of the bedroom, teasing him and making him think he should have just kept her right there in bed with him.

What had this woman done to him?

Many good things.

Despite his last-minute decision to hop on a flight to spend a single day with her before she was coming to him for a weekend, being here with August settled Beni in a way nothing else could. All his worries, the shit keeping him up at night, and busy in the daytime, well, none of it mattered when he was with her.

That's why he did this.

Why he was *here*.

Before long, August was back in the bedroom, phone in hand. He did his best not to leer as she climbed—beautifully naked and on display—back into the bed. And failed like the fucker he was, because *shit* ... how could he not stare at that woman?

And she was *his*.

Because yeah, Beni decided on that.

He just had to make it clear to her.

"Okay, here it is," she said, settling down into the bed beside him on her stomach. She flipped through the mock-up digital spread of her article showcasing the urban areas of Chicago, the brands that had come out of the city, and the impact it had on the culture. "All in all, it has the tone I wanted, and showcases what I intended for it to display."

"But?"

Because he heard that.

Her unspoken *whatever*.

Felt it, too.

August frowned as she pressed the button on the side of the phone, blanking out the screen. Tossing it aside to the table next to the bed, she stared at the print on her silk pillowcase, shrugging those delicate shoulders he loved to bite when he fucked her from behind.

Head in the game, Beni.

Right, right.

"I wanted to include other things, too," she said, "initiatives for the communities, and whatever else might encourage the reader to want to be involved with, well, if not Chicago, maybe their own community. Especially youth, and whatever else."

"I didn't see anything in there for that."

"Because it isn't. They *vetoed* it. Not on brand for Bared Brands, apparently. They're not in the business of showcasing what *could* be better, only what is good for them, and what looks perfect on a magazine rack. It's very likely the team will veto a lot of that kind of thing from my pitch by final print."

Ouch.

She didn't even try to hide her bitterness.

"Sorry," he said.

August rolled to her back, staring at the white ceiling above them as she replied, "It wasn't a bad thing … or I guess, something good came out of it, right? Because this whole experience made me look at my career in a different way. More what I wanted from it, and what I wanted to do with the platform I was creating for myself, and less about being the tool someone else uses for what they want."

"And what did you figure out?"

"I was going to wait to tell you …"

"Tell me what?"

She had *all* his attention now.

Not that she didn't have it before.

August grinned, peeking over at him through those dark, long lashes that framed her brown eyes. "I gave my resignation yesterday."

"*What?*"

"Yeah, and when I get to Chicago, I plan to meet up with Alessa again. Take that job … I still have to get some logistics figured out like moving and where I'm going to live, or whatever, but I would rather work for a company that will let me be great and do great things at the same time, than one that only wants to harvest my talent for their own gain."

He heard a lot in there.

The most important was the loudest.

"You're going to move to Chicago."

That didn't even sound like his voice.

August nodded once. "I am—"

Beni didn't even let her finish her sentence fully before he was *on her*. Her laughter melted into something lower, and *sexier* as he settled between her opened legs, his hands skimming over the curve of her waist, while he leaned in to kiss her. He wished he could take all those sounds of hers and keep them on repeat in his mind for the rest of his fucking days.

They were *that* addictive.

"That," he said, kissing her smiling lips, "is fucking *awesome*."

"Yeah?"

"So much."

She gave him a look. "So, what about *your* issue, hmm?"

Yeah, shit.

He knew what she meant.

"My twin, you mean."

August shrugged, but said nothing.

Beni understood.

"We're working on it," he said. "It's not as bad as what it was, but it's not perfect, either. He's got some shit to work on —being separated hit him harder than it did me, that's all, and he had it confused on what he wanted to blame for it."

"You mean *me*."

"No, I mean he wanted to hurt me, and he used you to do it a couple of times."

"He thinks I'm taking you away from him."

Beni let out a slow exhale, letting her words have their impact. "At first, maybe."

"I guess—*maybe*, in a fucked up way—I can understand why he hates me, then."

"Absolutely not."

August's brow dipped as she peered up at him. "What?"

"He doesn't *hate* you. Not at all."

"He certainly acted like—"

"He can't hate things I love, August. He can be a lot of things about them—*jealous*, usually—but he never hates them. Including you."

She stilled under him.

Blinked up at him.

So, maybe he hadn't meant to say it like that. To just blurt it out, and let it hang between them. Except there it was, and here they now were.

"Because I do," he added quieter, "love you."

"Do you?"

"Entirely too much."

"Or just enough."

Beni smirked. "I like the *too much* better."

August's tongue peeked out to wet her bottom lip. "Me, too. Because that's how it feels for me—like I want to just love you crazy. Love you until you make me insane."

"Because you do …"

"Hmm?"

"*Love me*," he murmured, lowering until their lips grazed.

"Too much," she echoed.

≈

Beni's phone dinged *again* as he and August headed down the hallway to his apartment. The flight to Chicago was mostly uneventful, thankfully. Except once they landed, he swore his phone hadn't stopped ringing. Apparently, someone figured out he had left the city without letting anyone else know.

Too little, too late.

He was already back.

"Here," he said, handing August the keys for the apartment, "I gotta take his."

He lingered back a couple steps while she unlocked the apartment, and he focused on texting his boss back with a simple, *Back at my place tonight—no worries, I'll be back to work tomorrow.*

Tommas was not pleased.

Beni figured, eh, it was done now.

"Oh."

"Hey there."

Beni glanced up from his phone to see his reflection staring back at him just over August's shoulder. *Bene*, that was. In his hand, his twin carried a weekend duffle bag just big enough to hold a change of clothes, but not much else.

"Um." August glanced back at Beni, clearly confused. "I didn't know someone was inside, or I wouldn't have just opened the door."

"Oh, I'm heading out. Have a plane to catch, and all. There's some ribs in the fridge, though, just heat 'em up, and they'll be good to go."

August nodded. "Sure, thanks."

"No worries."

Bene stepped aside to let her pass, and she shot Beni a quick look over her shoulder before disappearing further into the apartment. He stayed in the doorway, waiting until he couldn't hear August's footsteps before he spoke.

"Thanks," he said.

Did he need to say more?

Shit wasn't perfect.

Bene had this *thing*.

They would figure it out.

"Yeah, no problem," Bene muttered, rubbing at the back of his neck with his palm. "You know she DVR'd that whole medical drama series? It filled the memory. I ended up binge watching it last night when nothing else was on. It's not so bad."

Beni chuckled. "Yeah, I know … figured I would leave it so she could watch it again. You know, if she came back around."

"That's Ma's favorite show."

"I know."

"She's going to love her."

Beni nodded. "Yeah, I hope so."

The silence stretched on between the two before Bene broke it first with, "I gotta head out, but I found that info you wanted on the gang … passed it along to Tommaso, and he'll fill you in. Cory knows, too."

"Was it what I thought?"

"Pretty fucking close."

Damn.

That was going to be rough news to deliver to the Capo.

"Be safe," Bene murmured, stepping past his twin.

"You, too."

Bene laughed darkly as he headed down the hall. "That is the last thing on my mind. It's full of too much other shit for me to be worried about that."

Yeah.

Beni knew all about that.

Or, it felt that way.

CHAPTER 18

The bay window in Beni's living room didn't give a good view of anything in particular except the large apartment building next to his, and yet August found she didn't mind that at all as she stared between brown brick, and a blue sky. It gave her something else to focus on other than the private conversation happening between the brothers down the hall. Not that they tried to tamper the level of their chat for her benefit.

She figured … Beni and Bene deserved their privacy. Whatever the two of them were going through, it was for them to figure out in their own time. If what Beni said was true, and Bene's issue wasn't really her in the grander scheme, then she didn't want to step in between them and make it about her.

Or make it worse.

It was the least she could do.

The longer she stood there, watching dust blow around in the alley between the two buildings because of the wind, and the cloudless sky overhead, the more she realized how much she missed Chicago. She felt it when they drove through the city after leaving the airport, too, but it was only now that she understood what that light, happy feeling in her chest had been.

To be fair, it wasn't *only* the city.

Camilla, too.

And *Beni*, definitely.

New York was comforting. Familiar, really. August knew, no matter what, she could return to that place, and fall right back in step like she hadn't missed a beat. She knew those streets, could walk them with her eyes closed.

Chicago felt *new*—something to explore and grow into her own. And yet, it also felt as though it had become apart of her life, in some way. It wasn't lost on her how something that had seemed scary to her before, a risk she wasn't sure that she wanted to take, was now something she looked forward to doing.

Huh.

It was only the vibrating of her phone that drew August from her thoughts. She didn't bother to check the caller ID before digging the phone out of her bag, and putting it to her ear, if only because she assumed it was her father calling back after not picking up her call earlier. She'd left him a message just to say she landed safely, but knowing him, he would still want to speak directly to her to make himself feel better.

It wasn't her dad.

"Hello?"

"*Are you here yet?*"

Camilla's excitement had her words coming out in a high screech. Or something very fucking close to it. Laughing, August pulled the phone away from her ear a bit to save what might be left of her eardrums.

"Yes, we just got to the apartment," she said, "and I was planning on calling you—"

"Not soon enough!"

"God, I love you, Cam."

"I know," her friend chirped happily. "Was the flight good?"

"Yeah, and my companion, too."

She swore she could feel Camilla's smirk when she

replied, "Listen, you know I wouldn't usually give out your info like that to people ... but it was *Beni*. And he's clearly on for you, if you get what I'm saying here. Besides, I also have ulterior motives for doing what I did—"

"Yes, making me move here."

"No shame in my game."

"*Cam*."

"Hmm?"

She was going to keep this secret until she had everything figured out, and could lay it all out on the table, but the thing was ... that wasn't something Camilla would ever care about. She didn't need details—she just wanted to *know*.

"I quit Bared Brands," August said.

It took Cam a second.

Then, two.

"When?"

"Yesterday before I knew Beni was there."

"Does that mean—"

"It means what you think it means."

This time, August was smart. She was learning from her mistakes, which meant as soon as those words left her lips, she pulled the phone away from her ear so that Camilla's responding yelling wouldn't give her a headache.

She could still hear it buzzing in the speakers, though.

Shaking her head, August pulled the phone back to her ear when she figured it was safe to do so. Although, that was a hit or miss when it came to Camilla. The girl couldn't be contained, and it was better not to try.

"I am so excited!"

"I can tell."

Camilla laughed. "Have you told—"

"You and Beni."

"Yikes. Not your parents?"

"They're not like you ... they'll feel better to know once I have everything settled out. A job to show them, a place to stay, you know? That's all."

"I get it." Camilla sighed, but it still sounded like a happy one. "And also, I mean a place to stay should be easy—I hear Beni lost his roommate and all, so …"

"Don't get me with the shit, Cam."

"I'm just saying!"

August laughed under her breath. "Nice try. I will call you *later*, or tomorrow. We'll figure out something to meet up."

"I am free all weekend, and even if I wasn't, I would just call in."

"You're terrible."

"Terribly lovely, you mean."

"Nope—just plain terrible. Love you."

"Love you, too."

It was the dark, sexy chuckles ringing out from behind August as she hung up the phone that alerted her to the fact Beni was leaning over the back of the couch, watching her with amusement coloring his handsome face. He didn't look the least bit ashamed to have been caught spying on her when she turned to face him with a raised eyebrow.

"Seriously?" she asked.

"What?"

"I literally ignored your conversation for the sake of privacy, and you can't even be bothered to try for me."

He shrugged. "I was enjoying myself. Watching you when you're talking with Cam—reminds me of me and my brothers, I guess."

"Does it?"

"Yeah."

"She's kind of like a sister for me."

"How long have you been friends?"

"Too many years to count," August admitted, "and she knows more about me than anyone else in the world."

That had Beni standing straight, his hands fisting into the leather of the back of the couch as he said, "We'll see about that ... you know, now that I'm around."

"Oh, don't start *that*."

"Start what?"

"I have one jealous person in my life—*Cam*. Don't make it two."

"Too late."

His joking tone had her grinning.

"You know, I hadn't realized the last time I was here, but the place is kind of empty without your twin's stuff, huh?"

Beni's natural expression scanned the living room, and the few empty spaces on the wall. "I never really noticed—I was more concerned with the fact he was gone, honestly. That was something that took a while to get used to. Still not feeling great about it, but what can you do?"

"Sorry."

"It's okay."

No, she didn't think it was.

Undoubtedly, being separated from his twin, who it was clear he was close to and loved, hurt him just as much as it did his brother. The only difference, perhaps, was that Beni was slightly better at hiding his emotions and dealing with them than his twin was at the end of the day.

August didn't like him sad.

Not at all.

She wanted that sexy smile back.

His jokes, too.

All of it.

He came around the side of the couch as she crossed the space to close the distance between them with a grin, determined to get him happy and feeling good in a way only she could. It was the way his lips curved at the edges, knowing and wicked, that said he knew exactly what she had in mind for them.

Him on the couch.

Her on her knees.

Sucking him off.

Yes.

"So, I promised Cam I would figure out something this weekend to hang with her," she said, hands coming up to find his chest before she pushed him down to the couch. "And I am *sure* you will help me work that out."

Beni's laughter came out dark, and husky. "You know, I have to go grab a pack of condoms because I'm out."

"I'm on the shot."

He grunted thickly. "What?"

"Mmhmm, and since you're the only person I'm fucking, and I had better be the only person you're fucking—"

"You know you are."

"Then, I think we're okay."

"Good to know." He swallowed audibly. "And something is already in the works to meet up with Cam, and the rest."

She dropped down to her knees between his spread legs, her hands working fast at his zipper and button to get them undone. Through the fabric of his slacks, she could already feel his erection straining against her palm when she stroked him.

"How so?"

"We were thinking a big party at a club."

"How big?"

"Open invite to a group of people."

August arched a brow when he lifted just enough to let her tug his pants and boxer-briefs down around his hips. *And there he was*—his cock was free for her hands to fist his length, and she did just that, stroking his dick hard and fast, tightening around the tip just the way she knew he liked, and then again at the base. There was nothing particularly beautiful about a man's cock, and yet, she loved the way his looked. It didn't matter if she was jerking him off, he was just getting out of the shower with a semi, or he was stretching her out and she could watch him do it ... she loved it, wanted it.

"*Fuck*," Beni groaned.

"And when are we going to this club?"

"Woman, stop talking and suck my *dick*."

August grinned. "*Well* ..."

"You're killing me here."

But *damn* ...

He looked so fucking good like this. All taunt, and tense, watching her with hooded eyes that both begged and demanded all at once that she get her mouth on his cock instead of just letting her lips hover over the tip ... *teasing*. The strong muscles of his thighs jumped under her palm when she placed it down.

"*August—*"

"When are we going?"

"If all goes well, tomorrow night. Now, stop playing with me, and—"

She took him into her mouth.

That long, deep groan never sounded better.

Beni hadn't lied; the club was packed. Considering he nodded and spoke to far more people than August could keep track of, she assumed that *open invitation* he mentioned the evening before had meant exactly that. Anyone who knew anyone was welcome to make a stop at the club owned by the Rossi brothers, have a drink on them, say hello, and party.

"Oh, look at *this* one," Cam said, leaning over in the booth to get close enough that August could see the screen of her phone. Even over the loud music, and all the people moving about in the VIP section, August could still hear her friend pretty well. She had already been up on the floor dancing—with Cam, and then Beni. Right now, she was trying to let her feet have a rest. "What do you think?"

"What do I need three bedrooms for?"

Cam shrugged. "I mean, I need two just for my clothes, so …"

"That's because you have a problem."

"*Rude.*"

August's laughter melted into a sigh when Beni slipped into the booth on her side, tossed an arm over her shoulders, and pulled her in for a kiss that he pressed to her temple. "Where did you go to?"

"A drink order."

"Tommaso has had enough to drink tonight," Camilla said loudly.

"Don't be like that, Cam," her husband shouted back from the other side of the room. Apparently, he had been watching and listening. "You know—"

His words were cut off by someone to his left that stepped in his line of vision.

August only shook her head.

"Did he drink a lot tonight?" she asked Beni.

He shrugged. "A little. Just enough."

"Enough for what?"

Beni winked. "To make it look good."

She had no idea what he was talking about.

"Well, an answer on this one would be great," Cam said, waving the phone.

August gave her a look. "I don't need three bedrooms."

"Besides, she'll probably be staying with me anyway."

Beni grinned when August swung his way.

"We didn't discuss that," she said.

"Do you really want to jump between apartments throughout the week? A night at my place, one at yours—that seems … like a waste."

He wasn't wrong.

At the same time …

"I've lived alone for years."

"And I slept alone for years," he countered. "But now I sleep better when you're in bed, too. What's the difference?"

Uh …

"I will turn your place into a girl's haven. You will have to deal with Cam *constantly*. I wake up at six every day because I need that extra time for my hair. You don't have nearly enough books in your place. Oh, and you snore."

Beni guffawed. "I do *not*."

Okay, so he didn't.

"And you know you're considering it because all those reasons you just gave are excuses. Admit it."

"Stop making good arguments for crazy things," she said, trying not to sound whiney.

Across the booth, Camilla giggled. She hid her face by looking down at her phone, but it didn't matter because August had still heard it.

Damn her.

"Later?" he asked.

August nodded. "Definitely coming back to this later."

"Works for me."

Of course.

Because he was getting what he wanted.

Possibly.

And maybe, so was she.

This was nuts.

"Drinks, drinks, drinks!"

Their conversation about her future living situation was put aside as the Rossi brothers approached the table, both carrying trays full of drinks.

"Was that your drink order?"

Beni chuckled. "Yeah, but I didn't think they would bring it."

"Good to make them work," Cam said, "keeps them humble."

"That's enough of that," Cory grumbled.

"Just saying."

More trays were carried through.

Cory slapped a guy on the shoulder that August didn't recognize, but a few others seemed to, including Beni. "Thanks for the help, Neil."

"Yeah. No worries, thanks for the invite."

"Of course."

The guy—Neil—glanced Beni's way, asking, "Where did you disappear to on Friday? Thought you were supposed to be working with the rest of the guys in the crew?"

"Something more important," Beni said. "Besides, you've got the crew handled on the east side, right?"

"Always have."

"*Right.*"

Before the guy could reply, Tommaso came up to the table with a grin, reaching for one of the lowballs of whiskey. Lucky for him, because he did look a little drunk—totally unusual for Tommaso; he didn't drink heavily in public— Camilla missed it until he was downing the drink, and it was already too late.

"Tom," she warned.

"Relax, I'm fine," he replied, glancing Beni's way to ask,

"and speaking of the east side, did they move that shipment of cocaine again?"

Beni nodded. "Yeah, sure did."

"The one he uses on the west end?"

"Looks like it." Beni reached for one of the red vodka drinks, handing it over to August with a wink. "But that's enough business for tonight—we're here to have fun."

Tommaso grinned. "Right, *fun*."

Neil slipped away from the table.

No one else seemed to notice, though.

August went back to her friends, her drink, and her man. Nothing else mattered to her except having a good time.

"I'm not *that* drunk," Tommaso grumbled.

"You overdid it a *little*," Beni replied, "and I only needed you to seem like it, you fucker."

"Yeah, but—"

"Time for bed," Camilla said loudly, clapping her hands and gaining her husband's attention in the process, "because I swear to God, Tom, if you make me clean puke tonight … you will live with your mother for the next month."

"Maybe she'd be okay with that."

Camilla smiled coolly. "But would *you*?"

August hid her laughter into her palm.

"*Fine*," Tommaso grumbled. "You all ruin my fun all the time."

"And that's a lie," Beni replied. "Do you need me to help you get him to bed, Cam, or …?"

Camilla took Beni's place at Tommaso's side as they headed further down the foyer of the large home. "No, I got him. As for you two … use the small guest house over the pool, okay? I know you can call an Uber, or whatever, but just stay off the roads altogether. We don't mind, and someone is going to have to drag his ass out of bed tomorrow with the hangover he's going to have."

Beni looked August's way.

A silent question.

She shrugged. "Sure, we'll stay here."

Why not?

"And the pool is cool to use, if you want," her friend added before she disappeared around the far corner.

"That could be fun."

August's brow dipped. "What?"

"The pool."

"Oh, my God, Beni."

"Why not?"

She had a million reasons.

Her hair, for starters.

The fact she was *slightly* buzzed.

More.

His stare kept her quiet.

"Race you," she whispered before darting down the hall.

"*Unfair!*"

Their dip in the pool only lasted as long as it took for Beni's self-control to snap. By means of his hands pinning her to the wall of the pool while his hot kisses found her throat. She managed to convince him to get out of the pool, and *away* from where they might be seen, but fucking *barely*.

And as much as she tried to keep her hair dry in the pool, the ends still managed to get dunked under the water. Not that she could think of that what with the fact Beni had found the closest flat surface he could to sit her on, which just happened to be the fucking *couch* in the sitting room that the pool house led into, and now he was between her thighs.

Eating her.

Or feasting, really.

There was something about the sight of this man on his knees for her, his tongue and lips and mouth loving her pussy while his eyes locked on hers that just drove her crazy. It made her hotter than ever. And to see her wetness on his lips, slick with her … *yeah*, damn, that was something else.

Never had there been a sexier sight to be seen than Beni between her thighs. He ate her like he was worshiping a god at an altar, and this was his very favorite way to pray.

He knew just what to do.

How to tease with his tongue to bring her right to the edge, and then quickly dive right back into her slit with firm strokes to soothe her back down. It was enough to make her want to beg for him to let her come, but *hell* … she loved the sight of him like this.

All of him, really.

"You ready to come?" he asked, tone husky.

God, that need.

It was great.

She could *hear* every bit of it.

"Gonna come for me?"

"Y-yes."

His grin was all she saw before his tongue replaced his two fingers rubbing hard circles into her clit. That steady, fast beat was enough to send her flying right back to the edge again. He knew exactly how to play her body for him.

"Oh, my God … *Oh, my God.*"

Her words came out in heavy pants, shoulders arching as that tingling wash of pleasure started deep in her womb, promising bliss was soon to follow. The softness of his hair tangled in her fingers, his thick approval coming out in a groan that vibrated against her slit.

And then she was coming.

Hard, fast, and so *unsteady*.

"Fuck, *yeah*," he murmured, kisses dotting up her stomach as he rose higher to hover above her parted lips. She hadn't stopped trembling, that orgasm was still echoing, and he looked so fucking pleased with himself for having done it, too. "What do you want now, huh?"

"For you to kiss me."

Beni grinned. "Wanna know how you taste?"

"I taste better on *you*."

That wasn't a lie.

He inched that fraction closer, letting her arch into his kiss and lick the taste of her arousal straight from his tongue. She was tart, but *hotter* on him. His hands slid from her waist up to spread across her ribcage beneath her naked breasts—he'd wasted no fucking time practically ripping her clothes off when they first entered the pool house, or rather, what remained of her clothes after their swim.

… to be fair, she'd done the same to him.

"Now," he said, the demand coming in clear, "bend over for me, baby."

August didn't even hesitate to stand from the couch, feeling his hands run over her ass as she turned around to kneel on the cushions. Now, her ass was high in the air, and Beni apparently appreciated that sight if the way he groaned and spread her wide was any indication.

"*God,* look at you. So fucking pretty, and wet." His hand smacked against her pussy, inciting a moan from her as he added darker, "Greedy, too."

"And *yours*."

He slid in behind her, the head of his cock pressing against her slit. "And mine."

One of his hands landed to her shoulder, and the other flexed against her ass a second before he thrust in. It was the only warning she got, but it was just enough for her to drag in one quick, shaky breath before she felt like she could no longer breathe.

"So *good*," she mumbled.

"*Yes*, fuck yeah."

The way he filled her.

So much.

And then he just *fucked* her.

Brutal, and fast. Wild, and unrestrained.

Every stroke of his cock inside her pussy, and each beat of his hips into her ass sent her flying closer and closer to another release. All those dirty words and wicked promises spilling from him behind her aided the need on.

Take that cock, baby, and *fuck, you look so good like this*, and *wait 'til you taste your come straight from my fucking dick, huh?*

Was it any surprise that she was flying high again before she even knew it was happening? It was uncontainable—the orgasm coming on swift, and there was no controlling it.

She had never felt higher.

Never been so happily *used*.

"Fuck, let me do that again," Beni said, bending down to kiss a sweet path up her spine, his hips slowing against hers as the aftershocks of that orgasm started to slow. He hadn't even come yet. "Love you, huh?"

Didn't he know?

She had never loved someone more.

August turned her cheek to the side against the back of the couch, feeling his lips glide along her cheekbone as he started a slow, steady fucking her. He kissed her again, saying, "Yeah, damn I love you."

His next thrusts came harder.

She arched into him.

"Come," she breathed.

He groaned against her cheek. "*Say it.*"

A little deeper, then, with his strokes.
"Come on, Beni, *come.*"
"Say it to me."
Fast again, taking her breath away.
His hands flexed on her hips.
"Love you," she whispered.
She got to say it, *and* feel him come.
That was her new favorite thing.
She decided.

CHAPTER
19

The switchblade Beni liked to keep in his pocket was a good tool to play with when bored, and he needed to fidget. He could still hear his father's warning in the back of his mind whenever he toyed with a blade—*don't play with knives, Beni, that's how people get cut.*

There was something about a knife, though.

He liked it more than a gun.

Sitting on a chair that he'd placed in the middle of the cracked cement floor of a warehouse, Beni used the tip of that very sharp knife to edge along the tips of his fingernails. It shaved them down in the smallest strips, a testament to how sharp the blade was, and his sharpening skills.

All the while, he watched the door at the front of the warehouse, waiting for what he knew was inevitable. In his search for the person causing issues within the crew, he had realized something that should have been obvious from the start.

It was always the person people thought it would never be. That's why the fucker doing it had gotten away with his shit for as long as he did because *no one* was going to look at the guy closest to the Capo, a man that Jerome had helped to raise, in a way, as the person fucking him over at the end of the day.

And why would he?

Why would anyone look at *Neil?*

He had a good position—he helped to lead an entire *crew*. Unheard of for men who weren't made. He had a lot of respect, was given status in his place, and for the most part, seemed happy to do his business as he was told.

Loyal, too, right?

Right.

The click of a lock across the warehouse, the deadbolt in the heavy metal door sliding open, had Beni lifting his head and coming out of his thoughts all at once. This was the last test, in a way, although he already had his answer on Neil, and what the guy had been doing to his Capo when Jerome's back was turned.

He had keys to everything.

Got inside info on *everything*.

That's how much he was trusted.

No one would look to him—it was easier for a man to overlook the people he put faith in to have his back, than it was to look at those same people with suspicion. No one wanted to look at someone they cared about for reasons that were less than kind.

A simple fact of life.

Shame, really.

Beni partly blamed the Capo for this. Had the man not been so caught up in his feelings, and willing to blame an entire crew for what was happening, instead of looking at what should have been the obvious choice, considering everything … then perhaps they could have closed the file on this a month ago.

Shit, maybe they wouldn't even have needed him to come in and figure out what the fuck was going on within the crew.

But here he was.

And it would end today.

"Beni?"

Staying on the chair, because he had little to no interest in ruining the navy suit he put on that morning—Guzzis had their flaws, and vanity was certainly fucking one of them—Beni lifted his head to give the man entering the warehouse a slight smile.

Cold, but *knowing*.

"Looking for something?" he asked Neil.

The door clicked behind him.

Neil hesitated like he was going to turn around.

Beni was quick to say, "Oh, don't worry about the door. I put a little thing on the arm over the top of it, so when it closes, it's not going to open from the inside again. We need to have a little chat, and it wouldn't be very helpful if you ran off before I could say what I needed to say, you know what I mean?"

The man's jaw hardened. "I don't answer to you, and I don't have to stand here and speak to you, not if I don't want—"

"No, actually you do."

Pride was a *bitch*.

Everybody knew it.

Neil's pride made him take a few steps forward, daring to come closer to the man toying with a knife maybe fifteen feet away. "Who the fuck do you think you are, Guzzi?"

"The guy who figured out you were stealing from the crew to fund your little brother's issue … and by issue, I mean the fact that he was smoking meth like it was going to keep him alive, and then when he got mixed up in the gang business, well, shit really went downhill for you, huh?"

"Shut your fucking—"

"I get it," Beni said quickly, shrugging his shoulders. "See, I've got *a lot* of brothers, but one specifically, my twin —shit, I'd do anything for him. Someone needs to die? Cool shit, give me a name, you know? So yeah, I get where your mind was at when he caused problems with the gang trying to get in with them, and you wanted to fix it."

Neil's shoulders stiffened. "I just wanted to make it go away."

Beni nodded.

That's what sucked.

Because *maybe*—fuck, just maybe—had he been honest with his Capo from the start, and told him they were in trouble, Jerome might have been able to help. Or, he could have brought in someone else from the Outfit to get these kids away from the gang.

Now, though?

Now, they stole from the Outfit. They fucked with a Capo's business. They allowed a gang into their spaces to cause problems, and take their profits.

There was no saving it.

No excusing it.

Only one thing would answer for it.

"My twin called in some contacts," Beni said, "people he knew around Chicago that had some beads with the Easties gang. At first, we were just looking for connections, but then we found your brother right smack in the fucking middle."

"He was a good kid."

"Yeah, weren't we all?"

And then *life* happened.

This fucking life.

Beni didn't regret it.

He wouldn't regret this, either.

"Anyway," Beni said, standing from the metal chair, and flicking the blade of his knife closed before pocketing it, "that's how we figured out it was you, and I kind of put two and two together to make four, so I had the gist of the rest. Unless, of course, there's anything else you might want to tell me. I'll let Jerome know—hope you know what this is going to do to him because he cares a lot about you. Like a son he doesn't have."

Neil's jaw trembled as he tried to shrug it off.

Didn't matter.

Beni saw the emotion.

"They didn't give me a choice," he muttered "it was fucking feed into their shit, supply them with whatever I could—money, or something to make money—or they were gonna kill my brother. And he—being young, and fucking stupid—didn't know anything about it because he thought *they* were his fucking brothers, all right? What was I supposed to do, Beni?"

He didn't know.

Didn't have those damn answers.

"I would have done the same thing," Beni admitted, "if that's any consolation here."

"It's *not*."

"You had to know this couldn't go on for—"

"*Fuck you*. I was doing just fine until you came onto the scene to fuck it up."

Yeah, there was that anger.

"Maybe I can fix it," Neil added quickly. "You know, work something out with Jerome, or—"

"Nah, that's never going to happen."

Apparently, knowing you were going to die was kind of like going through the stages of grief, in a way. Neil was running through the gamut of emotions—disbelief, pain, bargaining, and anger. All of it, really.

Beni let him have his moment.

Thing was, he was already over it.

A form coming out of the shadows on the left side of the warehouse, behind Neil's position, had Beni speaking up again to keep the man's attention on him. The less fight and trouble they had here today, the better this would be.

Shitty as it was.

"See, last night at the club," Beni said, "that was all orchestrated. Your new friendship with Cory? Planned, so you would be there with him last night. Tommaso drinking too much, and talking out of his ass about business, and the shipment being moved? Done with a purpose. Because if it was you, then you'd have the keys to the warehouse—you'd have to check before you would pass the info off to the gang, so they could steal it."

That form—*Joe* Rossi, also known as Shadow for his work as a hitman in the Outfit—now stood directly behind Neil, but the guy didn't realize it. He was seconds away from death, and it would not be an easy one for him, although it would be mostly clean.

Beni stuffed his hands in the pockets of his slacks, murmuring, "Sorry it had to go down like this, but when you play games with the mafia, just know you will *always* lose. Because we can't afford not to win."

Joe unwound the wire in his hand. Neil didn't even get the chance to react before it was wrapped around his throat, and he was yanked against the other man's chest. Fight or flight kicked in for him, but it was fucking useless. Like his feet kicking at the floor—Joe was unbothered—or his hands clawing at the wire at his throat.

His eyes bulged.

Skin reddened.

Lips went blue.

Choked, and fought, and *everything*.

Beni at least gave Neil the respect of watching him die, although he reclaimed his seat on that metal chair for the duration of the show. It lasted longer than he expected, but then again, this was the first time he witnessed someone die by a wire choking them out.

Damn.

Dying was hard work, apparently.

∽

"Are you on your way back yet?"

Beni chuckled as he wiped his hands on the paper towel that Joe silently offered to him. The single sink on the right side of the warehouse had come in handy once they were finished with business. Joe stepped up next to wash his hands.

"Well?" August asked on the phone.

"Almost," he said.

"Good, because I'm getting hungry, and I can't be held accountable for my actions at that point."

Beni grinned, giving Joe a nod—his silent thanks for the man's work here today, his help after, and all the rest. Joe answered it back with his own. "And what does that mean, August?"

"I'm just saying that I was planning on going back to your place after this movie with Cam, but if you're going to make me wait longer, then we might go out and have some fun."

Mmhmm.

"But then I can't bring you home that takeout you like from down the street."

She hummed under her breath.

"And we can't watch that series you DVR'd to binge, either."

"You make such good arguments."

Beni laughed. "Not really, you're just easy to please."

And he loved that about her, honestly.

"How's the hair?"

August sighed *loudly.* "Still a mess."

"It's not a mess."

"Listen, you always think it looks good. *I* know when it's a mess, okay?"

He knew better than to argue with her. She had managed to keep *most* of her hair from getting wet the night before—the ends of her length, however, not so much. It was the first thing she said had to be taken care of as soon as she woke up in the morning, which meant a proper wash, a bunch of products to manage and protect her curls, and brushing it all out.

He helped.

As much as she would let him, really.

Also, while he didn't say it to her because they hadn't come back to that conversation from the night before at the club, but having her at his place in the morning … doing her routine, and just being there with him only confirmed his resolve.

He wanted that woman *with* him.

In his life.

At his place.

Waking up in his bed.

Full stop.

You know, when they got back to that conversation.

"You good, Joe?" Beni called over his shoulder.

Joe nodded as he finished washing up his hands. "Yeah, man. I'll call somebody in to help me get rid of the … rest of it."

"Right, thanks."

On the phone, August said, "Well, I'm just about to go back into the movie. I had to lie to Cam and say I had to pee to call you."

"She's very possessive of your time."

"Yeah, good luck with that one."

"I can handle her."

Somehow.

"And," he added, "I will have your food, and the first episode up for you to start your binge when you get back to my place. Sound good?"

"Sounds *perfect*."

"All right, baby, I'll talk to you in a—"

His words cut off as he pushed open the door to the warehouse. They'd taken the lock off the top after they finished their business with Neil.

He hadn't expected to find the guy's kid brother standing in front of his brother's beat up car—they had to dispose of that later, too—when he stepped outside, though. Never mind the fact that the kid was pointing a gun right at Beni.

Beni blinked.

Holy shit.

He should have known, really.

It was a stupid mistake to make. He'd told Neil himself, hadn't he? If it was his brother, he would do anything for him. Follow Bene *anywhere*, if asked, or if he thought that's what his brother needed.

No question.

Beni factored Neil's love and bond in for his little brother to explain why he did what he did, but not once had he thought about the other sibling. Neil had said his brother didn't know about the fact that the gang was using him to manipulate him, but that didn't mean it was the truth. Or even that the guy's kid brother didn't suspect something was up.

Yeah, a *huge* mistake.

Beni knew … it was already too late.

"Beni?" August said, her voice faint in his ear.

Shit.

She was still on the phone.

"Where the fuck is my brother?" the kid demanded.

He was all of seventeen.

That was it.

A *baby* on these streets, really. Not that it made any difference to the gang that recruited him, if the tattoos on his neck were any indication. Those tattoos told a story, one of a kid who had officially been initiated, and had done his crimes to earn his spot. All dangerous things, although who was Beni to speak?

Look what he had done *today*.

"Listen," Beni said, his hand raising like that might help him, "your brother made a choice, and—"

The kid—Beni's mind was struggling to catch up, and remember his name ... Nathan, was it?—jerked the gun, turning it to the side as he forced through clenched teeth, "Shut the fuck up, man, and tell me where my brother is before I blow your fucking face off!"

"Beni!"

August, again.

He could see the gun was already racked back.

Safety off.

He stared down that barrel.

Ready to fire.

"I'm sorry about your brother, but—"

That was the wrong thing to say.

Nathan pulled the trigger.

Beni heard August's screams *long* after he hit the ground.

CHAPTER 20

"Beni! *Beni*!"

August held onto that phone tight enough that the sides bit into her skin. It was the only lifeline she had left to the man on the other end—the sound of a gunshot so unmistakable and loud. It hadn't shot her, but it certainly felt like something exploded through her heart with pain shattering it into a million and one little pieces.

"Beni!"

What was that sound on the other end?

Crunching?

Choking?

Both?

In her shock, August forgot that she was still standing in the empty bathroom of the movie theater. The last chick, who was taking *way* too long to wash her hands, although she just figured the woman was eavesdropping on August's conversation, had left seconds before.

Now, it was just her alone.

With her *fear*.

So thick, she could taste it.

So cold, she couldn't get warm.

She felt like a fucking lunatic yelling into the phone, with nothing to answer her back. *Could* he even answer her back? *Oh, God.* Was he even still alive?

Bang.

Was that … another gunshot?

August jerked on the spot, a wash of dread falling down her spine as she stared into the mirror across from where she stood. Those wide eyes didn't look like her. That chestnut skin of hers now had an ashy tone, devoid of her usual color.

That woman wasn't her.

That woman was fear.

Except it was her.

"Beni," she mumbled one last time.

August had never realized it was possible to feel so entirely scared, and useless at the same time. Like there was absolutely nothing she could do here to help him, and he was listening to her scream for him while he died.

And yet, she couldn't say anything else.

Just his name.

It was the only echo in her mind.

Something crackled on the phone before a voice filled the speaker—not an unknown one, his tone was familiar enough to her, but barely.

"No time to explain," Joe Rossi snapped, "he'll be at the clinic."

August finally found a way to make her mouth work, although how, she wasn't sure. "*What* clinic?"

"Who is this?"

"August."

The call went silent for three seconds, maybe just long enough for him to pull the phone away and check the screen. Then, he was right back on the call. "Jesus Christ … he took a bullet to the chest. I have to get him to the doc."

"*What?*"

"Are you with Camilla?"

"Yes?"

"She'll understand. If not her, then Tommaso. I have to—"

"Don't hang up the phone!"

"It's that, or he *dies*."

He didn't give August the chance to choose, however, before he simply hung up the phone. She stared at the dead device in her hands for what felt like eons, although it might have only been a few seconds at the most.

Her heart was gone.

That was the problem.

It disappeared.

Turned to dust.

Apparently, it was that moment that Camilla decided to come and find August. How long had she been gone from the movie, now?

Fifteen minutes, or so.

Too long for the bathroom break she had claimed to her friend so that she wouldn't follow her, and she could make that call to Beni.

"Aug—"

Camilla didn't even get to push the door open all the way, or finish whatever it was she wanted to say before August spun to face her. Maybe it was the absolute terror in her eyes that did it, or the lack of color to her skin. It could have been the fact that she was still holding that dead phone in her shaking hands like she couldn't let it go because her life depended on it.

It felt exactly like that.

Whatever it was that her friend saw, Camilla knew right away. Something was wrong. *So very fucking wrong.*

"What happened?" Camilla asked, rushing into the bathroom.

"He was shot."

"What?"

"Beni was *shot*."

Camilla's hands landed to her arms, grabbing tight before

she shook her just hard enough that her hazy vision cleared of tears that threatened to fall. "August, stop mumbling."

"*Beni was shot!*"

That made Camilla freeze.

"When?"

"Just n-now—or a couple minutes ago. Joe said a clinic, o-or something … I don't k-know what he m-means."

Great.

Now her fucking teeth were chattering.

Shock was a bitch.

Camilla hugged August tight, arms locking around her like bars to stop the sudden shivers that raced through her body. "It's all right … it'll be fine. We'll call Tommaso, okay? He'll know what they're going to do."

But would it make a difference?

Or was he already dead?

He couldn't be dead.

She just found him.

"This isn't a *hospital!* He needs to be taken to an ER somewhere and—"

"*This* is where we can bring him," Tommaso said sharply, quieting August almost instantly with the look he threw at her over his shoulder. All it took was the smack of his wife's hand against his side for him to correct his attitude. "Sorry, Aug, I know you're scared and freaking out … Listen, we can't bring him into a hospital. Not unless we just want to drop him off, and leave him there alone until they figure out who he is, and call people in for him. It'll be flooded with *cops*. He's a gunshot victim. And just his last name would be enough to tell them that he's—"

"Connected to the mob," she whispered.

"Yeah."

God.

That pissed her off.

It made her so fucking angry for Beni.

"Why," she demanded, "because you protect the Outfit first, and its people second? Is that how it goes?"

"August," Camilla murmured, "they're doing what they've always done. Beni would do the same, you know?"

No, actually.

She didn't *know.*

However, what she did know was that it would be better for her to just get in line, let them do what they were going to do, and hope for the best. There was nothing else she could do right now except hope and fucking pray.

"We have a trauma surgeon on call that works in this clinic," Tommaso said, holding open the side door to a rather *normal* looking brick building. She had seen the sign on the front that explained it was, in fact, a walk-in clinic. "He's handled this kind of thing for us before."

Great.

That was just perfect.

"So, it's a regular thing?"

Camilla gave her a look.

August just shrugged.

She couldn't help it.

When she was scared, she got *mean.*

The second they stepped inside the darkened hallway of the clinic, August could hear the shouting. It sounded like pure *pain.* She didn't need to be told to know it was Beni screaming like that.

"Hold him down, get him fucking still on the table! Let's get this controlled!"

"Oh, my God."

Camilla was at August's side in a second, an arm locked

around her waist like she was determined to keep her still. "You're not going back there."

"But—"

"It's a bad idea."

Did it matter?

Those tears were falling again.

"I'll be right back," Tommaso said, quickly added, "keep her with you, Cam."

"Okay."

She suspected they were in the back hallways of the clinic, if only because the darkened space didn't offer anything to suggest the regular patients would be using the area. The one door she could see a few feet down had a sign on it that said *STORAGE* in black letters.

The shouting continued.

August squeezed her eyes shut.

Not that it helped.

She didn't open her eyes again until Tommaso's voice echoed down the hall, reaching their spot where the two girls hugged one another before he ever did.

"Good news first," he said, "it missed his heart by two inches. Bad news—the bullet hit a rib, broke it, and he lost a lot of blood. Joe is O Positive, so he was on hand to donate direct. We just have to let them get the bullet out, and—"

"While he's *awake*."

It wasn't even a question.

August stared hard at Tom.

"They're not equipped here to put him under safely, that's all."

Jesus.

"They have the tools on hand to take blood from Joe for him, but not to put him under while they dig a bullet out of his chest?"

"One doesn't require a tube down his throat, given the

severity, and monitors on his heart and brain while they work, August."

Right, right.

She understood what Tommaso was saying. He made sense, too. It wasn't that she couldn't comprehend all of this, but rather … her mind was trying to deal with it all in the only way it knew how. By picking apart every little thing instead of focusing on all the things she couldn't control here.

This wasn't in her hands.

She couldn't *help*.

"Someone has to call his family—his mom and dad, his brothers. His *twin*."

Tommaso nodded. "We already have."

Good.

As for her …

Well, she was just going to stand here and feel like she was dead already. What else could she do at this point?

~

"*Hey*."

The greeting sounded like it came from so far away, but August felt the couch shift at the same time the word reached her ears. She felt the warmth of a man who looked *exactly* like hers a few doors down in the clinic, but nothing seemed real.

Now, she was just floating.

Sixteen hours later.

The whole clinic was closed for them. She wasn't allowed to leave the space that was used as a waiting area, lest she wander too far and ruin the sterile environment they had set up. It was all over, now, and she watched them tote pail after pail of bloody water from the room—where Beni was currently recuperating—from her current position on the couch. It allowed her to look right down that hall and watch them move in and out of the room.

"He stopped shouting like … twelve hours ago," she said, her voice aching. "Or something like that—I guess he passed out."

Bene rubbed at his chest with his left palm, wincing a bit as he let out a hard sigh. "Tom said you didn't do well with the whole … well, anything."

"Would you?"

He eyed her from the side. "No."

August nodded. "Yeah."

"Where's the doc?"

"Sleeping in the room on a chair."

Or, that's what she was told. That way, if the shitty heart monitor they had went off, he was right there to react. Problem was, he needed to sleep, too, so that was another reason why she wasn't allowed to go down the hall to see Beni quite yet. She might wake the doctor up before he had a solid stretch of sleep to recharge.

"When is he going to wake up?"

"Who?"

"Beni."

"When he's ready to," Bene murmured, "because that's just Beni. Nothing is ever on someone else's time, it's always on his."

Wasn't that the truth?

"I don't mean to interrupt, but would you like something to eat, sweetheart?"

August glanced up from where she folded her hands in her lap to find a beautiful, red-headed woman standing just a few feet away. At her side, a man stood stoic and quiet, arms folded behind his back as he nodded at a younger man across the room.

"I … I don't think so," August said, "but thank you."

Bene gave her a small smile. "August, this is our mother and father, Cara and Gian."

Oh.

Oh.

She stared at the woman again, her soft features taking on a more familiar quality. She could easily see where the twins had taken after their mother, with just a dash of their father's tall, dark, and handsome characteristics, too. They had her soft smile, but his dark eyes.

It was then that she noticed all the other people now standing in the waiting area, too. Shock really was something else—it could take someone to a whole different world, and make everything disappear while it took over.

Like now.

Next to the new people in the room, on another couch in the corner, Camilla had fallen asleep while her husband sat next to her. Joe, on the far end, hid under the weight of his leather jacket where he couldn't be seen, probably sleeping, too.

It was August who couldn't close her eyes.

Even if her body begged for the rest.

"And that's Marcus," Bene said, pointing at the man Gian had been nodding at, "our oldest brother."

"Hello," Marcus greeted from his position near the clinic's front door.

"And Corrado."

He gestured to the man talking in hushed tones to whoever was on the phone. Angled slightly away from them, all she could see was his profile. Although, the side of his face matched the man he stood beside.

"Chris, his twin," Bene explained, "our other brothers. We're missing a couple—Les stayed with Ginny because she's pregnant, but he's coming tomorrow. And Val, Chris's wife, stayed behind with their daughter."

The whole family was there.

And now they were staring at her.

Even the one on his phone because he literally turned around to stare.

"I hope you don't mind," Bene said quietly, "but I explained a bit about you and Beni ... so they would know. Figured, in case they wondered who this woman was that loved him, might be better to let them know ahead of time."

Right.

Because they hadn't really gotten that far.

Now, they would.

It was just the worst possible time.

"I don't mind," she said quietly.

Bene nodded.

Cara smiled warmly again. "Are you sure you don't want something to eat or drink? One of the boys can run out and get whatever."

"No, I'm okay. I just want him."

Silence covered the room.

Thick, and oh, so heavy.

It might not have been the right thing to say.

It was still the truth.

Cara cleared her throat, giving her husband a nod before coming to sit on the couch on the other side of August. "I hear you come from New York."

"I do."

All eyes were still on her.

She didn't mind as much with Cara talking to her.

"Which borough?"

"Brooklyn, when I was younger. Queens later."

The shock lessened as the conversation continued. The others joined in, making her talk, and filling the silence in between with stories about them, and their family.

It really was the worst time to meet them. August was

grateful that she did, though, because it was impossible to deny how strong the group felt huddled together in that waiting room of a clinic that was not meant for this purpose. Beni's family was welcoming, and oddly familiar to her, in a way she couldn't explain.

They felt like him.

And she needed that.

So much.

~

Eighteen hours.

That was how long August had been sitting in that clinic before she was finally allowed into the back room where not only had they operated on Beni, but they kept him to rest, too. She vaguely remembered the doctor coming out, blood-stains still coloring his dress shirt and pants a ruddy brown, to tell them they could visit Beni a couple at a time, if they would like.

She said his parents should go first.

Then, his twin with Marcus.

The other two brothers.

She went last … if only because August didn't know how she was going to react once she was in that room, and she didn't want a witness to her pain. Wasn't it bad enough that she already felt like she was staring down at herself from above, and not really *there*?

Now, sitting at Beni's bedside, watching his heavily bandaged chest rise and fall, she was finally starting to come back to reality. If that's even what she could call this … *feeling.* Everything became sharp and clear all at once, from her pain, to the thoughts screaming in her mind. For too long, sitting in that waiting room, she felt nothing, her vision cloudy from tears that continued to fall, and her ears feeling like she was underwater.

Someone had cleaned him up—thankfully.

White, crisp sheets covered him.

An IV had been put in his right hand and leads attached to his chest kept the heart monitor on the other side of the bed beating with a steady sound. All was well. It looked good, including him in his deep sleep, face relaxed, and unconcerned that his bandages appeared as though they would need to be changed again soon.

The room still smelled of bleach.

Joe helped with that.

Seemed he knew how to clean up blood …

She didn't ask how or why.

There wasn't much to see in the space, and even the bed Beni rested on wasn't really a standard, issue hospital bed. It was one of those hard, rubbery pedestal beds one would find in their family doctor's office. Not at all meant for healing, or a restful sleep, but as she had been told time and time again … they were making do with what they had.

Doing what they could.

She wasn't the only one unhappy about that.

Beni's mother didn't like this, either, but Cara was a lot louder than August about it. If only because she could be, maybe, where as August didn't think her opinion counted for very much where these made men were concerned.

Letting those thoughts, and her constant worries, drift away so that she could focus on Beni and the present, she slipped her hand under his. Careful not to squeeze, just in case she did something to his IV, she settled herself on holding his hand, and taking those few moments to herself before someone came to interrupt it.

"You know, I don't think he would mind if you took a moment to rest."

August glanced toward the door, finding Marcus leaning there. "I can't sleep."

She tried.

"Hmm. He's going to be fine."

"So everyone keeps saying."

She believed them, too.

It was just hard right now.

Marcus pushed away from the doorjamb, taking a single step into the room as he took a second to look over his younger brother in the bed. "Funny this happened *now*—six months ago, a year ago ... if someone called me and said Beni had been shot, I wouldn't have been surprised. Him and Bene, they're reckless and wild. Never could keep them under control, you know? Especially not when they were together and feeding off one another."

He sighed, folding his arms over his chest as he added, "And then he went to Chicago, calmed down a bit, and this was not the call I expected to happen. Not for *him*, anyway."

Beni was still wild, she thought.

Maybe not *crazy* wild, like Marcus suggested, but just enough for her. All she had to do was think back to their time together—how he could make *anything* fun as long as he wanted to do it. The way he made split second decisions or chased the idea of a good time just because. The club, carnival, and even the other night in the pool ...

All of it.

That was Beni.

Beni was *fun*.

"Anyway," Marcus said, shaking his head, "Ma wanted to come back and sit with him for a bit, but she didn't want to take you away, if you wanted some more time. I said I would come back and ask for her."

"She's his mother. She can come back whenever she wants."

Marcus smiled. "She knows … but that's not our ma's way, you know?"

Well, she was learning.

"Tell her it's okay."

He nodded, and then quickly left her alone with Beni again. It wasn't long before the click of Cara's heels announced her arrival, but August was already standing to gather her things as the woman entered the room.

"Where are you going?"

"Don't you want to sit with him alone?" August asked.

Cara smiled from the doorway. "I would love to sit with him *and* you, if that's what you would like, too."

"Yeah, sure, I would love that."

With everyone else, it felt like August had to constantly be strong. Not that they made her feel any other way, and they surely didn't say anything of the sort, either. Cara was different, though. Something about Beni's mother seemed … well, *motherly*.

"Sit," Cara said, gesturing at the one chair, "and I'll just use this one over here. How about that?"

"That's good."

It wasn't.

Nothing would be good until Beni woke up.

August went back to doing what she could, for the moment. Which wasn't much, but holding Beni's hand, and resting her forehead against his warm arm while she listened to the rhythmic *beep-beep-beep* of the machine on the other side of his bed grounded her. It kept her from floating away again where it seemed like she was watching herself from above, and not *there*.

She would much rather be there.

With him.

CHAPTER
21

A hard, but *dry* grunt left Beni's lips as the doctor peeled back the bandage on his chest, and with a gloved hand, pressed around the now-exposed wound. "This is not where I was before I passed out."

He knew that for certain.

This room … he recognized it. Familiar tapestries, and a large, four-poster bed with sheer curtains one could pull around it for a false sense of privacy. The artwork on the walls, he had stared at before in his lifetime. He remembered thinking the paintings were terribly big when he was a child and didn't understand at all why someone would want that, instead of bright colors like on cartoons.

It was a bedroom.

In his aunt and uncle's mansion.

"You would be correct," the doctor said, "now hold still so I can get a good look at this wound, and clean it again, if need be."

"When—"

"That includes talking, Mr. Guzzi."

"Your bedside manners are shit."

The doctor chuckled. "Your uncle doesn't keep me on call because of my bedside manners—he does so because I am one of the best trauma surgeons in this city."

He knew he wasn't supposed to talk. Even breathing

made his chest feel like it was going to tear open all over again. That didn't stop his curiosity, and he had never been known for following the rules set out for him, even if it meant it would hurt like hell.

"Is that the only reason?" he asked, ignoring the silent reprimand for talking in the doctor's gaze that turned on him. "I'm just saying … because being good at what you do doesn't explain why you jump at the demand of a mob boss, that's all."

"An old family debt, how about that?"

Ah.

"Good enough for me."

"Great, now hush."

"Are you going to tell me why I'm here?"

The doctor let out a hard breath and gave Beni another look. "You are as … *difficult* as the one that looks just like you."

"His name is Bene."

"Yes, he told me that."

"I have a lot of questions."

"So it seems." The man shook his head, and resituated the bandage back in place on Beni's chest. "Lucky for you, the wound looks good. Not to pat my own back here, but having done too many of these fucking things, I can handle a wound like this."

Beni was pretty sure that was the first time he ever heard a doctor swear while tending to him. That included the one he called a prick for resetting his bone when he was twelve, and had broken his ankle from falling out of a tree trying to climb as high as his twin had in the back yard. That shit hurt.

"As for your question about being here," the doctor said, pulling off the latex gloves and discarding them to a nearby trashcan, "as you can see from the monitor there …" He pointed at a machine showing Beni's blood pressure, and heart rate. "Your vitals have been stable from thirty-six hours in, so I gave your uncle the choice to move you to a place where you would be more comfortable waking up. He decided to do that, and here you are."

Beni remembered none of that.

"How long was I out?"

The man checked his watch. "Fifty-two hours, now."

Huh.

"You are very lucky, young man," he said, "and I hope you know that."

Beni nodded. "Yeah, I do."

"I removed the IV this morning because you were showing signs of waking up, and the quicker you start doing for yourself—eating, walking to the bathroom, drinking—the better. You were getting antibiotics to prevent infection through the IV, but you'll be taking it in pill form now. And you're going to be in a lot of pain for a while. Painkillers will only do so much, and you're going to have to be careful about how much you take. Understand?"

"I got it."

"You won't be doing very much for the next two months except resting. That includes work, picking up a broom … that pretty woman waiting out in the hallway with the rest of your family. Do you hear me?"

Beni's laughter echoed in the quiet bedroom. *God*, it hurt like hell. His chest felt like someone had taken a sledge-hammer and beat on him over and over until there was a giant, bloody hole left behind. But none of that mattered. Not one bit of it.

Why?

Because he was *alive*.

Maybe it was the sound of his laughter filtering outside the bedroom, but soon, the space was full of familiar faces.

They slipped into the room one after the other—all wore smiles, and he grinned back, gaze sweeping over them to find the one he wanted the very most.

He loved seeing his ma. Knew he scared his dad. All his brothers looked like they wanted to both kill him and hug him. His twin practically bounced on his fucking heels, only held back by his mother locking her arm around his at the elbow. His friends, and the rest of his family also came into the room, but they hung back.

With her.

August.

She smiled softly, waving two fingers as his gaze finally landed on her. More than anything, he wanted to get up out of that bed, and go to her. Or even, have her come to him. Both worked just fine for his purpose of getting her closer, as far as he was concerned.

That was hard to do with everyone talking at once, though.

Literally.

"Scared the hell out of us, Beni."

"Look at you, awake."

"How's he doing, doc?"

More questions.

More statements to him.

Beni just kept looking at August, though. She hung back near the far wall with his uncle and aunt, and Tommaso and Camilla. She let his family approach him first, and have their time, which he appreciated. He was sure the rest of them were grateful, too.

He still wanted her closer.

"Hey," he mouthed.

She nibbled on her bottom lip before mouthing back, "*Hey, you.*"

"Love you."

"Love you, too."

"Okay, two or three at a time," the doctor grumbled, waving his arms at the now *very* large crowd gathered in his room. "Everybody out—choose who is staying for a quick visit, and the rest have to leave."

Corrado gave Beni a look, and pointed his finger at him as he turned to leave, "Ma, Dad, and Bene can go first—but if you *ever* pull shit like that again, I will put you underground myself."

"Corrado," Alessio—his brother's lover—muttered, "be easy on him, now."

"I said what I said."

"Corrado!"

Their mother, that time.

Beni nodded at his brother. "I hear you."

"Good."

Marcus came just close enough to the bed to clasp a hand down to Beni's ankle under the sheets, so he could squeeze gently. "Glad to see you awake, yeah?"

"Yeah, Marcus."

They filtered out of the room one by one. Including August, but not before he gave her a wink. Not that he had the energy to entertain, or chat, but when the door closed and he was left with just his parents, and brother … they didn't ask for much.

Cara approached first, bending down to clasp his face, so she could press a kiss to his forehead. "Look at you, my boy."

"I'm okay, Ma."

"*Barely.*"

Well, he didn't argue that.

"Scared the hell out of me," his father added, finding the spot on the other side of his bed. His mother moved just long enough for Gian to run his fingers through the hair at the crown of Beni's head. "I'm going to need you to not do that again, son."

"That's fair."

At the foot of the bed, Bene rubbed his chest.

"Fucking felt that."

"Did you?"

Bene shrugged. "*Too much.*"

Cara squeezed his shoulder and gave Gian a look. "Come on, let's go find him something to eat and drink. I think Abriella has a stew ready for the rest of us."

Beni wasn't in the mood to eat. He didn't argue with his parents about leaving, though, and soon he was alone with his twin.

Bene wouldn't meet his gaze.

He understood why, though.

"Fuck you for doing that," Bene muttered.

"Didn't really plan it, you know?"

"Put me to my knees, Beni, on a fucking *sidewalk* in Toronto. Thought you were dead—like my heart was coming right out of my chest into my hands. I know I've been an asshole lately, and shit, but that doesn't change anything."

No, it didn't.

Not between them.

"Anything you want?" Bene asked. "Other than soup, or water?"

Yeah.

He didn't even have to think about it.

"August."

Bene nodded. "Sure, I'll get her in here for you."

"Thanks."

"And take those fucking painkillers. My chest still hurts."

Beni laughed, as weak as it was. "Will do."

～

Beni was just beginning to drift into a light sleep when the bedroom door opened again, and the woman he wanted more than anything slipped into the room. His twin hadn't been gone more than five minutes. Probably just long enough to find August, and let her know she could come see him whenever.

It was a testament to his exhaustion.

"Sorry," she whispered, "do you want me to leave so you can—"

"No," he mumbled, rubbing the heel of his palm to his eyes as he tried to roll sideways a bit on the bed. *Fuck*, that felt like pure hell. It had him groaning under his breath, and twisting to his back way too fast. "*Holy shit*, that hurts."

August crossed the room faster than he could blink, her hands finding either side of his naked torso to lay flat like she was trying to steady him just long enough for him to get comfortable again.

Strangely, it helped.

It calmed his heart, too.

"Easy, easy," she said softly.

Those hands of hers drifted over his form.

He watched her through his lowered lashes.

"I'm sorry," he mumbled.

August dragged in a shaky breath. "*God*, for what?"

"That you heard it. That I scared you. All of this."

"It's okay, I'm just happy you're here."

No, it wasn't okay at all.

He would do his best to make sure it never happened again.

It was the best he could do.

"You know," she said, moving the blankets aside so that she could sit on the edge of the bed beside him, "your family is pretty amazing."

"Are they?"

They'd always just been *his*.

"And overwhelming."

Beni laughed.

It still hurt.

"They are definitely that," he muttered, resisting the urge to rub at the deep ache in his chest. "But that's what makes them great."

"It does, you're right."

He managed to find the strength to reach over and grab onto her wrist. He didn't need to say anything, simply tug on her arm to get what he wanted. Which was her resting beside him in the bed, her head resting on his shoulder, so he could feel her heartbeat and hear her steady breaths.

He had been the one who almost died.

It was her that he wanted to feel *alive*.

Funny how that worked.

"Everyone knows, by the way," she said quietly.

"Knows what?"

"That I'm staying here in Chicago. I called my parents a couple days ago. I chatted with Alessa before I went to the movies with Cam that afternoon, too, and told her I would take the job and start whenever she needed me to."

Beni found himself grinning. "Oh?"

"Mmhmm."

"What did your parents say?"

"They're going to help me pack up my apartment, so I don't have to fly back right now."

"So …"

August leaned up just enough for him to see her smile, before she leaned in and pressed a quick kiss to his lips. Even though she pulled away far too soon for his liking, he still felt that kiss fucking *everywhere*.

"So," she said, "I'm not going anywhere unless I'm going with you."

"That sounds perfect to me."

More than, really.

"Oh, and we should come back around to that conversation now, too. Remember?"

He blinked, trying to bring back whatever it was she was talking about, but his brain failed. Not surprising, considering how goddamn tired he was at the moment. Once he fell asleep, he bet he would stay that way for a good day or more.

A healing body took a lot of energy.

"What conversation?"

"Your place. *Me*. Moving."

Ah.

"Yeah," he said, not hiding the happiness that was thick in his tone. "That one. Not sure now is the right time ... me being in a bed, injured and all."

August laughed lightly. "Why, because I might feel manipulated by the situation, and that's the only possible reason I would choose to—"

"You said it, not me."

Her cheek rested against his. "Who else is going to take care of you for the next two months, huh?"

Well ...

"When you put it like that," he murmured.

Her smile curved against his jawline before she kissed the same spot. "That's settled, then."

Like it had ever been in question?

"Love you," he said tiredly, voice faint.

August's fingertips drifted through his hair, lulling him closer and closer to sleep with every passing second. He bet it would be far better to sleep with her beside him, though. "Love you, too. Always, Beni."

On his back, with a bullet hole in his chest, drifting off to sleep while he watched her as long as he could, and her voice filled his mind …

Life was looking damn good.

Even if right then, it also hurt.

Beni wasn't sure when he woke up again, but when he did, he found August sleeping beside him in the bed. Turned on her side facing him as he laid on his back, her forehead pressed against his arm, warm breath tickling his skin, and her hand stayed tightly tucked in with his.

"She's been sleeping about an hour, or so."

The familiar voice had Beni looking to his left. There sat his father, reading a newspaper—The Tribune, it looked like —on a recliner in the corner of the bedroom. He might have been annoyed that someone was in the room with him and August while they slept, except he couldn't find it in himself to drudge up the emotion, all things considered.

He scared the hell out of his family.

It wasn't a shock they wanted to stick close.

"Good," he replied, "she probably needed the rest."

"Yes, like your mother, she wouldn't sleep while you were out. Corrado and Les headed back to New York—they send their love, and Corrado … his threats, you know, it's how he shows he cares, but they have to get back to Ginny."

Right.

"How far along is she now?"

"Twenty-nine weeks pregnant. Did we tell you it's going to be a girl?"

"No."

Or if they did, he couldn't remember.

"Beni?"

"Hmm?"

He met his father's gaze.

Gian smiled. "You know what I promised your mother a long time ago, don't you? I've told you before, son."

Yeah, he had.

Every time he and Bene went nuts.

"That she wouldn't bury one of us."

"You almost made me break that promise."

"Didn't mean to, Papa."

The hard line of his father's jaw tensed, before that tremor worked its way through. Like his father was holding back his emotions because that's just not what Gian did. He was always strong—forever in control. Nothing else would do.

"I can't convince you to move back to Toronto, can I?"

Beni shook his head. "Chicago is better for me."

"Well, at least sending you here did something right, yes?"

"More than one thing."

Gian's gaze drifted to August, and then right back to Beni. "Yes, more than one."

"Dad?"

"Hmm?"

"Bene is going to be okay, right?"

He left a lot unsaid there.

He'll be okay with me staying here?

He'll be fine without me, won't he?

It'll get better for him, won't it?

A sigh answered him back.

Seconds ticked by.

"Eventually," Gian murmured. "He's still learning what it's like to be him without you, Beni, and right now … I'm not sure he likes who that person is."

～

Four months later …

"*Happy birthday, to you, happy birthday, to you … happy birthday, Bene and Beni, happy birthday, to you.*"

"And to many more," his mother said, raising a glass to her twins from across the room.

Beni held up his, too.

Bene had already downed his.

Not unusual for his twin lately, if everyone else and what they had to say about Bene was to be trusted. Seemed his brother was partying a lot more, but it was hard for Beni to keep track of what his twin was doing when he was in a whole other country. He got the information from his family because Bene sure as hell wasn't saying anything was up.

Tonight, though, was not about that.

It was their birthday.

And he had plans.

"Are you doing that now?" his brother asked.

Beni nodded, peeking over his shoulder to search for August in the large foyer of the Guzzi mansion. It doubled as a good party room when his parents didn't want to open up *more* of the house to the guests because it gave them access to the sitting room, the dining room, and kitchen. Lots of space to move.

He found his girl holding an almost two-month-old baby girl—happy as could be with the newborn Guzzi in her arms. Unsurprisingly, Corrado and Alessio were not too far away as August rocked the baby and chatted to little Maria at the same time. Ginevra didn't feel the need to hover over every single person who held her daughter like the baby's fathers did.

August bent down, letting Maria fix baby Caroline's big bow on her crown of dark hair. The two shared matching smiles, in love with the baby just like everybody else in their family. Although, to be fair, Maria *really* adored August. Her *Auntie A* as she liked to call her.

"Yeah," Beni said to his twin, "I'm going to do that now."

"Good. Maybe while everyone is all over you two, I can sneak out and nobody will notice."

"*Bene*."

He was worried about his twin.

Acting out, and shit.

Bene just laughed, and clapped him on the back. "I'm kidding, relax."

He didn't believe that.

Not for a second.

Still, tonight was not about Bene.

Or his issues.

They had all the time in the world to fix that.

Right?

"I'll go steal the baby from her," Bene said, "since you're going to need her hands free, and all. Swear it's like once a chick picks up a baby, they won't let it go."

Not a lie.

Beni and August enjoyed the time they spent with their nieces, but they weren't even at a place yet where they were considering kids of their own. Shit, they were *young*. They had time to figure that out, even if baby fever, as his mother put it, was thick in the air.

"That would be helpful."

"It's what I do."

Yeah.

That, and a hell of a lot more.

He clapped his twin on the back before Bene made a beeline for August where she had moved across the room with the baby—Caroline's fathers were close behind, of course—to talk to Cara, and swoon over her little dress, it looked like.

Beni searched for his father, but it didn't take him long to find Gian in his usual corner. Sitting on what his brothers had affectionately dubbed the *throne* because of the chair's high back, and ornate design, his father watched his family and the other guests enjoying the party. As soon as his gaze landed on Beni coming his way, however, his father's smile softened.

"Is it time?" he asked as Beni neared.

"Now or never, right?"

Gian chuckled, shifting a bit in the chair to dig into his suit pocket. He produced a small, black velvet box for his son to take, saying, "Do you want a *good luck* or …?"

"You know what," Beni said, flipping open the box to stare at the ring he had designed with his father's jeweler, using gold from one of Gian's rings, and diamonds from his mother's, "I think I got this, Papa."

"I think you do, too."

August was already looking his way from across the room when he spun around, keeping that velvet box hidden in his palm at his back. She smiled wide, coming in his direction when he took one step toward her.

She was a little different from that first night they met. Her hair was back in braids, but she'd lost the Frankie Zombie jacket, and jeans for a sleek black dress that hugged her curves, and showed off those fantastic legs of hers, and the red-soled heels he'd given to her to match the red choker at her throat.

So, not the same.

And yet, still perfect.

Entirely his.

She met him in the middle of the room.

He was already bending down on one knee, velvet case

opened on his palm for her wide eyes to find, and his grin growing deeper at her surprise. She liked that, though; his surprises kept her on her toes, so he planned to keep it up.

"If you'll take me," he said quietly, though the room had grown silent around them, "then I would be honored to be yours forever, August, if you'll be mine, too. Marry me?"

She didn't even hesitate.

"*Yes.*"

BETHANY-KRIS

Bethany-Kris is a Canadian author, lover of much, and mother to four young sons, two cats, and three dogs. A small town in Eastern Canada where she was born and raised is where she has always called home. With her boys under her feet, a snuggling cat, barking dogs, and a spouse calling over his shoulder, she is nearly always writing something ... when she can find the time.

Find Bethany-Kris at her:
www.bethanykris.com

BOOKS BY BETHANY-KRIS

Always

Revere

Unruly

The Companion

Naz & Roz

Guzzi Duet

Unraveled, Book One

Entangled, Book Two

DeLuca Duet

Waste of Worth: Part One

Worth of Waste: Part Two

Donati Bloodlines

Thin Lies

Thin Lines

Thin Lives

Behind the Bloodlines

The Complete Trilogy

Filthy Marcellos

Antony

Lucian

Giovanni

Dante

Legacy

A Very Marcello Christmas

The Complete Collection

Seasons of Betrayal

Where the Sun Hides

Where the Snow Falls

Where the Wind Whispers

Seasons: The Complete Seasons of Betrayal Series

Gun Moll Trilogy

Gun Moll

Gangster Moll

Madame Moll

The Chicago War

Deathless & Divided

Reckless & Ruined

Scarless & Sacred

Breathless & Bloodstained

The Complete Series

Maldives & Mistletoe

The Russian Guns

The Arrangement

The Life

The Score

Demyan & Ana

Shattered

The Jersey Vignettes

Standalone Titles

Dirty Pool

Effortless

Inflict

Cozen

Captivated

Dishonored

Find more on Bethany-Kris's website at www.bethanykris.com